THE LAST RESORT

RICHARD NEER

A RILEY KING MYSTERY

OTHER BOOKS BY RICHARD NEER:

FM: THE RISE AND FALL OF ROCK RADIO

SOMETHING OF THE NIGHT

THE MASTER BUILDERS

INDIAN SUMMER

(COMING)THE PUNCH LIST

FOR FRANK NEER

ONE

"I'm not giving you more than three shots a side, no way José," Rick Stone said. "If I didn't know better, I'd say I was being hustled."

For the last couple of weeks, Rick and I had been doing a golf tour of Hilton Head. There are over thirty courses on the twelve mile barrier island. Stone's career as a sports talk show host on WJOK, a powerful station out of Toms River, New Jersey, had provided him with great contacts. We could get on even the most exclusive private courses at a moment's notice, usually gratis.

"I can't get a rhythm going, Ricky. I'm just not adjusting to this period of idle play time like you are."

Stone had recently lost his talk show gig but the specifics on how it went down were still only coming out in drips and drabs. The conglomerate that had purchased his radio station was slashing expenses wherever they could and his salary was considered excessive by the bean counters. When his contract expired, they turned his midday show over to syndication.

Rick was trying to stay upbeat though it all. He said, "For you, shankasaurus, this is idle play time. For me, it's working toward my new career. If I can clean up a few things in my game, I can qualify for the Senior Tour. Then, the sky is the limit."

"Davis Love, Fred Couples, Phil Mickelson, Rick Stone. Which of these does not belong?"

"Phil. He's still on the regular tour, idiot. Here, check out this drive." He proceeded to split the fairway with a 280 yard tee shot, the slight draw he employed setting up a perfect approach. Even though I'm taller and stronger than Rick, I can't hit a ball that far in my dreams.

I plunked my drive into the right rough, not more than 230 yards from the tee box. We walked down the verdant fairway which led to the Atlantic Ocean, the waves crashing over a dune just a few yards past the green.

"Who were you on the phone with this morning, Mr. Golden Bear?" I asked.

"Geez, even at 77 years old, Jack Nicklaus can out drive you. FYI, I was talking to your next client. Trying to get your lazy ass in gear."

"You're always trying to push me, Ricky. Maybe toward places I don't want to go. I guess you mean well."

He said, "Like when I persuaded your girlfriend Jaime to give you another chance after you blew it with her? On account of that hot country singer you shacked up with?"

"I appreciate that little intervention more than you'll ever know. But I'm a big boy when it comes to my work. I can drum up my own business."

All I got from that was a wry grin. I said, "Okay, so I won't make the Senior Tour with you, Ricky. Who's this prospective client you're talking about?"

"You've met her. Alison Middleton. The lady who was on after me on WJOK."

"What's her problem?"

"Allie does afternoon drive with a guy named Wally Josephs. The *Allie and Wally* show, they call it. She knows her shit when it comes to sports; Wally's the sizzle."

I said, "I remember meeting both of them a few times back in my Jersey detective days. But I thought you hated Wally Josephs. You've never had a good word to say about him."

"That's because he's an asshole. My main problem with him is that he shoots from the hip and doesn't seem to care if he makes sense or not. He specializes in putdowns. He can eviscerate pro athletes like no one else in the business --- very negative and unfair. Hurts a lot of good people without giving it a second thought."

I found my ball in the rough and it was sitting up nicely. I said, "Can't say I like the show the few times I've heard it. Alison has the common sense and he's the young crazy one. A Mad Dog Russo wannabe."

"But nowhere near as good and Chris Russo is not mean spirited. The audience respects her, loves/hates him. The suits think the dynamic between the two of them is what they call *must-listen* radio. Their ratings are good, but now they're on a downward slide along with the rest of the station."

I said, "Why would Alison need someone like me? She's not married, right? So there's no cheating hubby."

"I wouldn't waste your time with trivial shit like that, kemo sabe. She's flying down here tomorrow after she gets off the air. She'll tell you everything you need to know."

"Here you go again, my devious friend. I'm a little wary about getting involved with people at that station after what happened last year with McCarver. And now they've fired you. Why would I want to help anyone there?"

Stone said, "The McCarver case paid off big time, didn't it? You and I got an oceanfront house here on Hilton Head and he paid you enough so you never have to worry about money again. Not a bad payday for a couple weeks' work."

I dug my next shot out of the short rough and somehow managed to connect perfectly, its high arcing trajectory cutting through the ocean breeze and landing twenty five feet from the flag.

Stone wasn't impressed. "Nice shot. Lucky, but nice. By the way, Alison is staying with us here Friday night. Make sure the guest room is ready."

"Come on, Ricky, don't leave me blind on this one like you did with McCarver. What's going on with this Alison Middleton?"

He lined up his next shot and proceeded to place a gorgeous nine iron well inside my ball. He turned to me and said, "Wally Josephs has been missing for three days. He might be dead."

TWO

After the golf, Rick and I went our separate ways. He said we'd meet at the house later and he'd tell me more about Alison but never specified exactly when. That made me think that he was hooking up with one of his young nubiles, planning to make the nineteenth hole a late afternoon delight.

I made a quick stop to pick up my golden retriever Bosco at the groomer. The boy loves the attention they lavish on him there, and he wasn't all that eager to get back in the car with me after his spa day. I've spoiled him rotten but they must do it in ways I haven't thought of.

I was greeted at my front door by a naked woman.

"Where's Stone?" I asked, seemingly oblivious to the glorious sight before me.

My girlfriend Jaime Johansen was tall, tan, young and lovely but not from Ipanema. A natural redhead, her present state of dishabille leaving no doubt.

"So I come to the door wearing nothing but a smile and your first question is where is your golf buddy. I guess the thrill *is* gone, Riley King."

Riley King is the birth name I share with the late bluesman B.B. King, a fact my parents never mentioned until I was in college and discovered his music on my own. Jaime's allusion was glib but apt. I've become so preoccupied with a lot of extraneous noise that my libido takes a distant second. That's not to say that all romantic ardor has left me, as I hoped to prove in the next few minutes.

I said, "Not that at all, Jaime. Just wanted to make sure there were no witnesses to what's about to happen."

She shrieked as I swept her off her feet and onto the nearby sofa, proceeding to show her that the thrill wasn't gone. In fact, I'm afraid I proved it too quickly.

"I suppose it's too soon to request an encore?" she said, when we were finished, or should I say, *I* was finished.

"I keep telling you I'm too old for you, sweets. Takes me a few minutes to recharge these ancient batteries." More like a few hours, but why spoil the illusion. Jaime is a shade under forty, which I often boast gives me the advantage of more than a decade's worth of experience in these matters. It is a hollow boast, as I just showed again.

She said, "Those batteries still have plenty of life in them. I can wait. Where's Bosco?"

"Oh shit, he's still in the car. I wasn't expecting to be surprised by a nekkid girl at the door. I came up to get his walking harness and I forgot about him. It's not just the batteries that are getting old."

I pulled up my pants and rushed back to the driveway to fetch the dog. My seven year old pup was sound asleep in the cool back seat of my Audi. Age was becoming a factor for him too, evidenced by how gingerly he jumped out onto the pavers.

"Front door, pal. Mommy's inside."

That didn't get much of a response from him until I uttered the magic word, "Cookie."

With that, he mounted the stairs as quickly as his four legs would allow and sat panting at the front door. As I let us both in, he immediately charged over to the sofa and started sniffing. After deciding it was a disgusting human scent, he lit out for the kitchen where his cookie jar resided.

Jaime had put on a robe and was making dinner. When Bosco spotted her, he forgot everything we had been trying to teach him and jumped on her with the full force of his seventy pounds. Rather than scold him as she usually did, Jaime dropped to the floor, massaged his ears and gave him a biscuit. He showed his gratitude by bolting away from her, chewing noisily as he pounced onto his corner dog bed. I entered the room a moment later and he leapt up to greet me as if he hadn't seen me in weeks. Short memory must be contagious.

"It's nice that both my boys are so happy to see me that they couldn't wait to jump my bones," Jaime said. "I wanted to surprise you. Did I do wrong?"

Jaime and I have a complicated relationship. I used to be an intrepid private investigator in Toms River, New Jersey, where our paths first crossed. The winter weather and a couple of bad case outcomes pushed me south. We were apart for almost a year. She was heading a tremendously successful literary agency up north and could not abandon it during its growth phase. With Stone's intervention, she had recently agreed to move in with me on the proviso that she would need to travel to New York and the West Coast a couple times a month.

I said, "No, I was just worried that Rick would catch us in the act. He does occasionally share the house with us when he's not out with one of his chippies."

"I made sure he wasn't here before I ambushed you at the door. I'm not that brazen a hussy."

"Not that he'd mind seeing you in the altogether. What male with a pulse *would* mind that?"

THREE

That night, I awoke at three a.m. and couldn't get back to sleep. Existential thoughts began invading my brain instead of sweet dreams and flying machines. I thought about gently caressing Jaime to stir the embers from earlier but she looked so peaceful, I hadn't the heart to disturb her. But as I started to get out of bed, she turned to me and said, "Are you all right?"

"I'm fine. Just can't sleep."

"What's on your mind, babe?"

"I don't know. We can talk about it some other time. You go back to sleep."

"No, I'm up now. Tell me."

"It's just that Stone's pulled one of his typical radio tricks again. The tease. He throws out a headline. *One of our deejays is missing*, like that old Kinks song. He refuses to tell me any more until tonight and then he never shows up."

As a successful agent, Jaime was wise to the ways of the media. "It's what they call quarter hour maintenance. They need you to stay tuned, so they entice you with promises that something exciting is about to happen next, but never get too specific. Local TV news does it all the time. So you sit through those endless commercial breaks and more often than not the payoff is something totally lame or misleading."

"I know. I guess when you've been schooled on something your whole professional life, it's hard to teach an old dog new tricks. Sorry, Bosco. I just don't get why he'd want to revisit the scene of the crime. They fired him barely a month ago. He hates this guy Wally Josephs. Why does he want me to get me involved to help WJOK? Why not just let the police handle it?"

She reached across and massaged my bad knee, a remnant of my last college basketball game at Georgetown. "You'd think he'd want the whole place to go up in flames after the way they dumped him. But you know Rick. Beneath that tough Marine exterior, he's a sentimental softie. He and Ted McCarver built that place up from a little dump in the swamps of Jersey into a major sports station, second only to WFAN in New York. He still has great memories from those glory days."

"I get that, but it's not the same station anymore since McCarver sold it to that big conglomerate. When I was working up in Jersey last year, I could barely stomach listening to it when Rick wasn't on. The Allie and Wally show is a travesty. Josephs sounds like a late night drunk at the end of a bar, with his bullshit theories about sports and life in general. Nothing to back them up but his own resentment and bile. If he's missing, I say good riddance."

"What about this Alison Middleton?"

I moved closer to her side of the bed, trying not to disturb Bosco, who lies between us when the mood strikes.

I said, "I've met her a few times. She's smart and a real tough cookie. She's a breast cancer survivor and she does great work for the cause. Uses her radio platform to promote all kinds of fund raisers. I don't know how she tolerates Josephs but the show is popular and it's taken her career to new heights. I guess she holds her nose and takes the money."

"We all have to do that sometimes. Hey babe, you're having doubts in the middle of the night about jumping into a situation at a place where they screwed your best friend, I get that. But he's the one who wants you to do it."

"There's a lot he didn't tell me about how they fired him. That might be the key. I need to know more about that before I take this on."

"Now that money's not a factor, you're thinking about your legacy, your place in the world. You only want to accept work that serves the greater good these days. I think that's admirable. McCarver paying you all that cash and a half share of this oceanfront house was supposed to be a blessing, not a curse."

"Good old Ted. He dealt with his issues by running away to a monastery."

Her gentle caress had moved north from my sore knee. "I hope you're not considering the same thing. Those monks are celibate, no? You'd miss what we did this afternoon. At least I'd like to think so."

I said, "I feel kind of petty for whining about this, especially given Stone's problems. All those years on that station and boom, it's gone in a heartbeat."

"I know. It's sad. But he'll be all right. We all will. Come back to bed, sweets. I bet Rick's sleeping like a baby somewhere now, dreaming of winning the Masters or something."

"Knowing him, he's not alone and he's not asleep either."

"Neither are we. I have an early plane to catch. Are those batteries up to speed yet?"

They were.

FOUR

Jaime took off for the West Coast that morning to work on a new deal to bring some of her clients' books to the big screen, or more likely in today's environment, the small screen. It seems that major motion pictures hold less appeal for her stable of serious writers than binge-watchable series from the likes of Netflix and Amazon. It was territory that my upwardly mobile other was eagerly mining --- the potential being as infinite as the web itself.

So instead of my frisky paramour, Rick and I were drinking late on a Friday night with a lady whose career was already at its zenith. In her mid fifties, Alison Middleton was still a handsome woman, who reminded me of the actress Charlotte Rampling. Despite her well documented battle with breast cancer, her face was relatively unlined and had good color.

Rick and I were well into our second single malt; she opted to nurture a light Bacardi rum and ginger. We'd been making small talk since she arrived --- the weather, sports, her flight from New Jersey.

"So Alison, let's get down to it. What happened with Wally?" I said, when we ran out of chitchat.

"He didn't show up for work Tuesday. No sweat, it's happened before. Overslept, hung-over, whatever."

"Wait. Your show starts at two in the afternoon. He oversleeps for that?" I asked, not bothering to hide my antipathy at his lack of professionalism.

"He's just a big kid. He's thirty six years old but parties like a frat boy. He drinks, snorts, gambles, screws anything available. Whatever gets him through the night."

Stone chipped in, singing, "Yeah, *it's all right, it's all right.*"

She glared at him, in mock anger at his annoying habit of referencing rock songs at every opportunity, appropriate or not. "Anyway, I called Wally's cell and it went to voice mail. No surprise there either. I did the show solo and covered for him."

I said, "I know that you media people aren't like the rest of us working stiffs. Jaime's told me stories about her writer and actor friends. But how does your boss tolerate this stuff? I have to think that the show suffers without Wally."

She stiffened. She is a New York City girl but her speech bears no vestiges of the street. Off the air now, her demeanor was somewhat gentler than the aggressive style she needed to keep up with Josephs. "I can see we're not going to pull any punches here, King. Good. I don't tolerate bullshit either."

Stone tried to play mediator. "Alison, I think what Riley meant was..."

"I know what he meant and he's right. I'm not some green little girl. I worked solo for years before they teamed me up with Wally. Had a nice little career going but nothing like I have now."

I got up to refill our glasses. Alison shook me off. Rick was leaning back on the sofa. His days of 36 holes of golf in the sun were taking their toll. I'm sure he'd spring to attention if I told him what Jaime and I had done on that very spot the day before.

I said, "Okay, Alison, even though I think you're enabling him, I get it. So why is this different than his other binges? Maybe he met a girl and they shacked up at her place."

"It's happened before. But regardless, he always calls me back after a day or so. He's been AWOL for four days now and I'm really worried."

"Have you called the police?"

She took a sip of her drink and shook her head. "I know they say that any publicity is good publicity, but if I call the police, it'll be all over social media and the local papers. The public knows that Wally is a wild child, but if they knew chapter and verse, it could be bad for the show."

Living with Jaime had taught me otherwise. "I think you're wrong, Alison. That bad boy shtick plays well these days, always has. Millennials especially love it."

Alison said, "Maybe, but I'm old school and I draw bright lines at certain points. I know we fight constantly on the air and sometimes it carries over when we get off. There have been times where we don't speak much off-mic."

Her dirty blond hair was streaked with gray but her hazel eyes twinkled. I didn't know much about her personal life, only that she had married young and had been divorced forever. I had heard rumors linking her with a few well known athletes over the years and the inquisitive public speculated that her relationship with young Wally was more than just business.

As if reading my mind, she said, "I really care about Wally. I feel like his mom. Given the age difference, I guess I could be. He's got a lot of talent and despite how he comes off, he's very bright and has a good heart. And before we were teamed up, when I was going through chemo, he was the only one at the station who came to see me on a regular basis. That counts for a lot and I don't want to reduce him to Johnny Manziel."

She hadn't mentioned Stone by name, but by his guilty look, I knew that he hadn't been supportive enough of his colleague in her hour of need. I broke the uneasy silence. "I understand your concern. Look, I know a cop with the Ocean County force who's a standup guy. I can put you in touch with him directly and I'm sure he'll keep it under wraps."

"Does that mean you won't help?" She was getting annoyed with my reluctance to dive right in. She'd flown all the way down here only to have me tell her she could have done better by staying home.

"That's not what I'm saying. It's just that I work alone these days and my cop friend McCullough has the resources of the whole department at his disposal."

"That's just it. You may trust this cop and I'm sure you're right about him. But the minute he enlists any of his colleagues, the cat's out of the bag. I need to handle this privately, case closed."

"My advice is the opposite. You can trust McCullough's discretion. This is a police matter."

"Rick said you were the best but that you've been gun shy lately. I can stay at a hotel tonight and fly back in the morning. I can see this was a waste of time, King."

FIVE

Rick managed to talk Alison off the ledge and she agreed to stay over and re-open the subject in the morning. I went to bed convinced that if the story did happen to leak, it could only benefit the *Allie and Wally* show.

I generally get up before Stone and that Saturday morning was no exception. I took Bosco out for a quick walk on the beach at dawn, and returned to find Alison in the kitchen, drinking coffee.

"I hope you don't mind me serving myself, King," she said. "I assumed it was there for the taking."

"Of course. And call me Riley. Look, I'm sorry we got off on the wrong foot last night. I *would* like to help. But if your fears for Wally are legitimate and something happened to him, the police are going to be involved at some point no matter what. And if not, he'll surface on his own soon and you'll feel silly for worrying."

Looking at her in the bright morning sunlight, I no longer saw the hard driving sports know-it-all, but a woman in her fifties clinging to her last shot at glory. Her existence centered around her job, and after years laboring as an anonymous journeyman, she had finally hit the big time. Achieving success in that all-boy sandbox hadn't been easy and I imagined she lived in the constant fear that it could all be taken away on a corporate whim.

She had seen how quickly they had dispatched Stone, and he had been the previous owner's golden boy.

"The timing bothers me," she said. "Usually when he goes on his benders, it's over a weekend. This happened early in the week."

"So he did the show with you Monday. Anything different about him then?"

"Well, I suppose I should have said something about this first thing. We got into a big fight on the air about football. Not about the game itself, but about how these guys act like fools, celebrating after every decent play and God forbid they do something extraordinary. They act like they've won the Super Bowl every time they make a first down. Of course, Wally defended them and that's fine but then he called me an old dyke who doesn't like to see young guys having fun. At the break, I said that he had made this personal by attacking me and I didn't like it. He said 'chill out, bitch'. That hurt. I said some harsh things after that and before the show ended, he just stomped off."

"So you think he's mad at you and that's why he didn't show up for work?"

"That was my first inclination. This type of thing has happened before and he's always apologized the next day when he realizes he's clearly in the wrong. And we move on. I don't mind him arguing with me on the air, that's what makes the show fun to listen to. If we agreed on everything, it wouldn't work. But I draw the line when he lies about my sexual orientation and attacks my age."

"Do you ever attack his age?"

"Sometimes in jest, but that's different. Calling someone a callow youth implies that someday they'll grow up and learn the error of their ways. An old dyke? There's no recovery from that, you only get older and dykier."

This was a smart lady. Even though Alison is on radio, she has to present a youthful image to appeal to the young male demographic that the station seeks. She can't be perceived as *Lesbian-Grandma-Talking-Sports*. So she hangs out with a younger crowd, picks up their slang and tries to absorb their culture while trying not to appear as a poseur crone. I wouldn't be surprised if she even sleeps with some of them --- strictly for research, of course. She needs to project herself as a cool older woman, or to be more vulgar about it, what they call a MILF. *Old dyke* doesn't mesh with that.

"Do you think he's dodging your calls because he knows he went too far this time and is ashamed to face you? You think if Rick called he'd answer?"

"Rick's the wrong guy. They never got along. Stone despises Wally, thinks he's reckless and irresponsible and he almost cold cocked him one day over something Wally said about him on the air. Wally knows that Rick is mi amigo. That's the only reason he's doing this, not to help Wally."

"When they paired you guys up, why didn't they put you and Rick together?"

"I'd be more comfortable working with Stone, but we agree on most everything. It would be easier on us both but the dynamic wouldn't play nearly as well."

"Well, Rick's set on becoming Jack Nicklaus in winter so that can't happen."

Bosco snuck up to Alison and gently placed his snout on her lap, as if sympathetic to her laments. She caressed his ears as we spoke. My dog had naturally gravitated to the human who most needed his attention. Or was it that he sensed the new lady in the house would lavish more attention on *him*?

"Like I said before, Alison, if he's just holed up somewhere, he'll get over it and come back, right? But you didn't fly all the way down here because you're having a little spat with your partner."

She looked out toward the Atlantic, which was a constant presence given its proximity and the tall windows facing the dunes. "No, I didn't. I came down here because I'm afraid. If Wally is gone, the show goes with him. There's no way they'd let me go on solo. Not with someone who comes off as an old dyke."

"That's not true and you don't know that for sure," I said.

"You may be right, but there's no one I can talk to about it. Rick was my best friend and confidant at the station and since he's been gone, I'm sort of at sea. I feel strange moaning about my problems at the station when he was the one who was fired. I'm alone there now and I don't know who I can trust."

SIX

If I need to clear my head, I do something physical. I run, play golf, cycle --- anything to get the blood pumping.

What do most of the women I've known do?

Shop.

Okay, or maybe go out to lunch with a friend.

So when a distraught Alison Middleton needed to blow off some steam, she took off for the two outlet malls just off the island in Bluffton. There's Ann Taylor, Ralph Lauren, Coach and a bunch of hip names that mean nothing to me but get female shoppers salivating like Bosco at the Dunkin' Donuts drive-thru window.

So when Allie suggested taking a break from her worries about Wally to cleanse her mental palate, I welcomed the time-out.

Rick rolled out of bed and stumbled into the kitchen a few minutes after Alison departed. I told him of her itinerary and he shrugged. "So King, are you going to work with her or make me look like an asshole for telling her to fly down here? Big markdowns on fall frocks will only go so far."

"I know that I'm supposed to be Superman and Batman all rolled into one, but what can I do? I keep telling her if her guy is room temperature, there's no hiding that fact from the world. The cops get involved; the show goes on without him."

"But I'm thinking we just need to do what she asks, for now at least. Allie is really a great lady and a good friend. If she were twenty years younger, I'd be over her like..."

"Stop right there, fool. She's your age. You need to get off this twenty years younger thing."

"Just emulating you, Riles. Jaime's your *September Song*, let me have mine. That hot country singer Charlene was your age and that didn't exactly work out, did it?"

In a nutshell, that was why my lectures to him always fall on deaf ears. He plays the Jaime card whenever I bring up his habit of tearing through younger women like Kobayashi with hotdogs on the Fourth.

"All right Rick, enough about me. I think I've been pretty patient about not pressing you on what happened the day they fired you. But if I'm going to get involved with this Wally Josephs deal, I need to know how everything went down."

"Why? What does my situation have to do with Wally?"

"Maybe nothing. Maybe everything. The thing is, I don't know. It sounds like I'll be going up to Jersey to investigate and it's pretty likely I'll have to stop at your old place of business. I need to know who I can count on, and who hates you and knows I'm your friend. I need to know who I can trust up there."

He half smiled, showing no teeth. In addition to helping me with the Wally Josephs story, letting it all out might be therapeutic to him.

He said, "If you insist. Here goes. It was a pretty shitty day, pardon the pun."

"Pun? I don't get it."

"When you hear my story, you will."

SEVEN

"I felt like a fool."

Since he was finally ready to tell me the story, I just let him ramble on with minimal interruptions.

"I flew up to New Jersey at my own expense, ostensibly to go to my own career funeral. You remember Donna Parker, my good friend, who goes back to the days when Ted McCarver owned the station? She said I should plead my case in person. She was hoping that her boss might reconsider and offer me some crumbs, like a weekend air shift or two."

"Who's this guy who made the call to let you go?" I asked.

"The program director/general manager. I mean this guy is so devoid of human emotion he's called 'The Tin Man' around the shop. But Donna kept at him and he agreed to give me the news in person and to listen to what I had to say."

"This Tin Man have a name?"

"Brian James Campbell or BJ as he insists we call him. He's just a soulless corporate executioner. His only mission is to make the bottom line look good from quarter to quarter. He's a sales guy, no idea of what makes good radio. Any idea that doesn't instantly increase revenue he has no use for."

Ted had told me that encroaching technology is a beast that radio has yet to tame and that many pundits believe that there is no long term future for over the air broadcasting. Ted McCarver had created WJOK thirty some years ago from almost nothing. But he foresaw the tough times ahead for the industry and had sold a few years ago, cashing in his millions.

Rick went on. "So BJ Campbell was the man Cirrus Partners brought in to chart the future for the station. He sees the road to survival as an accounting exercise: pare expenses to the bone and broaden cash flow. The first part was easy: fire anyone who was making more money than the union minimum. That was the part that directly affected me."

He finished his coffee and went to the breakfast bar to refill his cup. "The second stratagem involved accepting advertising for *Gentleman's Clubs*, (aka Houses of No Repute), get-rich-quick 'investments', and internet gambling schemes. Male enhancement products, sleazy bait-and-switch car dealers, and porn sites. No standards of taste or credibility. The limit for commercial minutes went from fourteen an hour to thirty. How do they expect listeners to put up with that?

"At first, I argued with Campbell about those things that hurt the station. He listened without comment, then blew me off. Never addressed any of my concerns. So after banging my head against the wall, I got the message. The company intended to bleed the place dry."

"So what happened at the meeting the day you flew up there?"

"I didn't expect they would let me to do a final show. They were afraid I might embarrass the company. When I got there, I saw Sean Falcon at my desk and that cinched it."

"I've heard Falcon on the air. He seems like a decent guy."

"Oh, he is. He's syndicated.

I said, "Sounds like a nice kid. At least there'll be a few extra bucks in it for him, I guess."

"Are you kidding? He doesn't make a dime more when they add stations to the list. In fact, I'm sure when his deal is up, he's in for a healthy pay cut. It's just the way it is."

"You know, I still don't get why you didn't take that job at WFAN when they came knocking a couple of years back. That's a great place to work and they've stayed true to the mission."

"Commuting to Manhattan is not my thing. I guess I'm just a Jersey shore guy at heart. You wouldn't believe what WJOK looks like now. Sterile. Plastic and foam cubicles in what used to be a classy work space. You wouldn't believe how many new faces there are. I was just in Jersey a month before, but it seemed like half the staff was different this time and the leftovers seem completely demoralized. Even my old friend Donna Parker looked beaten down."

"She's a sweet lady. I know how much you liked her. Too bad she's your age or else you'd have made a nice couple."

"She's been married for thirty years, dickhead. She told me Campbell sent her a text. He wouldn't be in that morning. He said to send me to Herb Keane in the business office. It was Campbell's birthday and he was out celebrating last night and wouldn't be in today until lunchtime."

"So you're saying you flew up there from Hilton Head for nothing."

"Yep. Donna said I should blame her. She felt awful about it. She thought that after being there for twenty five years, he might listen to me. He told her he would do that. But she obviously overestimated the bastard."

"What a prick."

"The place is sucking the life out of her. My nickname for her was Moneypenny. I always thought Donna Parker was the one essential employee of WJOK, like Moneypenny was for MI-6. She knows all the secrets including where the bodies are buried. It wasn't like her to have misjudged the situation, but that's how low they've sunk."

"So the guy didn't even have the guts to tell you to your face."

"I needed to pick up my Mustang and drive it south anyway, so it wasn't a total loss. And talking about song titles, before I walked out, I said to Donna that with shitheads like Campbell, the *Song Remains the Same*. And she came right back with '*Led Zeppelin, Houses of the Holy*, circa March 1973."

He was about to lose it, thinking about Donna Parker but the Marine couldn't let that show. "After signing the docs and getting my severance check, I stood on the street for a while, just looking back at that old Painted Lady where I'd spent so much of my life."

I said, "Rick Stone emotional. Who would have guessed?"

He sniffed. "There's a dog park a block away from the station where I used to have lunch sometimes after my show when the weather was nice. It's a nice little green space, with all kinds of dogs, many of them walking with smoking hot female owners."

"You're not going to tell me you found a bored housewife that could be seduced into offering a famous radio host some comfort?"

"It wouldn't be the first time. But a different nasty idea crossed my mind and I acted on that one."

"Uh, oh."

"Donna told me about what happened an hour later. BJ Campbell gets to the office. On his big, immaculate desk, there was a large yellow envelope. Inside, a cheesy card with puppy dogs on the front wishing him a happy birthday. Signed Rick Stone. Beneath the card, there was a neatly wrapped gift box."

"You didn't," I said.

"Oh, but I did. 'Donna', he screamed when he opened the present. 'Get your ass in here right away. God damn it.' Moneypenny was hiding, but he wanted her *now* and didn't care if she was in Europe."

Knowing Stone as I did, I had a good idea what was coming.

"See what I meant before by a pretty shitty day, Riles? When he opened the box, Campbell found his birthday gift from me --- a steaming helping of dog shit."

EIGHT

Alison Middleton returned a few minutes after Rick told me his story. I was still dismayed by the lack of humanity in people like Campbell. Although they may have no real love for their employees, they at least owe loyal workers a shred of dignity. I couldn't quite find soothing words for Stone, except to say that people like that usually get theirs in the end, but that had to be cold comfort. Hot dog poop, notwithstanding.

Allie was upset. At first, I suspected that Off Fifth had showcased the perfect dress but didn't carry it in her size. It soon became apparent that tragic though that may be, she had larger concerns.

"I heard from Wally," she said.

"That's great," Stone and I said, almost in unison. I said, alone, "So he's not dead. That's got to be a relief."

"You don't understand," she said. "It might be even worse."

Tempted as I might be to engage in a religious discussion with her on the afterlife and what could be worse than being on the wrong side of the grass, I merely said, "Explain."

"Wally called while I was at the outlet mall. He sounded as shaken as I've ever heard him. This from a guy who takes nothing seriously."

Stone said, "I can vouch for that. So what happened?"

"Monday night, after our little blow up, he hit one of his favorite watering holes, looking for what he calls a *tension easer*. That's what Joe Namath used to call the ladies he, er, patronized when he was nervous about a big game."

Joe Willie had sex the night before a game? Who knew?

She continued, "He didn't have to wait long. This gorgeous blond sidles up to him and they're headed back to her motel room. The place she was staying wasn't exactly the Ritz and he was getting a little apprehensive. Before they got it on, he needed to eliminate some of the beer. But while he was in the bathroom, he heard the door to the room open and a man's voice."

"*She came in through the bathroom window*," Stone sang. "Only he left through the window. Is that what happened? Buck naked?"

"Yeah, the oldest scam in the book," I said, ignoring Stone's Beatles' reference. "Hooker sees a mark, invites him to a motel, pimp shows up and rolls him."

Alison said. "He did squeeze through the window, but lucky for him, he was dressed and had his wallet with him. It's also lucky he's so skinny, or he never would have made it out."

"So all is well in the end," I said. "He got taught a valuable lesson about easy women, maybe one Stone should learn, and he made it out unscathed."

Alison shook her head. "I wish. The man chased him, a couple of shots were fired. Finally Wally got to a convenience store and the man either lost him or just gave up."

"So where is Wally now?" Stone asked.

She said, "He wouldn't say. King, you said you know this scam. But if this was just someone trying to

27

roust him for a few bucks or his credit cards, why would the guy run after him and try to shoot him?"

I said, "Desperate measures sometimes don't make sense. If this pimp was frustrated by the mark's escape and wanted a payout no matter what, he might have chased Wally. These are usually low rent scumbags, not Mensa grads. The beauty of the scam usually relies on the victim not coming forward, too embarrassed to admit that he went with a prostitute."

Stone said, "So what does Wally want to do now? He's got a legitimate story to tell the police. It wouldn't hurt him if his fans knew he went to a bar and picked up a blond. He could say he didn't know she was a hooker. Who knows, he's so stupid, maybe he didn't know. It's not like he's married or running for office."

"He won't go to the police. And he won't show up for work. He's afraid they'll try to kill him again."

I pressed my case. "Why not tell the cops? Even if I do agree to help, it couldn't hurt to have the police on his side."

There had to be another reason. This reluctance made no sense, given her media savvy sensibilities.

She said, "Because Wally saw the face of the man who chased him. White guy in his thirties. He'd seen him before. He's a cop."

NINE

Stone, always one to seek humor in times of stress, thrust his arms upwards, splayed his fingers into a warped peace sign, hunched his shoulders and proclaimed in the deepest tone he could muster, "Now my fellow Americans, we need to compile an enemies list."

The hackneyed Nixon impersonation wasn't entirely wasted on his audience; it actually made sense. It was Stone's sophomoric way of introducing the age-old question --- who had the most to gain by eliminating Wally Josephs?

"Let's get the obvious out of the way so we don't waste time with it," Alison said. "Me."

Even Stone was taken aback. "You? You're his champion. You keep telling me that there was good in this jerk that I couldn't see."

She said, "Keep in mind a few things. I make a lot less than Wally does. Sexism, plain and simple and I've let the bosses know it. His contract is for six more years, mine is renewable at their option every thirteen weeks. And who gets all the ink and recognition for the show's success? Wally. I'm the straight man. They think anyone could play that role, I was just lucky it fell to me. Or did it, Rick?"

Stone blinked a few times, while trying to swallow the diatribe whole. "What are you talking about?"

"They wanted you first, didn't they? You thought I didn't know about that, did you?"

Rick is never at a loss for words --- normally off the air, he says whatever is on his mind, and deals with the consequences later. He'll readily admit his errors when proven wrong, but his instincts are usually correct. I could see him carefully weighing his next words, trying to walk the tightrope between dissembling and hurting Alison. Or was he just considering trotting out Tricky Dick again?

"Allie, I won't lie. They *did* approach me. I said that there was no way in hell I'd ever work with that asshole. I'd wind up killing him."

I watched with amusement as it played out with these two radio veterans.

Alison said, "Maybe you're right, but that's one reason they fired you. The new owners weren't very understanding when they heard you didn't go along with the plan. They branded you as *not a team player.* You were a relic of the McCarver era, and as soon as your old deal under Ted expired, you were toast. Maybe I should have told you that as soon as I knew about it. Campbell told me, maybe thinking it would get back to you and you'd quit or look for another job, knowing you were a lame duck."

I finally joined the conversation, trying to nudge it into a more productive direction rather than complaining about the state of their industry, however valid their issues were. "Alison, did you hire someone to kill Wally?"

How's that for a subtle nudge?

"No. I know how important he is to the show. My career was just toddling along before they hooked me up with him. And even though our pay isn't equal, I'm still making twice as much as I ever did, all the public appearances included. I need him," she said.

"I'm no expert when it comes to radio," I said, prefacing my remarks. "But in New York when Mad Dog left WFAN, a lot of so-called experts thought the show wouldn't survive with just Francesa. They were looking for a co-host but in the meantime, it reached even greater heights as a solo act. I guess what I'm saying is, don't look at Wally's survival as essential to your career. You've got the goods on your own, lady."

She said, "If I hadn't met Jaime once, I'd say you were just trying to get into my pants, King."

"We're way off topic here," I said, trying to un-hear that. "Let's get off this treadmill and get down to who really profits with Wally Josephs out of the way. Let's assume this supposed cop is a hired gun. Unless you can enlighten me otherwise."

She considered that for a second. "Well, not discounting someone with a personal grudge, like maybe Wally slept with the man's wife. I can't see the police in general having a gripe with him. He hates Springsteen because of that song about the guy the cops shot when he was reaching for his wallet. That's not a very smart position to take in Jersey because Bruce is a god there, not to mention that Springsteen has explained many times that the song is not anti-cop. Whenever law and order stuff comes up, Wally always supports the authorities. We had an argument on the air about *Black Lives Matter*. He said it stirred up trouble with cops and that black kids should be more respectful to the police."

Stone said, "But Wally does mess with married women, I bet. That could be motive for some jealous husband to go after him."

"Words you should heed yourself, Ricky-boy," I said. "Wally will need to give us names of these women, if they exist. Let's go global here. What about powerful enemies? People rich or corrupt enough to pay an assassin. Competing stations?"

"That's a non-starter, Riles. You were right before when you said you knew nothing about radio," Stone said. "WJOK is a virtual monopoly when it comes to sports talk in Jersey. No other station in the state has the signal to compete. The New York and Philly outlets are doing fine; they may see us as a minor annoyance, but not to the extent that they'd kill Wally. If anything, they'd try to hire him away."

"All right then. What about at the station? Anyone there jealous of Wally or other than Stone, have a personal beef?" I asked.

Alison said, "The morning show guys aren't fans of his but neither of them would want his job. They're successful on their own and when they rip Wally on the air, it's mainly to cross-promote, to get him to talk about them. The rest of the place is a few old guys happy to have a job, not anyone gunning for afternoon drive. Really, if I had to make a case for anyone in radio, it would be Rick. He was just fired, hated Wally. Was a Marine. Through you Riley, he probably has contacts with the Jersey underworld. Rick's the man, if you're looking internally."

TEN

"Okay, you're right, Allie. I paid to have him killed so I could come back to WJOK and work as your partner. Campbell will forget about me leaving that pile of dog shit on his desk after he fired me. He's that kind of forgiving guy," Rick said.

Alison burst out laughing.

"Okay children, enough," I said. It always amazes me how people in show-biz can act goofy in the middle of discussing serious matters. Kind of like cops cracking jokes at gruesome crime scenes --- a defense mechanism. "For argument's sake, let's rule Stone out for the moment. Who else would want Wally gone?"

"If you read my twitter replies, about half our listeners. Not to denigrate our audience, but there are some real psychos out there. Could be someone Wally dissed or hung up on," Alison said.

Stone said, "That narrows it down to a few thousand. Really, I don't know what a pro hit goes for in Jersey these days, but let's say ten grand. Some offended caller is going to shell out that much risk getting nailed for it because some jerk on the radio blew him off?"

Alison and Stone rose simultaneously, almost as if on cue, and started pacing the room, deep in thought. This game was being played on their turf, since I hadn't lived in Jersey for several years. I sat on the sofa, rubbing Bosco.

Stone had a thought. "Allie, what about that media critic in the Toms River Trib, that guy Rasputin who's always ripping Wally? Is that just part of the game or is it real?"

I expected Alison to shrug off the idea Stone had advanced, but she gave it some credence. "No, they really do hate each other. They got into a shoving match one day at a charity golf event."

"No shit? I never knew that," Stone said.

"You weren't around when it happened. You were probably sneaking in a few extra holes. Both bosses, Campbell and the publisher of that rag, convinced them to hush it up. Lucky it happened in the men's room and there were no witnesses, other than Campbell."

"Who exactly is this guy?" I asked.

"He goes by the pen name of Rasputin but his real name is Chuckie Schwartz. Young punk, thinks he knows everything about today's media. Long black hair, goatee, looks a little like the Russian monk. He rips Wally in just about every column, whether he deserves it or not. If Wally flubs a line or gets a prediction wrong, Schwartz is all over it. He never really wrote about you much, did he Rick?" she said.

"For that, I'm eternally grateful. Talk about a poison pen. So you're saying this wasn't just part of the act. Are you sure it's not just for show, Allie?"

"If it is, Wally has me fooled. You should hear the things he says about Chuckie with the mic off. Makes what he says on air sound like NPR. In fact, if it was Schwartz who was threatened, my number one suspect would be Wally. No, they really do hate each other."

"Interesting," I said. "But even so, they're probably smart enough to know they need each other in a weird way. Like Rick says, I bet this Rasputin's readership benefits from Wally's digs, and vice versa. It's worth looking into, though. Anybody else come to mind?"

Stone said, "Only one I can think of would be the ex-starting Giants quarterback, John Henry Brown. Wally did a number on him when they drafted him and hasn't let up since. When he got hurt and the backup took over and won a few games, Wally kept hammering and said the coach would be an idiot to reinstate Brown."

"You think that had an effect on the coach's decision to keep him on the bench?"

Stone and Alison looked at each other, like kids in a classroom who both have an answer but weren't confident enough in their conviction to go first.

Stone took the lead. "I will say this. Coach Mackris is on the hot seat. Wally has enough sway with the fans to make them hate the kid. Coach would be sticking his neck out if he defied public opinion and brought back Brown. Unless Newman gets hurt or stinks up the field for three games in a row, I believe it's his job and they'll cut Brown at the end of the year. No big guarantees on his contract so I'd say he'll lose millions. I don't know if another team will give him a chance, not as a starter anyway. Motive for murder? People have killed for a lot less."

ELEVEN

Alison was perched on one of the stools in the breakfast area. The house that Ted McCarver left Stone and me has a wide open floor plan, with floor to ceiling windows facing the Atlantic. There are incredible views from every room.

All of our speculation about potential killers amounted to lobbing grenades in the dark, hoping to get lucky. Who had motivation to eliminate Wally Josephs? A jilted lover or husband of same, a newspaper columnist, a pro quarterback, or just a random crazy with some imagined slight.

A more promising approach would entail getting up off our collective asses and tracking down the assassin. For that, we needed to enlist the assistance of the victim, Mr. Walter Josephs himself.

To that end, I asked Allie, "Can you get in touch with Wally? We need to talk to him."

"Does that mean you're in?"

"Depends on what he says. How do you know he didn't just go on a long bender and made up this story?"

"Of course I thought of that, King," she said. "I know he's a multiple addict. Drink, drugs, gambling and women --- that I know of. He sounded upset but sober when he called me this morning and he made me swear not to tell anyone else about what happened."

Stone said, "I wouldn't put it past that weasel to cook this up as a publicity stunt. Your last ratings book was down. The show could use a jolt."

Allie turned red. "I know you don't like him, Rick, but how can it be a stunt if he doesn't want anyone to know about it? And if you guys won't do this for him, do it for me."

I've always seen Alison Middleton as a strong woman. She battled her cancer alone, never asking for sympathy or advantage because of her illness or her gender. Her face bore no ravages of her struggles; she remained an attractive lady. Until today, I'd never seen her less than completely put-together --- made-up and dressed to the nines. But now she appeared as her unvarnished self and I like this version better. She isn't a tall woman, but her outsize persona projects a stature beyond her physique.

I could clearly see her vulnerabilities now. She seemed lonely, conditioned by a lifetime of playing by rules set by an old boys' club, most of whom were not her equal. The fact that she had acceded to their strictures was not weakness, but superior discipline at disguising her assertiveness when it imperiled her greater goals.

There was a bit of Jackie Robinson about her. She had once told us about an experience as rookie beat writer, when three large football players cornered her in a locker room, waving their privates at her, accusing her of voyeurism. There was a semi-organized boycott involving a baseball team which refused to speak to any media person until she was banished from their ranks. Rather than appeal to team authorities or her boss, she confronted the aggressors head-on and won them over with a superior knowledge of their sport and her disdain at their feeble attempts to intimidate her.

Despite her courage, she never achieved the status of many of her less talented male counterparts until the *Allie and Wally* show. Deemed too old and not sexy enough for television, she worked twice as hard to merely remain on the career treadmill. But now that she was finally reaping the rewards of all her hard work, her crazy co-host put it all in danger due to his unreliable character.

I couldn't turn my back on her now. "We need to talk to Wally."

"I promised him I wouldn't get anyone else involved. I tried to tell him that he could trust you, but he knew you were friends with Stone and wouldn't buy it. I can't go back on that."

"Has he ever lied to you, Alison?"

"Many times."

"Then this will be the first time you lie to him. Get him on the phone."

TWELVE

Stone made himself scarce for a while, ostensibly to take a shower and groom up for the day. In a rare show of discretion, he left the room so that Alison could speak to Wally privately, without concern for Stone's negativity.

"Wally. It's me."

"Why are you on speaker, Alison? Is someone else there? I told you not to trust anybody. I'm hanging up now."

"Wait," she said, too late. The line was dead. She redialed, this time off speaker, but his voice was so cutting that I could make out his words.

"I told you, Allie. You can't trust anyone."

"I know what you said, Wally. But you need help. I told you before that I've found a man who can help you."

"Not that Riley King schmuck. He's tight with Stone and for all I know, that putz is the one who wants me dead. Forget it."

I generally don't engage clients who refer to me as *that Riley King schmuck*, but I've grown more tolerant as I've aged. I briefly considered seizing the phone and instructing Wally on the facts of his life as they stand right now, but as I said, I've become more tolerant.

"Listen to me, Wally," Alison said. "King knows Ocean County inside and out. He knows cops there. He knows a little about radio because of his friendship with Stone. I flew all the way down to the Carolinas to meet with him and he agreed to help. Pro Bono. That means for free."

This was news to me. Alison had effectively shut down my ability to protest, since a discussion about compensation at this moment would upset Wally. But then she gestured toward herself while rubbing her fingers together, which meant that she'd pay out of her own pocket. I wouldn't take her money but the offer was appreciated.

"Why would he do that? Maybe he's working with Stone and using you to find me. Ever think of that, Allie?"

I decided it was time to intervene. Alison clicked her phone onto speaker and I said, "Listen Josephs, it's because of Stone that I'm doing this. Alison asked for his help and he recruited me. He has no stake in this other than to help a colleague."

"Frigging asshole hates me."

"You two will never be best men at each others' wedding, that's true. But as much as Stone might not like your style, he doesn't want to see a coworker in danger. And besides, he's tight with Allie. If anything happened to you, it would hurt her professionally, not to mention this misplaced affection she seems to have for you."

That stopped him in his tracks. "Give me a few minutes to think about this. I'll call you back."

"You'll never know how grateful I am for the opportunity to help save your life," I said, hoping the sarcasm was as obvious as I intended, but he had already hung up.

A half hour later he did call back and seemed more receptive. I said, "Look, I need you to be honest with me about what happened the other night. If you want Alison to leave the room, it's okay."

"No, I told her the truth about everything that happened." He recapped the story as she had related it, including the pertinent details.

"And you don't want to go to the police because you think they're involved? How sure are you of that?"

"I recognized the motherfucker who chased me. I seen him at that bar before and he was usually with a bunch of guys who I know are cops. He was definitely one of them."

"That's it? Nothing other than he hung out with some cops?"

"Birds of a freaking feather, man."

This was a good lead, whether the man was actually on the force or not. If Wally had seen him before at the bar, others had as well, and some of them must know who he was. But it also meant that rather than some conspiracy to kill Wally Josephs, this might just be a case of the shooter observing that Wally was a horndog and therefore vulnerable to getting rolled by a pretty face.

I said, "You want to tell me where you are now?"

"No way. They might be listening. Those cops can hear every call you make if they want to. I'm not going to tip them off."

Just because you're paranoid, it doesn't mean that they're not out to get you. There was truth in the old cliché. The cops use a device manufactured by Harris Electronics called Sting Ray to monitor and locate cell phone users. The courts are still in the process of deciding whether its use is constitutional and if a warrant is always necessary. They are keeping it quiet since it is an effective weapon against terrorism and if too many details are made public, the bad guys might generate technology to circumvent it.

"What about your radio show? Alison can't keep covering for you. Aren't you worried about losing your job?"

"They'd never fire me. They huff and puff all the time, but I have a rock solid guaranteed deal. I'm golden there."

Alison jumped in, "Wally, be smart for once in your life. You saw how they got rid of Stone and he'd been there for over twenty years."

Stone came down the stairs, freshly showered, his hair still wet. He made a grand gesture of holding his nose while Wally spoke. He sat on the sofa next to Alison and massaged her shoulder affectionately. Bosco looked jealous.

Wally said, "How the fuck you expect me to show up at the studio? That dude could be waiting in the parking lot. And don't try to sell me on some sort of bodyguard. A hotshot sniper could pick me off, no matter how careful I am."

"Are you sure he fired shots? That it wasn't just a car backfire or kids playing with fireworks?"

"I know what a gun sounds like. But no, I can't say for sure he was the one who fired, but he was chasing me and who else could have done it?"

Alison and I looked at each other without expression. Stone raised his index finger, like a reluctant student who wanted to be called on for an answer no one else had thought of. I shrugged and gave him a nod to speak up.

"Wally, it's Rick Stone. I know we've had our differences, but I want to help. You know that you don't need to be physically present at the station to do your show. I've been doing mine on the road more than half the time the last few years."

"Yeah Stone, I know. Kept me from having to stomach seeing your ugly face during changeovers."

"Ahhhh, Wally," Stone said, looking away and mouthing the word 'scumbag'. "What if we could find a safe place for you to do the show away from the studio?"

Wheels were turning on the other end of the line. Stone had stumbled on another good idea --- twice today, a new record for him. There were hazards with that scenario. If Wally came to Hilton Head, we'd have to fortify, meaning I wouldn't want Jaime or even Bosco to be around for the duration. If I journeyed to Jersey to find the hit man, Stone would have to stand guard.

"I'm listening, Stone. But this better not be a trap."

"You watch too many movies, Walter. You can either trust King and me or not, in which case, you're on your own, pal. No skin off me either way."

THIRTEEN

"Even if I trust you dickwads, how do I get to this magic place?" Wally said.

I said, "You have such an endearing way of asking for help. Find a safe landline. A pay phone would be great if any still exist. Someplace off the beaten track. Then call us back."

I cut the connection.

Alison needed some background. "Why did you tell him to call back from another phone?"

"Your cell has a 201 area code, and if they were listening just now they would be trying to track where he is, not where you are."

She still didn't follow. "If Wally's right and his phone is being monitored, how do we get him here?"

I'd been in a similar situation a few years back. The feds were looking for me, boasting exponentially more resources than any renegade cop could hope to acquire. I managed to get away with it for a few days, after which they gave up the chase to focus on the genuine culprit. Their technology has advanced since that time, but not so far that the same principles wouldn't apply.

I explained. "First thing is, he needs to get rid of that phone. And he has to get hold of a different car."

"He drives a Porsche, King. I can't see him dumping that," Alison said.

Stone was familiar with my little sabbatical and the techniques I employed. "He doesn't need to get rid of the Porsche. He just can't drive it here."

"Can't he fly or take a train?"

I said, "Flying is out. Any LEO worth his salt will be checking flights. And even if we could whip up a new identity with false papers at a moment's notice, if he gets caught, he goes on the terrorist watch list. They'd be less likely to track trains and buses, but it can be done so that's out. I know a guy who runs a used car lot on Route Nine in Forked River. I'm sure he'd be willing to store the Porsche and provide your friend with a reliable old beater. One without a chip."

Stone was on the same page. "The big thing is cash, right Riles? He can't use credit cards. No E-Z pass on the toll roads. A burner phone, or actually a few of them."

"Absolutely. It's probably a twelve hour drive here from southern Jersey. He can stop somewhere near Richmond on I-95 if he needs a break." Alison was as perplexed by our spy craft as I get when she and Rick talk about a baseball player's WAR.

Rick added a broadcast wrinkle I hadn't thought of. "Allie, I think you need to go back to Toms River tomorrow to anchor your Monday show from the station. That would mean that all the live reads and continuity would be in your hands. When I worked out of King's pad in Charlotte, I got the paperwork emailed and the caller list instant-messaged to me but that would be traceable. You'll have to run interference with Campbell. I'm sure he'll be curious as to why Josephs can't be in the studio with you. Maybe you should tell Campbell about the attempt on his life."

Alison shook her head. "No way. Campbell can't keep a secret. Like you guys were thinking before, he'll see this as a chance to get cheap ink. I can guarantee you it'd be in Rasputin's column the next day."

Stone said, "Then we've got until Monday to come up with a cover story. In any case, I can set up the equipment from here so at least they can't fire him for not showing up. Although, Wally seems to think he's bulletproof on that score anyway. Is he?"

She hesitated. "I'm not sure. You know when Imus left WFAN with that Rutgers scandal, a lot of people thought it would be a big blow to the station. But the new team they hired is doing better than the old guy did. So no one is irreplaceable. If Wally's out, they'll be looking to replace the whole show, including me."

As altruistic as her desire to save Wally might be, it also was rooted in self preservation. If he was eliminated, she likely would hold down the fort for a few weeks until they put together a new team or found a hot solo act. It was unlikely she'd survive the cut when her thirteen weeks expired.

Her cell buzzed. Wally had found a safe landline. I explained the drill to him and he went along without comment, raising only one objection.

"What happens with the Porsche? If they can track it as you say, aren't you putting your car dealer BFF in a tight spot? They trace the car to his lot and they pound it out of him, like where he got the car. Then they track me from there."

"My guy can disable the tracking chip. And if somehow they find it anyway, although I can't imagine how, he says that you sold him the car for cash and grabbed an UBER from his lot."

"And that'll hold up under torture?"

"It won't come to that. Look Wally, I need you to understand something. These are extreme measures we're taking, belt and suspenders. I very much doubt some local cop has the wherewithal or expertise to find you."

"Easy for you to say, fuckface. It ain't your life on the line."

At that moment, I felt like telling him to shove it and fend for himself. I was exposing those around me to danger if someone was skilled and relentless in their pursuit of Walter Josephs.

But I restrained the impulse and said, "Just do what I told you. Make sure you pay cash for the tolls and it'd be a good idea to wear a hoodie and sunglasses when you go through the booths, in case they have to ability to check the cameras. Pay cash for everything. Don't engage anyone on the way down. Gas up off the main highway, preferably at a small, off-brand place. Ditch your phone and only call me on the burner. See you tomorrow."

FOURTEEN

Stone and Alison took Bosco out for a long walk on the beach. With our strategy locked in place, a relaxing excursion on a warm sunny day in early autumn would be therapeutic, especially for Allie. Hilton Head is very dog friendly; they allow pets on the beach but the local ordinances do levy fines if you fail to clean up afterwards, so I handed Stone the green plastic glove-bags they provide for pet refuse, something that Bosco offloaded in abundance. Maybe he would ask Allie to leave some more of it on Campbell's desktop as an additional parting gift, although the airline might object.

I had some calls to make: The first was to my car dealer friend in Forked River, Paul Esposito. After assuring him that nothing I needed from him was illegal, I asked to him store Wally's Porsche for him and disconnect the battery, if that's what it took to make it untraceable. Next, would he loan Josephs a reliable but nondescript vehicle that didn't have a tracking chip? Treat it like a short term lease and charge the going rate. Paul actually thanked me for the business. I told him that the Audi A5 he'd sold me years before was a great car but it was getting outdated and I was looking for a newer ride. He said he'd keep his eye out for a similar model.

My next call was to Jaime, who had texted me that her business on the coast would probably be finished by Sunday. After some verbal smooching, I got down to business.

"It might be a good idea for you to fly back to New Jersey for a while, Jaime. Got some problems here." I explained the Wally situation and the fact that he was going to be at the house for a bit.

"So you think that whoever tried to kill him will track him all the way down to Hilton Head and try again and you don't want me in the way? That about it?" she asked.

"Not that you'd be in the way. I don't want to put you in any danger, that's all."

"Babe, I know a lot of what you do is dangerous. Aren't you forgetting how we met?"

Who could forget? Jaime's mother, an attractive woman named Paige White, was the founder of a successful literary agency. She hired me to locate an author who had submitted a manuscript that showed great promise. It turned out that the writer, frustrated by her many rejections of his previous work, murdered her. I took it upon myself to find the killer, and subsequently became involved with her daughter Jaime during the search. Along with Stone, we tracked the man to a remote cabin in Vermont, where the madman cornered Jaime and me and was about to add us to his list of victims when Rick saved the day, taking a near fatal bullet in the process.

"Yeah, we both almost bought the farm. I never want you to have to go through that again."

"I'm sorry but that doesn't work for me. I fell for a private investigator. I was fully aware that sometimes that puts you in dangerous situations. I'm not going to run and hide every time you're in a jam, just like you didn't walk away when my mom was killed. You stood by me then, even though you didn't have to."

"Jaime, this may be a whole lot of nothing. This threat could be a figment of Josephs' imagination. But I can't risk you getting hurt if it's not. This just came up out of the blue. It'll probably never happen again where we have to worry about some killer stalking me or a client."

"You willing to put that in writing? Come on Riles, it's what you do. I don't want you to stop working on the side of the angels because of me. And I can't tuck tail and retreat hundreds of miles away whenever the heat is on. We're apart enough already with my business. I'm not going to let yours push us apart even more."

"I couldn't live with myself if anything happened to you."

"I'm a big girl and I know my way around guns, in case you forgot."

She had won some target shooting competitions in college but taking careful aim and shredding a piece of paper is a whole lot different than center-massing a human with bad intent.

I conceded the point, rather than prolong a battle I was destined to lose. "Okay, here's what I'm thinking. Once we get Josephs set up here, I'll fly up north to see if I can get a lead on this hit man. Given that he was a regular at Wally's bar and that he hung out with cops, it shouldn't take long. Why don't you head back to New Jersey and we can meet at Newark Airport and fly back down here together, probably no later than Wednesday."

"That'll work. What about Charlotte? When do you think we can go back there? Most of my stuff is in that house."

I said, "If we fly into the Hilton Head airport instead of Savannah, all the flights change in Charlotte anyway. Can you look into it, so we have time to stop at the house and pick up some things during the layover?"

"Sure, I'll get right on it. I won't book anything until we know more."

"Sounds like a plan. Love you."

"You too. Let's talk tonight. I'll head east tomorrow."

Just because Jaime had talked me into letting her stay on the island, it didn't mean I was going to let it lie there. If someone was going to come after Wally, I'd need reinforcements. With that in mind, I made my next call.

I dialed Moses Ginn.

FIFTEEN

"**Y**ou been under the radar screen lately, King. What up?"

"Sounds like you've been hanging with some younger brothers these days, Moses."

Moses Ginn was hired muscle. I had used him a couple of times as a stand-in when someone tried to hire me as a bodyguard, a gig I have no interest in. His six foot four, wiry presence was certainly intimidating. He was close to seventy now, but could pass for a man two decades younger. A black man who had grown up in North Carolina at a time when members of his race were considered sub-human, his experiences as a young man had toughened him up enough to withstand just about anything life threw at him thereafter. I didn't know him well, or any of his history, other than he said he had served in Special Forces during the Vietnam era. I don't remember who recommended him in the first place, but he had always come through the couple of times I needed him.

He said, "Well, you know, even though you a few years short of me, you get a little age on you, you tend to have more time at liberty."

"Funny you should mention that. I have a job for you, if you're interested." I told Ginn about Wally and how I needed someone to stay at my place and protect him, in case the shooter tracked him down South.

When I was finished, he said, "You see this as a real job King, or just a onetime only deal?"

Since moving to Charlotte, my operation has strictly been a one man show. I hire independent subcontractors as needed. My stable consists mostly of computer geeks, my BS squad, although recently I have come to depend on only one of them. He's a man or woman, I can't really say which, who stands out from the rest in terms of efficiency and discretion. Jaime helps me on occasion with advertising on social media and such, but other than that, I am self contained and have never considered taking on regular employees. I went that route in New Jersey, leading a full-fledged agency, and it almost bankrupted me.

I said, "I don't know, Moses. Lately, the work coming to me is helping out friends or friends of friends. What are you asking? Are you interested in teaming up?"

"Thought had crossed my mind. Don't need much money. But what you do ain't so far away from what I be doing my whole life. I mean extracurricular like."

"You do know that this business relies less on muscle than smarts these days. And by smarts, I'm saying a lot of that is digital."

"You think my skills limited to just being some big old menacing nigger?"

"That's not what I said. Look, I can't hire you as a steady employee. The work is too sporadic and a lot of it doesn't pay much, if at all."

"So how 'bout this? You get a good paying case, you slide a little my way, as you see fit. I be there to help when you need it, out of your face otherwise."

Ginn's proposal really didn't redefine anything we hadn't been already doing. I am no slouch in the muscle department, but having a man like Ginn on call when I need reinforcements is attractive. His intimidating physicality has been useful in the past. Stone can kick some ass too, but he is bent on being a pro golfer which is a much safer profession than what Ginn and I were used to. People don't die on the Senior Tour, unless they stroll up the fairway too aggressively for their aging tickers.

But why argue the finer points? Ginn wasn't asking for a retainer or a signed contract, just offering his services on an ad hoc basis as he always had. I asked if he could come to Hilton Head for a couple of days to watch over Josephs. He readily agreed and said he could be down by Tuesday after he cleared up some errands in Charlotte.

"And King, this one's on the house," he said. "Just so's to make sure you be comfortable working with an old grizzled vet like me."

"You know Moses, this could be the beginning of a beautiful friendship."

SIXTEEN

Allie, Stone and I dined that evening at a place called Pomodori, one of the many fine restaurants on New Orleans Road. It was a small bistro carved out of a storefront in a strip mall, and it was the closest thing to authentic Italian food outside of Tuscany. Dark stained concrete floors, a rustic barn wood bar topped with marble, low copper ceilings and seating for fewer than fifty patrons gave it a cozy and welcoming ambiance. The pervasive aroma wafting from the kitchen, rich with garlic and olive oil, made me miss New Jersey. I'd be there soon enough.

We ate heartily, downing two bottles of pinot while talking sports, politics and music --- anything but Wally and his troubles. The next morning, Alison took an early flight out of Savannah. She thanked us for our help, including a subtle scold aimed at Rick to treat Wally kindly during his stay. She said she'd call when she got settled in back home.

After she left, Rick said, "You know, you could have flown back up with Alison, Riles. I'm capable of holding down the fort here."

"I know. I just want to be here when Wally arrives so I can talk to him in person. I need a more detailed description of this alleged gunman and the girl, amongst other things. Although the more I think about it, the more it sounds like a pimp roll gone sideways."

Rick said, "You might be right, but if this was a typical scam, wouldn't they have scouted the place out? I mean, if there was a bathroom window big enough to serve as an escape hatch? Why let him use the bathroom in the first place?"

"Not to sound too gruesome, but if it was a sanction, it makes it easier to clean up the gore. Cut up the body in the tub and haul out the parts in plastic garbage bags. That's how the pros do it. But see, that's where Wally was really stupid and something you should think about, too. I know that motel. It's a notorious hot sheets joint. Cheap, rooms by the hour, none too sanitary or romantic. In short, not the kind of place a businesswoman would be staying. My guess is that he took her for a hooker all along but figured she might throw him a freebie since he was a celeb."

Stone said, "He was so consumed by his lust that even when he smelled a rat, he still went along. I bet the girl thought this was just another scam and she didn't know upfront that murder was," he sang, *"part of the plan."*

Another one of his song references at the wrong time. "I suppose, Dan Fogelberg. Let that be a lesson for you, pal."

"Just so you know, *pal*, I never travel in those circles. All my conquests are clean cut girl-next-door types, preferably co-eds. No sleazy motels for me."

"You're class all the way, Ricky." I'm sure he missed the sarcasm. "I'll probably fly up first thing tomorrow. Too bad McCarver's not around with his plane. He'd have me in Toms River from the airport here on the island in no time. I guess they don't let monks fly around in private jets up at New Skete."

We were sitting on stools at the huge granite breakfast island that dominated the kitchen. The travertine floor gleamed and the European cabinets blended seamlessly into the tumbled marble backsplash. McCarver had outfitted the place with top grade appliances --- a six burner Wolf range, the requisite coffin sized Sub-Zero fridge with accompanying freezer and a Thermador double oven. The appliance Stone and I used most was the microwave.

The spare contemporary style was a bit sterile for my taste, but when someone bequeaths you a half share of a three million dollar oceanfront manse, it's considered bad form to nitpick about the decor.

Stone said, "Uh, there's something I meant to tell you but in all the clamor about Wally and everything, it slipped my mind. The other day there was no hot water in my bathroom. I know that it's all electric and Ted sometimes turned the water heater off when he was gone for extended periods. So I called New Skete to ask him where the shut-off was and as an excuse just to say hello. They told me that Ted was no longer there and hadn't been for six months."

"Wow. It doesn't surprise me that he didn't stay there with the monks and their dogs. I knew he'd be bored. The guy was into his creature comforts and as upset as he was about his fiancée getting killed, I didn't think he'd be beating his chest forever about it. Even though he gave me a crazy generous fee and left the two of us this house, he did make sure there was a pretty sizable chunk of change available to him in trust. He gave himself an option if he changed his mind, which it seems he has. I *am* a little surprised he didn't tell us. You think he wants the house back?"

"If he does, he's welcome to it. I love this place but it's way over the top for my needs. What about you?"

I said, "I'd be on board with that, if that's what he wants. He gave it to us furnished so it's his stuff anyway.

But if he wants it back, wouldn't he have asked us before this? You say he's been out of the monastery for half a year? Maybe the place has too many memories."

"I guess. Even though Stevie was killed in Toms River, they did spend a lot of time here. Anyway, let's add that to our to-do list. Finding Ted. I just want to make sure he's all right. Mentally and physically. I owe him a lot," Rick said.

As did I. But a terrific woman named Stevie Perry had been killed in the process. If I could trade all my good fortune for her life, I would. In a heartbeat.

SEVENTEEN

I had met Wally Josephs a couple of times in the past while hanging with Rick. The last time happened was several years ago and I barely recalled what he looks like. We have never had a real conversation, nor did I yearn for one, based on Stone's relentless negativity about the man whenever his name comes up.

My friend is not a hater by nature. I can't even get him to bad mouth the woman that caused him so much pain, football sideline reporter extraordinaire Lisa Tillman. If she turns up on some sporting event we're watching, I usually make a catty remark, which he counters with a comment about how good she still looks and how it was partially his fault.

If I didn't know him well, his hatred of Josephs might be attributed to professional jealousy. Josephs' stock at WJOK had soared past Rick's over the years, and his salary had advanced in direct proportion.

I was trying to keep an open mind about Wally since he'd be living in my house for an indeterminate length of time. On a hunch, I called my cop friend in Charlotte, Peter Shabielski and after we had chatted a while, I brought up my current case. Pete had been on the job in central Jersey for almost twenty years before moving south so I took a shot.

"Hey Peter, before you go," I said. "Rick and I fell into a case which may turn out to be nothing." I gave him the Cliff Notes version of the Wally Josephs tale, with an appeal not to share any of the story. I trust Peter completely on that score.

As I finished, he burst out laughing. "That fuckup? I go way back with him. Do you know what his real name is? It's Hamilton Fish. No wonder he changed it. We picked him up a bunch of times in Bayville, like twenty years ago. Parents always managed to bail the little shit out. DUIs mostly. The big one was sex with a minor --- he was 17, she was 15. Lucky he didn't get put on the sex offender list for that little kerfuffle. His folks were tight with my boss. Gave big bucks to the police benevolent association. Somebody wants to shoot that little prick? All I can say is, it'd serve him right."

I thanked my friend for the background and hung up. It was lunchtime and there was nothing much to eat in the house. The NFL was about to monopolize the next twelve hours of our time, and we'd require some kind of sustenance. A call to New York Pizza was in order.

Even after talking with Pete, I felt ill prepared for Josephs' visit. I hoped Stone could put his hostility aside and provide something more insightful. "Rick, before he gets here, tell me more about Wally. Why do you hate him so much?"

"Hate's a strong word. I've done radio for a long time. I always considered it to be a privilege to talk to hundreds of thousands of people. I owed the listeners the best part of me. You know me, I use pretty explicit fucking language when I'm off the air, but when I'm working, I rarely even say *damn*."

"Bottom line is, you're old school."

"Campbell said that I was the building they razed to build the old school. That line was too clever to be his; he must have stolen it from somebody. But he was wrong."

"I figured you just spouted your random thoughts on sports for three hours a day. I didn't really catch any deep philosophy behind it."

He smiled. "That's a compliment. One of the keys is never letting the structure show. There's nothing more boring than a lecture. But if you sketch out a situation and let the listeners' imagination do the rest, you've created a great interactive environment."

What Rick had done for a living up until a month ago seemed so simple. I figured with a little practice, I could do it. But I had thought that about golf as well and Stone dusts me every time we play together. On the surface, Rick Stone is a middle aged Lothario, in feckless pursuit of wine, women and song. I'd never really seen this thoughtful side of him when it came to his job.

I said, "But back to why you detest Wally so much."

"You see, Wally is the total opposite of what I'm all about. He just looks to be outrageous so he can to get a rise out of his listeners. He makes up shit. Says stuff he doesn't believe. Never apologizes when he's wrong. Insults the world. I mean, how do you call a lady like Alison an old dyke on the air? You know when they first started working together, she used to show up in tears at my door at least once a week. Something he said, on or off the air that hurt her. He was like an abusive husband. He'd rip her a new one, then apologize and say it would never happen again, get all lovey-dovey and then start in the next day with the shit."

"So why does she put up with it?"

Stone was on his third beer already and it was barely noon. He never drinks this much this early, and I have to chalk it up to his dread at seeing Wally.

He said, "You heard her. She thinks he has a good heart. But she also worries about herself if he's gone.

Truth is, he needs her as much as she thinks she needs him. Whenever she's on vacation and he works solo, the numbers go down. He has no governor then, no one to balance the craziness --- he just pushes the envelope further and further until people can't stand it and turn away."

You would think after twenty years, your best friend would lack the ability to surprise. Good friends become as comfortable as an old flannel shirt.

But listening to him today, he let me see he faces the same anxieties I do when the lights are out. Marine strong, he'd barely flinched when his career went up in smoke barely a month ago. He just accepted his fate and moved on to his next dream, becoming a pro golfer. The only time I saw him crumble was when Lisa Tillman dumped him. Then all his fears coalesced into an ugly bundle that he carried with him for almost a year. It took a near death experience to shake him loose from the demons she had unleashed, and they still come back to bedevil him when some young hottie rejects my aging pretty boy pal.

I said, "You know Rick, I think you're in your sweet spot. You've had just enough alcohol to lose your inhibitions about sounding semi-intelligent and not enough to act like the crazy asshole you become when you've had too many. You think you could self medicate to this level every day?"

"You ask a serious question, you get a serious answer."

"I'm just busting on you, partner."

He sighed. "That's what our business has become. Whoever yells the loudest or sells the most outrageous line of bullshit gets all the attention and reaps the rewards."

"And that describes Wally to a tee," I said.

"There's no place for me on the radio anymore. But damn, I loved it while it lasted. Ted saw the writing on the wall, he got out and took his millions with him. And he hooked me up with his money guy early on so I'm set for life financially. But if I needed to earn a living in radio? I'd be eating Bosco's food when he wasn't looking."

"There's no chance of that. As much as he loves his uncle Rick, that kibble is off limits. I think you sell yourself short, my friend. Alison told me that the station was deluged with angry calls and emails and tweets after they let you go. She thinks if you hadn't let your childish revenge get the better of you with Campbell, he'd be calling to see if you'd work weekends."

"Prime golf time, my man, prime golf time. I'm going to light up the Senior Tour."

"I have no doubts. Maybe my next career is your caddy. They take ten per cent, no?"

There was someone at the door. The legendary Walter Josephs was here, in the flesh.

EIGHTEEN

"The Wally Show is in the House," he said, announcing his arrival with a boisterous flourish.

I hoped that Stone would at least attempt to welcome him, for the first five minutes anyway. Was there any chance his deeply held beliefs regarding his former profession could make some headway with this jerk while they were forced to breathe the same air?

Stone said, "Isn't it the Allie and Wally Show?"

Wally smirked. "I don't see the old cow here. Did she hop on her broomstick and fly back to Jersey?" When neither of us broke the slightest smile, he said, "Just kidding."

To look at him, you'd never think that Wally Josephs was a radio star pulling down seven figures. He was wearing what appeared to be paisley pajama pants, a ragged Metallica tee shirt and several days' stubble on his face and head. A lot of young guys shave their heads to look cool, but Wally was a natural, losing all his hair save a fringe around his ears. There were multihued predator tattoos adorning his neck, and I imagined, or rather tried not to imagine how the rest of his scrawny physique was ornamented. As he drew closer, it was obvious that his journey hadn't included personal hygiene, causing the normally exuberant greeter Bosco to keep his distance.

"Why don't I show you your room, Wally," I said, trying to appear accommodating while hinting that his personality wasn't the only reason he was unpleasant to be around. "You can freshen up and then join us to watch football."

"I'm cool. Got any hooch? This is some crib you dudes have here. Allie said you both own half. Hey, I can respect that. I never knew you were a fag Stone, you did a good job hiding it."

This was not going well. I needed to set boundaries, before things got too far out of hand. I said, "Hate to disappoint you, but we're both as straight as a Kansas Interstate"

"Hey man, like I said, no offense. Live and let live. Cornhole forever, that's what I say. Just kind of weird a couple of elderly dudes are shacking up without any female types present."

This was behavior I'd never encountered before and I've met plenty of psychos in my day. Here was a man, chased out of his home and business fearing for his very existence, insulting the people who offered him a lifeline with no tangible benefit to themselves. Stone had been willing to put aside his loathing to protect this idiot. What should have been a grateful Josephs was unable to squelch his need to constantly take the offense. He had been in the house less than five minutes and I was already tempted to give him the boot. If he was this crass with his defenders, I could see how someone less tolerant might engage a killer to rid the world of the pustule that was Walter Josephs.

Bosco overcame his initial reticence and wandered over to Josephs, sniffing the floor as he approached. Josephs lashed out with his foot, missing the dog's jaw by inches.

"Get that mutt away from me."

I overcame my aversion to the stench and bolted over to Josephs, grabbing him by his sweat stained shirt.

It ripped from collar to waist as I shoved him up against the wall, knocking over a chair in the process. I pinned his neck hard with my left forearm, exerting enough pressure to keep him from spouting any more shit.

"You hurt that dog and it'll be the last thing you do. Now go up and take a long shower, asshole. You stink like a tent full of bean eaters. And when you come back down, bring some decent manners with you or I'll tell the whole world where they can find you. Either that or I'll kill you myself."

NINETEEN

When Josephs emerged from his room, the physical transformation was not complete but it did nudge the needle into the barely acceptable range. The stench was gone, replaced by some overbearing aftershave. He'd showered and changed into a clean orange tee shirt and madras shorts, which although hideous from a fashion standpoint, was a marked improvement over his previous attire. He'd taken the time to shave and looked almost respectable. Almost.

The more notable change involved something other than his appearance. His manner had softened to the point where we might be able to talk without Stone resorting to a steel cage match. He didn't exactly apologize for lashing out at Bosco, but when my dog gingerly approached him, he gave him a perfunctory nod and let him sniff. Bosco wasn't impressed by the perfume and turned away, snorting.

I tried to play gracious host. "Can I get you something to drink, Wally? Pizza should be here soon. They operate on island time, which means no one is in a hurry to do anything." I tried acting as if our confrontation had not taken place and hoped he'd let it go as well.

"Just a coke if you have one. The drink that is. I'll save the real thing for later."

Stone said, "Jet game starts in five minutes, Giants play tonight."

"You think I don't know that?" Wally said, an uncalled-for edge to his voice. "Of course, you know I know. I guess you were worried I'd be out of touch. My bad."

That was the closest thing to an apology we could ever expect from him. I hated to think I'd have to get physical with him every time he got out of line, but it seemed to have worked.

I said, "Let's watch some football then. And we can talk about our next move." I outlined how I planned to travel north the next day and try to find the man who assaulted him. "Among his other talents, Rick is pretty good with Ident-i-Kit software. If you can describe the guy, it might be good enough for someone to give us a lead."

Wally said, "I can do that. Like I said, I got a pretty good look at him under the street light. And I seen the frigging bastard before at the bar."

Stone went upstairs to get his laptop. When he was out of earshot, I said, "You know Wally, it's obvious that you and Rick don't like each other. But he's sticking his neck out for you. I've got a guy coming from Charlotte to keep an eye on things, a big black dude named Moses Ginn. But he probably can't get here until Tuesday. So once I head north, it'll just be you and Rick for a couple days."

"A moolie? You couldn't find a white guy?"

"You use that word around Moses and you won't be worrying about somebody from Jersey killing you. What the hell is wrong with you?"

"I didn't think some southern yom would know what that means."

"I don't know who you're used to hanging with Wally, but that shit doesn't cut it here."

"I figured since I was in South Carolina, it'd blend right in."

"Blend in with who exactly? The few redneck idiots who still hang on to that crap? You want to be one of them?" I said. This man never failed to amaze me with his ignorance. "I'm surprised no one has tried to kill you before."

"See, you and Stone don't get it. I speak for the common man --- the fan. I just say what they think. I don't judge. That's why I get double digits on the radio. I'm not some politically correct phony." He poured his soda into the glass I'd set out, letting the foam overflow onto my coffee table. He made no attempt to sop it up. "I *am* careful on the air to avoid some words or else my ass would be grass with the corporate assholes. And FYI, I get threats every day."

I wanted to pursue the threats and make him clean up the mess but Stone was on his way down the staircase. Bosco greeted him as if he'd been gone for weeks, almost causing him to drop his computer. Rick responded by removing a dog biscuit from his pocket and tossing it toward Bosco, who retrieved it and gobbled it down.

I said, "You realize that you just rewarded him for bad behavior. Good thing Jaime's not around."

"I just thought I'd get into the theme for the day. I couldn't help but hear some of the shit you were dishing, Wally. All it proves is that you *are* a phony. I know you're not a racist. You're friends with more black dudes than white guys in Jersey. A lot of ex-jocks. They'd smell you out in a heartbeat if they thought you were really a bigot. But you play to the lowest common denominator on the radio with your dog whistle crap and coded messages.

One of the reasons I can't stand you," Stone said, leaving no ambiguity.

"Fuck you, Stone," Wally said. "You think because listeners call you the *voice of reason* that I can't see through your act. I've seen your temper. You're a maniac, not like the pussy you play on the radio. You're a bigger fraud than I could ever be, with your weak-ass, phony intellectual bullshit."

With that, Stone set down the laptop and rushed Josephs. I got between them, taking a wild shot from Stone that drew blood. I pushed him back onto the sofa, and spun to restrain Wally. I grabbed his arm and twisted it behind him, careful not to break anything but intending to inflict some pain.

Stone stayed put where he had landed on the couch --- breathing heavy, trying to calm down. Maybe the sight of blood dripping from the corner of my mouth helped bring him to his senses.

It was going to be a rocky couple of days until Moses arrived to keep the peace.

TWENTY

"I am sick and tired of breaking up fights like a high school principal. Grow up, you two. Josephs, you come with me, we're going for a long walk. Stone, you and Bosco, enjoy the Jets game," I said.

"I need to see that game if I'm on the air tomorrow," Wally said. He was shaking, but not out of rage. He knew that I was his last line of defense against an angry Marine who had already drawn blood.

"It'll be on the DVR," I said. "Now move!"

I pulled him up by a belt loop, not wanting to spoil another one of his tee shirts. I was being selfish, because I didn't want to lend him one of mine if he had packed short. Stone glared up at me but complied, perhaps guilty that his best friend had been caught in the middle.

I shoved Wally toward the French doors facing the Atlantic. It is ironic that his punishment for being a dickhead was a long walk on a beautiful stretch of white sand, still inhabited by tanned bodies, some of which were spectacular. No one would consider time spent on Hilton Head Island punishment, although Stone probably sees it that way now, sentenced to live under the same roof as Josephs. The lush setting was scant reward for his burden.

Wally and I walked over the dune and there was the Atlantic Ocean, in all its sundrenched glory. "Let me put it to you this way," I said, as we reached firm sand, steps from the breaking waves. "The quickest way toward fixing your problem is for me to start in New Jersey. But I'm thinking of not leaving until Moses Ginn gets here rather than leave you and Stone alone. So it's your choice. You behave like an adult, or I stay here until Wednesday and more time passes for the shooter to vanish."

"Your shithead buddy pushes my buttons. You heard what he said. Called me a fraud when he's the one who bullshits his listeners."

"You two will never agree on your approach to radio, but so what? He's moving on to a new career and you're riding high in his old one. He was just fired from a job he did for over twenty years. Put yourself in his position. How would you feel? Someday it'll happen to you. For your sake, I hope it won't be for a long time but it's the business you've chosen. What's cool and hip today is old and in the way tomorrow."

That shut him up for a bit as if it was the first time he had ever considered his media shelf life. Guys in their thirties are like that.

I focused on the matter at hand. "Wally, it would help if we could narrow down the list of people who might want you gone. First thing we thought of was a jealous husband or lover. Are you doing any married ladies?"

"Never. No need to. There's lots of available quim for me out there. I don't need no jealous dudes coming after me for something I can easily get elsewhere. So I never fish in those waters, man."

"Okay. But understand, I'm not here to judge. Tell me the truth. If there is someone out there who thinks you're doing his woman, best let me know now."

"Nope. I'm clean."

"Stone says you've been trashing the Giants backup quarterback. He's got money and motive. Make any sense?"

"Shit, no. He's a friend of mine. You can't tell anybody this but he *wants* to be traded. Hates New York, hates the media there. So the plan is for me to get the fans against him and he's going along with it. The Giants are an uptight Catholic organization. They weren't happy that their placekicker turned out to be beating on his wife, especially after they signed him anyway. If they get the feeling their fans are staying away because they hate the quarterback, they'll move him. Jerry Jones is interested down in Texas, where he's from. It's tampering so don't tell no one I told you. If the Giants cut him, he'll get snapped up by the Cowboys in a minute."

I try not to be cynical about sports. I try to believe that the playing field is fairly level and that these guys represent the best of us, but when I hear stories like this, I feel foolish for paying the games any mind. Cross the Giants' QB off the list. Next.

"How about that guy Rasputin who's always ripping you in the paper?"

"Now that little faggot, I really do hate his guts. Little wimpy fucker still lives with his parents. Never accomplished anything on his own so all he can do is rip others."

"Lives with his parents, eh? So would he have enough money to hire someone to knock you off? And does he really hate you that much?"

"That simpering little queer hates me more than Stone does, if that's possible."

I shot him a dirty look.

"Okay. I mean, you can check him out but if I'm gone, who else would he be able to rip a new asshole in his column three times a week?"

"Anyone you think could be a candidate?"

"Aside from Stone?" Another hard look from me didn't stop him. "I'm not kidding. You saw that way he came at me. Same thing happened more than once at the station. Your pal has a thin skin. I made fun of him on the air a few times, the fucker didn't understand it was good cross promotion for his boring show. He takes trash talk personally like the old fart he is. Are you sure this isn't some plot he came up with so's he could be alone with me down here?"

"That's not the way Rick thinks. If he has a bone to pick with you, he comes at you directly. Yeah, I know he has a temper but he's not a killer. And don't kid yourself. You're no more than a pimple on his butt. Especially now that he doesn't have to see you every day at the station."

"I'll give another name that you'll scoff at. But it's something I thought about at first and still do a little."

"Who's that, Wally?"

"Alison. You should have heard her when I called her an old dyke. She gave it to me, both barrels. Threatened to cut my balls off. Then that night, a guy takes a couple of shots? Just sayin'."

"So you think she has a killer on her speed dial and could set that up within the hour? Or called *Killers R' Us*? She came to Stone and me to help you. She wanted to pay out of her own pocket for me to find you and keep you safe."

"You just don't learn, do you King?"

"Okay, Wally, I'll bite. What don't I learn?"

"You think Alison is some naïve little pup? Did you know she sleeps with Campbell, the boss? She didn't survive in this biz as long as she has without some Machiavelli in her. Bet you didn't think I knew that word, did you?"

"I'd ask you to spell it but what's your point?"

"Simple. Last year, you got hired to find that Stevie Perry chick for my old boss. It was in all the papers. You did your job and she winds up dead. You don't think since she knows where I am now that she wouldn't tip off the killer she hired?"

"God, it must be hard to live in your world. She thinks that you're her meal ticket. If you were gone, she'd be out in a heartbeat. I don't agree with her but she believes it's in her best interest to keep you on the right side of the grass. She was afraid that you were dead. It wasn't until you called yesterday that she knew otherwise."

"Holy shit man, you just proved my point. I talked to her the day after it happened. She knew damn well I was alive. She pulled the wool over your eyes, shamus. Bet you didn't think I knew that word either."

He walked away from me, snickering.

TWENTY ONE

Stone and I were alone in the house just before sunset, between football games. Even though Wally had not been his hyper-obnoxious self while watching the Jets, his comments were so insipid it seemed as if he had never seen a pro game before --- as if he'd just gotten off the boat from Romania and the only English he spoke was "hit him again, harder, harder."

"Wally's out taking a run on the beach. No harm in that unless someone tailed him all the way down here," I told Rick, when he returned from his room after making a few calls, no doubt in search of a *tension easer*.

Rick managed to maintain his cool throughout the game, but it put a strain on him. He and Wally sat on opposite sides of the room and never interacted. I had gotten them to declare a truce and shake hands after the beach walk, but Hezbollah and Israel stand a better chance at keeping a lasting peace than these two.

Stone said, "Thank God he's gone for a while. I think I'll watch the Giants' game tonight up in my room. I can't take his bullshit. If you listened to him, you'd have thought the Jets lost instead of winning by two scores. Wanted them to throw deep when the defense was in dime coverage and go for it on fourth and nine from their own territory. I thought he just said that idiotic stuff on the air and he really knew better. Obviously, he doesn't. So what did you boys talk about on your little walkie?"

"Couple of interesting things. I must admit, the kid's in pretty good shape. Says he runs three miles every day rain or shine and you can tell by his calves he's not lying. I can see how he could outrun the guy who was trying to kill him."

It was Bosco's dinner time and I went to the kitchen to put out his kibble. Stone said, "You might give him a little less supper, Riles. He hit that popcorn pretty hard during the game. All that salt, he'll probably be thirsty as hell."

"I can see *you* were. The beer supply took a pretty good hit."

"Between the game and putting up with Wally, I needed it. I'll make a run later if we're short."

"I have extra stashed in the garage." I dished out a cup and a half of dry food for Bosco instead of his normal two. The warm late day sun was streaming through the clerestory windows, reflecting off the waves to create soothing patterns on the whitewashed walls. Whoever had designed this place knew what he was doing. The bedrooms were oriented toward the morning sunrise, and the wide overhanging eaves shielded the living space from the harsh afternoon rays. The main floor was open and welcoming, ideal for entertaining intimate gatherings. A spacious screened porch faces the ocean, inviting the breezes that grace the island as the sun sets. White wicker sofas and low tables embellish the lanai, where Stone and I sat on overstuffed cushions, taking quiet pleasure in the indigo water view, only occasionally sneaking glances at the oversized flat screen showing football highlights.

"So you didn't answer me before," Rick said. "What did Wally tell you? Anything relevant?"

"Some things you won't like. He says he talked to Allie the day after the incident and checked in every day after that. So if that's true, she lied to us about worrying that he might be dead. He also says that Allie's been sleeping with Campbell. How you like them apples?"

Stone looked as if I'd just punched him in the stomach, digesting the little factoid about Alison trading fluids with his arch enemy. He said, "I can't think of a snappy line from a rock song about that image. It makes me sick if that's true. BJ Campbell is one of the world's biggest pricks and I'm not just saying that because the douche bag fired me and couldn't even do it in person. He's a weak-ass coward. I know Allie's worried about survival but I find that one hard to believe. She's got better taste than that."

"That point is debatable, my friend. Josephs told me that her first choice of men at the station ignored her advances. That's where his story strains credibility because I know for a fact that guy would boff anything with a pulse."

"I'm afraid to ask. Who might that be?"

"You."

TWENTY TWO

Wally had been out for almost an hour and darkness was approaching. Since I couldn't hail a convenient posse to send after him, Bosco and I decided to form our own search party. We sent Stone out for some burgers. I'm not sure which group Bosco would rather have joined, but I leashed him up, hoping that he didn't understand enough Human to know that Rick was headed out for beef.

As expected, Stone had played dumb when I passed on Wally's contention that Alison had the hots for him. He loved her like a sister, he said, but there was no sexual chemistry at all, at least on his part.

I carried binoculars with me as Bosco and I scuffled over the dune. It was hard to focus the spyglasses with a big dog tugging at me whenever I paused to reconnoiter. The tide was out and there was a lot of sand that a dedicated runner could put between himself and the house. After a few minutes, I spotted a lone figure a several hundred yards off, walking with his head down. It looked like Josephs.

I waved to him and when he finally looked up; he recognized that it was me and started a slow jog, reaching us within a minute. He said, "I should have sent up a flare or something. I must have passed by here at least twice. These houses behind the dune all look the same at dusk."

"No problem. The first few times here, I missed the path over the dune myself. It's a big beach."

He had a pensive look and his voice was minus the harsh rasp that defined his radio persona. "I've had some time to think on my run. Damn! I hate to admit it, but I'm scared. Nobody's ever shot at me before. Guy like you, I suppose you're used to it. But it scared the shit out of me."

For the first time since he'd been here, I saw someone other than the iron-ass insensitive lout he played to his public. He might act out like a tactless oaf, but underneath it all was a frightened child. Alison always maintained he possessed a basic decency and good intentions, which now were almost visible.

"Truth is Wally, you never get used to it. A couple of years ago, I was a few seconds away from buying the farm. A crazy man had a gun pointed at me and was about to use it. If Stone hadn't jumped in, we wouldn't be here having this conversation. But was I scared? You bet."

He kicked at the sand, then reached down to pat Bosco's head. The dog stiffened at first and then gave in. "This is so not my world," Wally said. "I've never even been in a fist fight. I always manage to talk my way out of whatever I talk myself into. That's one reason Stone scares me."

"My boy Rick does have a temper. He's impulsive but he's no fool and his common sense kicks in pretty quickly. He might lace you a good one, but he'd never keep pummeling once he had you down."

"Gee, that's comforting. Not. But the last few days, I feel like I'm in a movie living someone else's life. Who would want to kill me? I'm harmless. I never hurt anybody."

"You know Wally, *Sticks and Stones can break your bones* and all that. But don't underestimate the damage words can do. You talk into a microphone and a few dozen carefully screened listeners call you every day, but there are a lot of folks who hear your words and are hurt by them. You never see those people, they never reach out to you. But they're out there, and not all of them are a playing with a full deck. All it takes is one guy who's depressed about his life and resents you ripping his team or his favorite player. That could be all it takes."

"But it's all bullshit. You think I actually care who wins unless I got money on it? And I don't even bet much anymore. It ain't real, man. It's like this big play pen. I pick games on Fridays but what the fuck do I know? There's people out there who study like it's a science and they get it wrong all the time. It's like they say, opinions are like assholes, everybody's got one and they usually stink."

The sun was down and the ocean had turned pink in the afterglow. It felt ten degrees colder. Bosco, bored with our analysis, added his commentary by squatting and eliminating the popcorn Rick had fed him. I used a plastic bag to scoop up the smelly mess and deposit it in one of the large canisters that dot the beach at frequent intervals for that purpose. Whenever I complain about my job, remind me of those who are charged with collecting these bags, most of which are loosely sealed.

I said, "We'd better get in. Can I trust you and Rick not to kill each other if I leave tomorrow? The sooner I can track down this hired gun, the sooner we can put this all to bed."

"I'll try, that's all I can promise. The guy hates the sight of me. I hope you're right about his common sense. Does he have a gun?"

"He does. A few actually. If I'm to trust him to look after you, he'll need one. As I told you before, the chances this hitter tracked you down here are slim. We took a lot of precautions. No one up north other than Allie knows you're here. You should be safe and big Moses will be here by Tuesday. Trust me, there's no one I'd rather have watching my back than him, including Stone."

For the first time today, Wally smiled. I wouldn't consider him handsome by any stretch, but there was a boyish quality to his features that some might find attractive when he lit up. He said, "So I guess niggas with attitude jokes are out of the question? Don't worry, when my ass is on the line, I can be quiet as squelched fart on a first date."

To his generation, I guess that passes as wit.

TWENTY THREE

"That Wally dude or whatever his name, he get there yet?"

I had called Moses Ginn, hoping that he could drop everything and prioritize his work for me.

"He's watching the Giants' game now in the living room. Any way you can get here sooner? Stone and he are like the Sunnis and Shia. They've been at each other's throats since he got here."

He stifled a laugh. "Tuesday, best I can do. Stone's not exactly a mellow dude, but he ain't the agitator here from what you say. This Wally must be a piece of work."

"That he is. Maybe after you get here, Stone can get back into his natural routine --- out on the links all day and chasing tail all night. The less those two see of each other, the easier your job will be."

"Ain't nothing Moses Ginn can't handle. You got a sports package and a big mother of a TV down there?"

"DirecTV with a full boat and a seventy inch 4K Sony. You'll lack for nothing, big man. Just cut Wally a lot of slack. He's got a warped sense of humor --- and that's the nicest way to describe it. He thinks he's the white Eddie Murphy, if you take my meaning."

"He don't like no coloreds around, that it?"

"No, some of his best friends are... Just pay him no mind. He thinks he's edgy and he steps over the line trying to be funny when he's not. But it's not all tough duty, Moses. I shouldn't be long in Jersey. When I get back, you'll get to meet my girlfriend Jaime."

"Hot Damn."

"Careful, pal. You'd sooner mess with me than her. She's a tough cookie. Anyway, your name is at the gate here so you won't have any problems getting into the plantation."

"That be what you call ironic, ain't it? For hundreds of years, my people struggle to get off the plantation. Now I need permission to get back in."

TWENTY FOUR

I took the early morning flight out of Savannah to Newark. The plane was half full, mostly wise vacationers who knew that this was the best time of the year to enjoy Hilton Head. The crazed tourists were gone, the snowbirds had yet to arrive and the weather was still balmy and much less humid. There were occasional beach days when it reached the eighties, and the water was warm enough for those hardy enough to withstand the initial chill.

I booked a subcompact rental and headed toward the shore. Traffic was light on the Parkway going south. With any luck, I'd reach Toms River before noon, in time for lunch at one of my old haunts, the Starlight Diner on Route Nine.

But I wasn't headed there for the food or the uninterested service. It was because their most reliable customer was sure to be inhabiting his customary back booth. Sure enough when I walked in at 12:05, Ocean County Detective Flint McCullough was sipping ice water at his reserved spot in the rear of the diner.

"Long time, no see," I said, failing to come up with a more original greeting. "Where's the old chipped coffee cup? They have it bronzed in your honor?"

Showing no surprise at my unexpected intrusion, he merely motioned me to sit across from him and said, "The last physical, the docs told me I had to cut down on the caffeine. The old ticker had a couple of anomalous beats, they said. Only two cups of Joe a day. I can't tell you how much I miss it. Everything feels like slow motion now."

"I'm sorry to hear that. Nothing serious, I hope."

No reaction other than a shrug. I ordered coffee for myself, wondering if the mere sight of it would send him into withdrawal. I said, "You're not going to ask what brings me here?"

"I figured you'd get around to it when you were ready."

The Starlight hadn't changed much in the fifty years since it first opened. Bright chrome exterior, gold flecked laminate counters rimmed with aluminum, old-fashioned small juke boxes at every table. The music they featured was a mix of tunes from the Rat Pack, some fifties do-wops, and sixties/seventies classic rock. The benches in the booths were shiny red vinyl, cracked and inexpertly patched. The tabletops were scuffed past the wear layer in places. The place still smelled great, the result of an inadequate ventilation system in the kitchen. The short order cook attending the grill behind the lunch counter slathered everything with butter and the omnipresent onions frying adding to the succulent bouquet.

I said, "Damn, you still remind me of Scott Glenn. That craggy mug of yours never changes."

"Who's Scott Glenn?"

Every time I bring up the name, we go through this song and dance. I tell him he was the actor who played Alan Shepard in *The Right Stuff* and also had a big part as a submarine captain in *The Hunt for Red October*. He always just grunts in recognition. Since McCullough has amazing recall and can cite details from decades old cases, I know he is just playing with me, although I can never figure out why. I suppose it's just part of a ritual that old friends go through to reacquaint themselves. Although he and I have sometimes been on opposite sides, there is a mutual respect that remains unsaid. I help him when I can and he gives me tidbits that his superiors would rather keep under wraps.

After I told him for the tenth time who Glenn was, I got down to business. I said, "A friend of a friend was attacked the other night by a man he thinks might be a cop."

"Really."

"I was hoping you could help me identify this guy, if in fact he is a cop." I gave him the details of the assault, but left out Wally's name. It wasn't that I don't trust Flint to be discrete; I was just trying to honor Alison's wishes as best I could.

McCullough said, "Why didn't your guy report this? Why pay for a private investigator?"

"He was worried that if the guy *is* a cop, you guys wouldn't break much of a sweat looking into it. Also, word might get back to the hitter since you tend to stick together. My client's gone underground, he's so afraid the guy might still be after him."

We talked a little more about the assault until Flint's food arrived. In the past, he'd always ordered the same lunch --- an omelet of egg whites and greens but today the cuisine was even healthier, some kind of Kale salad, in deference to his doctors' orders. He still retained the wiry physique of a man much younger than his fifty four years, but his deeply lined face and grey crew cut added ten to that. He was past the service time when he might retire with a nice pension, but I couldn't imagine McCullough doing anything other than what he did. No real hobbies or interests, other than his job.

THE LAST RESORT

Flint looked at the salad with disdain, and said, "You say this guy hung out at the Iron Horse Tavern? A lot of cops do. The unmarried ones mostly, or the hitched ones who're bored. Lot of broads who go for men in uniform hang out there. Or so I've heard."

He had been married since he graduated the academy and had grown kids. He'd never shown eyes for anyone other than his wife, even on boys' nights out.

I said, "Stone did an Ident-i-Kit of the hitter and the girl from the vic's description, and I have copies on my tablet. You'd think a lunk like that wouldn't have any artistic talent, but he's pretty good at it."

The two boys had managed to remain civil during the sketching process, which gave me hope that they'd both be alive when I returned.

"Give him my regards. Tell him I'm sorry he got canned at WJOK. They suck even worse without him there. Jeez, I can't stomach all the commercials they run on that Allie and Wally show they put on in the afternoon. I love her, she's great. But if anybody deserves the old pimp roll, it's that Wally guy. What a jerk."

Little did he know.

I showed him the man's picture on my tablet and he shook his head. "Doesn't look like anyone I know. If he is on the job, could be from a different town. I could show it around, I suppose."

"I'm not sure that's a great idea, if you show it to the wrong guy. The Iron Horse is pretty much out of the way, so I can't imagine someone coming from very far away to drink there."

"Like I said, lots of available broads. Show me the picture of the hooker."

"My client says it's pretty accurate. Family man that you are, I didn't think you'd know anything about her."

RICHARD NEER 88

Flint munched on a heart of palm stalk that he dug out from under the kale. "Nah, I don't recognize her but if she's ever been arrested, we'll have mug shots I can look at."

"I figured I'd take a run over to the Iron Horse tonight. See if anyone there can help. Apparently the guy is a regular."

"Why don't I join you? It might help to have someone legit with you, just in case. Still not gonna tell me the name of the victim?"

"Confidentiality. I know I hated that when I was a fed, but like you say, the guy is a victim. He didn't know the girl was for hire, just thought he got lucky. Not something he'd want out there, if you take my meaning."

"Ah, a married man."

I just raised an eyebrow. Given McCullough's earlier comment about Wally, it would serve him better not to know. After arranging to meet him at eight near the tavern, I slapped a ten on the table for the coffee and a tip, even though I hadn't eaten. He shoved it back at me.

"You can buy me a beer at the Horse," he said.

TWENTY FIVE

On the way to WJOK, Paul Esposito called. The Forked River car dealer and I are friendly, but other than exchanging cards at Christmas, we haven't been in regular contact since I moved South. After not speaking for over a year, two times within a couple of days meant something was up.

"Hey Riley, got a minute? Got a couple of things for you."

"Sure, Paul. Everything okay?"

"Yeah, everything's fine. When we talked the other day, you said to let you know if someone came in asking about your friend's Porsche. Well, a guy was here first thing this morning and he was pretty interested. I told him it wasn't for sale, but he insisted on checking it out."

"What did he do specifically?"

"See, first thing, he asked me if could see the title. I said no, that the transfer hadn't been finalized and the new title hadn't cleared yet, you know, shit like that. But he bullied me into letting him look under the hood, then he went through the interior, opened the glove box. I tried to be polite, I mean, I thought the fella could be a serious customer someday so I didn't want to cheese him off, but he really gave it the once-over. Even looked underneath, felt around the wheel wells for rust. Weird to spend that much time on iron that ain't for sale."

"That is strange."

"He asked me for the key, said he wanted to see how the nav system works. I told him that the battery had been disconnected while we do some work on the electrical system. He pushed me to re-connect it. I didn't, but he was pretty insistent."

I wasn't sure about that particular model, but some hard drives store your telephone directory for voice activated calling. And the nav system would have a log of previous destinations.

I said, "So what was your take? Just a quirky car guy, like 'The Count', Danny Koker, or something more?"

"I told him that this particular car wasn't available but that I knew of one just like it if he really wanted a Porsche. He said, no, it wasn't in his price range. King, I've seen tire kickers before but this guy takes the cake. He must have spent a half hour with a car he couldn't afford."

"This is going to sound like a bizarre favor. Paul, do you have surveillance cameras at your lot?"

"Of course. I've never had any of my cars jacked, I got good locks and stuff but yeah, I got a couple in the showroom and outside on the lot. Why you ask?"

"You think you might have this guy on one of them?"

"Likely."

"Tell you what, I'm actually not far from you now. I'm in Toms River, I just flew up this morning. Are you around later this afternoon, if I drop by to look at that footage?"

"I am. What's going on?"

"I'll let you know when I see you. It might be nothing."

"Suit yourself. I'll be here all afternoon 'til about six. Hey, got something else you might be interested in.

You told me your old Audi was ailing down there in the Southland. I just happen to have a sweet S5 Quattro, came in last week. Less than two years old. Low mileage, loaded."

"Sure, I'll take a look. Maybe a test drive if you'll let me."

"Are you kidding? Of course. This baby is cherry. One ride and you'll want it in your carport or whatever you got down the old dirt road to your double-wide."

"Keep thinking that way about the South, my friend. I tell everyone we already have too many Yankees moving down, spoiling the vibe."

He whistled. "Listen to you, Jersey Boy. Bring your checkbook. I'll see you later."

TWENTY SIX

$\mathbf{W}$JOK-FM is located on Main Street in Toms River. A century ago, the wide thoroughfare gave rise to sprawling Victorian style manses on large tracts. In the sixties, the town fell on hard times and the homes into disrepair. They were eventually bought up at bargain prices by developers and gentrifying professionals, intent on refurbishing the old painted ladies into trendy office/residences for doctors, boutique businesses and attorneys.

The radio station has occupied the same old building on Main Street since its birth in the sixties, when it was originally conceived as an easy listening outlet. It provided background music with few commercial interruptions for upscale suburbanites and survived as such until the novelty wore off. The desperate owners began to lose substantial money, and were ready to shut the whole mess down in the late eighties. That's when Ted McCarver, always on the lookout for opportunity, bought it for a song.

McCarver was able to turn his modest investment into a broadcast entity worth tens of millions by upping the power and changing the format to sports talk. His timing was great on the other end as he bailed out of the terrestrial broadcast business just before the internet began to erode its value.

Lucky for him, the conglomerate Cirrus Communications was taking advantage of loosened federal regulations to expand its radio empire, purchasing dozens of stations on credit.

McCarver walked away a very rich man but was ridiculed by most financial analysts as a fossil who had lost touch with modern sensibilities.

He had the last laugh.

WJOK's hard-won appeal kept it in the black as internet streaming and the Great Recession started to exact their toll. But the numbers started to erode as the austerity measures kicked in. The state of the building was a metaphor for the downward slide.

When I arrived at the station shortly after one, I was taken aback by how the facade had changed. The once magnificent lawn was now spotted with weeds and was badly in need of mowing. The cobblestone drive had been ripped out and sold off, now replaced by cracking macadam. Several of the majestic oak trees had died and were reduced to ugly stumps. The paint on the building was peeling and the once gracious lemonade porch was checkered with rotting floorboards held in place by popped nail heads.

Inside was even worse. Donna Parker was at lunch, so it was left to a gum chewing receptionist to inform me that Alison Middleton was in the jocks' lounge on the third floor. She didn't ask for identification or the purpose of my visit. I climbed two stories worth of rickety stairs, careful not to put any stress on the wobbly banisters.

Alison wasn't in the lounge. There were a couple of college interns inhabiting the "bullpen" area who merely shrugged when I inquired as to her whereabouts. One of them suggested she might be in the tech area, toward the rear of the building. That's where I found her, exasperated by another youngster's lack of technical expertise.

"Damn it, Jim," she said to him as I entered. "What's so hard about hooking Wally up? They did it for Rick Stone all the time when he was on remote. I'm sorry Riley, I'm in the middle of this but we do need to talk."

"Yes, we do Allie. What's the problem?"

The kid engineer or whatever he was, sulked. Allie said, "Jimmy here is new and doesn't know how to hook up the line to Wally. The main guy is on vacation and apparently had a system of his own that he didn't pass on before he left."

"Well, it's your lucky day. Stone did so many shows from my place that I know how this works. He showed me in case he got in late and the techies needed to check the system before he went on. A couple of times, he slid in right before the show started."

"Let me guess why he was late. Have anything to do with women half his age?"

"Possibly. I thought I might have to fill in, which of course I would have done masterfully. But then they probably would have let him go and hired me and he needed the work. Anyway, let me look at this."

My attempt at humor didn't warrant a smile from her or the kid, who looked to be fresh out of high school. The Comrex instrument booted up within a minute. A second later, it lit up with an incoming call. It was Rick, his smooth radio voice counting down from ten, using a microphone eight hundred miles away on Hilton Head Island. The miracles of modern technology.

"You are a lifesaver, King. Is there anything you can't do?" Allie said as she led me toward the vacant studio.

When she closed the door to the soundproof room, I let her have it. "Allie, you lied to me. I'm trying to help you and the first thing out of your mouth is something easily disproved."

"What are you talking about?"

"Wally told me he called you the day after he was attacked and every day up to the weekend. You knew he wasn't dead. Why did you lie?"

Her face lost color. "When I first called Rick, he said you weren't looking to take on new clients. And he hates Wally, as you've seen firsthand. But I know Rick's a decent man and that if I told him that Wally might be dead, he'd prevail on you to help. So I exaggerated a little. I'm sorry, but it worked. Here you are."

"Yeah, here I am. But your little ruse now has Wally suspicious. He told me that you might be behind the attack and he thinks you might have lured him to South Carolina so that you can tell the hitter his exact location, since he wouldn't tell where he was hiding up here."

"How can he think that? After all I've done for him." She looked genuinely hurt by the suggestion.

"You lie to me one more time and I don't care who gets hurt, I'm gone. I like you Alison, but this is no game we're playing. I got a lead today that tells me there really is someone out to get Wally."

"What lead? What did you find?"

"I'm not telling you anything yet. It's too early and like I said, you've lost my trust. For better or worse now, Wally Josephs is my client."

"Please, Riley. I'm sorry. We're on the same side here. Surely you don't think I would ever want to hurt Wally."

"There's another thing. Wally told me you're sleeping with Campbell."

She looked down, a surefire tell that I had hit home, but then she looked up at me in defiance. "I don't see where that's any of your business or what that has to do with this case."

"It has to do with how you characterized this whole affair right from the start. You said if anything happened to Wally, you'd be fired as soon as they lined up a replacement. Obviously, sleeping with the boss might buffer that a bit, wouldn't you say?"

She walked away from me, toward a compact audio console that alerted her as to who was calling and what they wanted to address. She pushed a couple of buttons and adjusted a knob or two.

She still didn't face me as she said, "I lied to Wally about that. I told him I slept with Campbell once to protect him. Campbell was raging about how Wally had insulted him on the air. Wally does that for the working people in the audience who hate their boss They love the fact that Wally can complain and the bigwigs can't do anything about it. But Campbell wanted to suspend him without pay. I got him to go out for a few drinks to explain and calm him down. That's as far as it went."

"Anything for the cause, eh?" I said. "Just don't lie to me again."

I didn't know what to believe. So far she had admitted she lied twice about things that might have a bearing on the case. Did she sleep with the boss as she had told Wally, or was the sanitized version she gave me the truth? Did she still hold onto secrets that I might have to pry out of her?

Other than Stone, was there anyone honorable in this business? So far, I'd come up empty on that score.

TWENTY SEVEN

"Like the floors?" Paul Esposito said, as I looked around. "Terrazzo. We did ourselves over a couple of days last winter. Looks classy, no?"

"I like everything you do, my friend. The place is impressive."

Esposito Motor Sports had taken a step up in class. Founded a dozen years ago, it started as almost as a pawn shop for cars, taking trade-in vehicles that were destined for auction. Paul Esposito, a mechanic by trade, could offer cash slightly above wholesale but far below private sale assessments. He used the skills of his team to sweeten the cars up to a level where they could be sold at a premium.

Paul had a genuine smile that made me feel welcome in his updated surroundings. He said, "My guys are the best. You know I don't pay them a ton, but they all get a little piece of the action. Makes 'em take more pride in their work. I read it in a book by Bill Gates."

"Hey, Microsoft started small, too."

In order to start the business, he'd mortgaged and re-mortgaged his house and every other item of value that he possessed. He'd taken advantage of the easy money at low rates that the banks were offering before the recession hit. As time went on, he began to specialize in late model luxury imports ---Mercedes, Lexus, Audi, Jaguar, and BMW. His lot became a nexus for those who were unable to keep up payments or the high maintenance costs that these brands demanded, and he formed a cozy relationship with the local banks who alerted him to potential bargains. He had sold me my beloved Audi A5, partially in barter for some work I'd done for him.

I said, "So where's that Porsche? Is it nice?"

"Fair to middling. The guy didn't keep it up the way he should. I detailed it for him, although he didn't ask. I figured a big time radio dude like him could afford it."

"He told you who he was?"

"Didn't have to. I listen to that guy every day. He tells it like it is. Recognized him first time he opened his yap."

"You didn't tell anybody, I hope."

He smiled that infectious grin of his. "Herkos Odonton. We paisanos know how to keep a secret."

"I always thought that was Greek. Anyway, can I see the car?"

Esposito is in his late forties and in an attempt to keep up with his business's cosmetic enhancements, had some restoration of his own done since I'd seen him last. A slightly reshaped nose, firmer jaw line, and implanted cheekbones. He had attended to his receding hairline with a row of transplants that had yet to fill in, which the comb-forward barely disguised.

Although his showroom didn't rise to the level of the top branded dealerships, it was clean, well laid out and professionally appointed.

"Right this way, monsieur." I suppose between Greek, Italian and French, Esposito was affecting a continental demeanor for his sophisticated clientele. I wanted to tell him that anyone with more than a tenth grade education would see through it, but he did it in such an innocent, childlike fashion that it worked. Kind of.

THE LAST RESORT

The car was in a back corner of the shop and it shone like a ruby. Sporting a deep crimson exterior, the tobacco leather interior was burnished to a high gloss. Its mere stance reeked of speed even while standing still. Ten years ago this would have been the ride for me, but ten years ago I couldn't afford to keep it in gas. Now that I could, Jaime would shoot me if I tooled around in such a mid-life crisis buggy. She'd pass a comment about a small penis that I wouldn't find amusing.

I said, "Can you show me what this guy was looking at underneath?"

"He seemed real interested in the wheel wells, I guess checking for rust. Folks think it's a problem here down the shore with the salt air and all, but this whip ain't got no tumors."

I knelt and checked out the wheel wells, looking for a tracker. Although I didn't find the device, I did notice something. On the rear passenger side, there was a small area not larger than a playing card that was spotlessly clean. In order for a bug to stay in place under all driving conditions, they are normally attached with 3M tape adhesive, which demands a pristine surface. It seemed likely that the hitter removed the expensive bug while inspecting the car, satisfied that Wally wouldn't be back anytime soon.

I said, "Can I see that recording of the guy? Did you get a good shot of his face?"

"Not bad. A little fuzzy, but see for yourself. You wanna tell me what's going on?"

"Well, herkos odonton. This guy is interested in Wally. Don't know why. Maybe he owes him money. Wally does like his wine, women and song, you know."

"You think he needs dough? I'd be interested in the car, if he's got clear title, I mean."

"Again, I don't know." He led me to a small glassed-in area just off the showroom where the firm's only secretary sat. Blond, buxom, a carbon copy of his wife but ten years younger. I hoped she wasn't a trainee for the position.

"Cherie, get lost for a minute. Mr. King and I have business."

She looked up at him with adoring eyes. "Yes sir, Mr. Esposito."

After she left I said, "You'd better watch out for that one. She digs her boss."

"Got the real thing at home. Not messing with any amateur stuff. One divorce is enough, cost a fortune."

Paul withdrew a full size keyboard from under the desk and after a couple of strokes, a small gallery of pictures appeared. It took a few minutes but Paul found the correct timeline and then pointed to the monitor. The man in question looked like Stone's Ident-i-Kit rendition.

"Mind if I copy these, Paul?" I asked.

"Go right ahead. Is that your guy?"

I fired up my tablet to show him Stone's work as I made my copy. "Does that look like him to you?"

"Same guy. And you don't know who he is?"

"Not yet, but I will. You have no idea where he went after he left you?"

"Nope. Headed north on 9. Once he checked out the car, he blew me off pretty quick. Like he was in a hurry to go somewhere."

"Okay. You can tell Cherie, she can have her desk back."

"Her name is Suzanne. Cherie is French, it means darling."

"You don't say."

"Hey, so you wanna see that Audi I told you about? It's a cool set of wheels, brother."

"I didn't really come here for that but since I'm here, why not?"

A winning smile enveloped his open face as he shook my hand. My friend, Paul Esposito --- always the used car salesman.

TWENTY EIGHT

"Hi, Jaime. I might buy a car," I announced.

"Whaaaa? Hold on a minute. I thought you were coming to New Jersey to investigate this Wally Josephs deal. You never said anything about buying a car."

I was hooked on this ride, as Paul Esposito had predicted. "You knew that I'd have to replace the old Audi sooner or later. And Paul had this great car that had just come in. His guys went over it with a fine tooth comb and tweaked a couple minor things. I'm in it now and loving it."

"So how does it get down to Hilton Head? Can Paul arrange to ship it to you?"

"Well, that's something I wanted to run by you. He lent it to me for a couple of days, sort of an extended test drive. Insisted on it rather than the cheap rental I was driving. If I do buy it, I was thinking of driving it down. I thought you might want to come with me. We could break it up into two days, stay someplace romantic overnight. Maybe stopover in Charlotte and get some of your things."

"When would this all happen? I do have work, you know."

"Depends. I've got a lead on this shooter. I'd be surprised if I can't ferret him out in a day or so. But if the car trip doesn't appeal to you, you could always fly down whenever it works for you and I'll drive straight through when I can."

I heard some clicking as she referenced her schedule and checked flights on her desktop at work.

I said, "Listen to this description from Paul's website: *GLACIER WHITE METALLIC, S5 PRESTIGE PACKAGE, ADAPTIVE LIGHTS, SIDE ASSIST, BANG & OLUFSEN SOUND SYSTEM, AUDI MMI NAVIGATION PLUS PACKAGE, BLACK OPTIC PACKAGE, QUATTRO SPORT DIFFERENTIAL, SUPERCHARGED BADGE.* This buggy rocks."

"You know I don't share your enthusiasm for cars. I'm sure it's pretty."

Jaime said things like that but she wouldn't be caught dead in the Korean subcompact I leased at the airport. I left that car at Paul's and he said one of his guys would return it to a local branch of the rental agency if I kept the Audi. Service above and beyond and he gave me a great price, just a few hundred over his cost after prep. I was stoked.

Jaime said, "I'm checking flights now. I know you don't like me sticking my nose in your business unless you ask for my opinion, but you don't seem focused on this Wally case. You're talking about long romantic car trips and you're really more into this new Audi than telling me anything about your investigation. Did something happen?"

She could read me like a book. "You picked up on that, did you? Well, a couple of things. Wally himself is a jerk of the highest order. I always thought that Stone's hatred of him was irrational but now I see why. And Alison lied to get me involved in the first place. She isn't who I had her pegged for either, although I'd rather not get into why that is now. So yeah, I'm not so gung-ho on this."

"Maybe you should tell her that and recuse yourself. It's not fair to give them anything less than your best, especially since the man's life might be on the line."

Jaime has a rock solid set of ethics. In her cut-throat trade, it has cost her business on more than one occasion when she refused to cross certain lines. She knows that I sometimes cross those lines, and will to do so again. If I am to do my job, I have to. But I'm thankful that she's never shy about voicing her convictions when I get lost in the dense ethical forest of what I do.

I told her so. "Thanks for the reminder, dear. That's one of the reasons I keep you around. You always steer me true when I need a mid-course correction."

"It's what I do with my writers when their book is going off course. Get them to straighten up and fly right, as they used to say. So, are you thinking you're going to quit?"

"No, I just have to get my head back in the game. I've worked for a lot worse people than these two. The thing is, that was for money when I really needed it. When I came into the big bucks, I told myself I'd only work if I believe in the cause. I can't say that I like the man, but Wally doesn't deserve to die because I think his show stinks."

"I'd agree, the penalty wouldn't exactly fit the crime. Too bad the Geneva Convention prohibits torture, because I could think of some appropriate punishment for this creep. All right, I won't book anything yet and maybe we can drive down together. Even if we don't stay over at some cozy B and B, we need some alone time. A long car ride might be just the ticket. We've been apart an awful lot lately and I don't like it."

"I'll call you tonight if it's not too late."

"No such thing as too late, babe," she said. "I'm yours 24/7."

"You deserve better than a broken down old P.I.."

"There isn't any better, my love."

This was getting too mushy for me. I was much more comfortable thinking about how cool my new car was. "Love ya. We'll talk later," was all I said.

TWENTY NINE

I had some time before meeting McCullough and since Flint hadn't offered to share his luncheon salad with me, I was getting a bit peckish, as the Brits say. The food court at the Ocean County Mall seemed like a convenient spot for a quick bite to tide me over. Not sure what I was in the mood for, I was ripe for an impulse buy, something unhealthy that Jaime wouldn't approve of.

In our consumerist age, I don't know how it had escaped my attention that tonight was Halloween. As a kid, it was my favorite holiday, more so even than Christmas. But as I entered the shopping plaza, I was completely unprepared for the zombie invasion that greeted me. Teenage boys were roaming the area with torn clothing and mutilated features, some with macabre masks, others with grotesque and skillfully applied make up. I'm not up on zombie code, but it seems that all the women have been liberated from conventional morality and are free to display their wares. This was one of those times when I was thankful I never had a daughter, because the abundant displays of green tinted and pseudo-rotting flesh left little to the imagination. Zombie sluts on parade!

Of all the exotic offerings in the food court, the exhibit of marauding youth unsettled me enough to opt for a safe, boring choice --- a Wendy's Northern Pacific Cod sandwich. I don't know why schools of fish from that

---

part of the sea are considered special; maybe they've taken advanced placement. I picked the quietest table I could find away from the moaning brigands and called Stone.

He sounded disgusted, and he hadn't even been haunted by the undead. "You know, Riles, I should have done the world a favor and pretended I didn't know how to hook up the Comrex so that Wally could do his show."

"That bad, huh?"

"Here, listen for a second. I'll be right back."

I don't know how he did it but the next voice I heard was Wally, wailing away about the Giants. They had beaten Washington last night by a wide margin, but Josephs was giving scant attention to the game itself.

Wally: Who gives a crap what a bunch of wahoo Indians think of the name Redskins? Hell, we gave them the casinos so Tonto can gamble all he wants and drink firewater on the backs of the taxpayers.

Allie: They find the name offensive, Wally. What if they called you paleface?"

Wally: Not with the tan I'm sporting, Pokey-hontas. You politically correct liberals can't let anything traditional stand, can you? Hail to the Redskins. Redskins, Redskins, Redskins. There."

Allie: But why go out of your way to offend people?

Wally: I'm not. That's their name. Put that in your peace pipe and smoke it, Injun lover.

Thankfully, Stone came back on the line before I was exposed to any more of this puerile dialogue. "See what I mean, Riles?"

"What was it Voltaire said about disagreeing with what you say but defending to the death your right to say it?"

He gave a deep sigh. "Voltaire never listened to Wally's show. I'm sure Wally would call him a pussy socialist Frog anyway. Thing is, I don't necessarily disagree with Wally's point about the team's name. It's the ugly way he makes it."

I told him about the car and my meeting with Alison. When I was finished, he said, "Well, I'm not sure she'd admit it to you if she did sleep with him."

"Alison might be lying, but if she'd go to those lengths to save Wally's job, I seriously doubt she'd be the one trying to have him killed."

"Yeah. By the way, with you staying at my place in Mantoloking tonight, I have a favor to ask. I don't know your plans for tomorrow, but there's a showing at nine a.m., so maybe you could tidy it up a bit if you have time."

"King's maid service, at your command. No problem, I'll make sure it looks presentable." After Rick had lost his job at WJOK, he had put his beach house on the market. He hadn't decided where he wanted to live --- maybe the place we shared on Hilton Head or in some other warm climate where he could work on his game all year.

"You might want to look presentable, too. My realtor is a real looker. Take it from one who's been there. Legs right up to her neck," he said.

"Gee, thanks. Well, hopefully McCullough and I will get a lead on the shooter tonight at the Iron Horse. The faster I can track him down, the sooner the talented Mr. Josephs will be out of your thinning hair. I've got to go. Enjoy the rest of the Allie and Wally show."

THIRTY

Bay Head is pretty quiet this time of year. The benes, (the Jersey shore term for summer tourists from the north, who come to soak in the *bene*ficial rays of the sun), have gone back to their igloos. The full time residents are largely seniors, who make very little trouble.

The Iron Horse Tavern dates back to the fifties and shows its age. They don't sell hot food, even typical bar fare. The menu consists of nuts and chips, nothing that requires a kitchen or any degree of preparation. It is strictly a drinking establishment that caters to cops and their followers, both wannabes and wanna sleep-withs.

It's a block away from the ocean and the salt air has taken its toll. The owners have long since given up trying to keep paint on the worn wood siding, letting it crack and peel in the name of crusty authenticity. The knobs and fixtures are rusted and barely functional. There is a buzzing neon sign announcing the *I-n Ho-s-*, which some of the hipper LEOs have taken to calling the joint.

I met McCullough a block away from the tavern. Remnants of damage from Sandy were still visible on the streets and sidewalks, but the town was slowly recovering from the devastation. Unlike the Iron Horse, many of the buildings lining the street were either new or recently rehabilitated, gleaming with fresh paint and brightwork.

"Nadine doesn't mind you being out this evening?" I said as he approached. He was dressed more casually than I had ever seen him. Replacing the nondescript off the rack suits he favors were black jeans and a dark turtleneck topped by a worn leather jacket. He could almost pass as a civilian.

"She couldn't care less, either way," he said.

I waited for him to elaborate. I knew very little about his private life, other than he'd been married a long time and had two grown kids.

"She left me six months ago, King. We waited until both boys were out of the house. We thought that maybe once they were gone, things would change but they only got worse."

"I'm sorry to hear that."

I'd met his wife and kids once --- they seemed like a typical All-American family. The boys had played high school basketball; one was now just out of college, the other following his father's line of work up in Bergen County.

He said, "Nadine just couldn't take the hours and the neglect that comes with what I do. It sounds like a cliché, I know, but I'm married to the job. The good thing is that now we're apart, she taking care of herself better. Enrolled in a gym, gone vegan. She looks great, almost back to her high school weight. I hate to say it, but she's better off without me."

I didn't know what to say. "What about you? Are you dating?"

"Who would date this ugly mug? Nah, I wouldn't impose this life on anyone. Maybe someone who's been there and understands. I don't know if there's a website for female cops or military looking for love." He winced at the thought. "I'm sorry to lay this on you. Let's drop it and get on with what we came here for. We can walk into the place together. Just don't hold my hand or people might get the wrong idea."

THE LAST RESORT

We tough guys rarely lower the shield with those we don't know extremely well. Fact is, even with close friends we don't often share. It's a sign of weakness, or so we were taught. The unwritten code of the West.

We entered the Iron Horse together through the aging front door, which suffered from too many coats of black paint and no prep work in between. The interior had survived the years more or less intact --- the long mahogany bar is varnished to a high sheen. The black and white marble floors will outlast the next two generations of owners. The booths and tables are scarred but shine through multiple coats of polyurethane. If the health department ever visits, it is merely to enjoy an afternoon of drinking on the house. Vermin have been spotted there, both the two and four legged variety. The human sort rarely stay long, once they realize that there are more guns present than at a Trump rally.

I was taken aback by the lack of patrons: there couldn't have been more than a dozen men and no women. The men, who didn't appear to be active cops, were clumped in small groups in the booths. All the barstools were unoccupied.

McCullough answered my unspoken question. "It's Halloween, King. Most of the locals are out on nuisance calls. Minor vandalism. It's probably the busiest night of the year down here --- writing up reports for insurance purposes. Also July Fourth with the fireworks accidents. Next would be Super Bowl night, mostly domestic violence. The place will start to fill up around eleven when most of the delinquents are home, I'd imagine."

There were two men behind the bar. The older of the two was probably sixty, corpulent and half asleep. His doughy features were crowned by a full mane of white hair, swept back from a high forehead. The other was in his thirties, and walked with a pronounced limp. He didn't seem in much of a hurry to take our order.

I knew from the quick research I had done on the place that they were father and son and that the younger man's limp was caused by an IED in Afghanistan. The lower part of his right leg was missing and he had sustained severe burns on the other. His face had not been affected by the blast. He was handsome --- dirty blond hair worn long, blue eyes and a lantern jaw. He resembled Viggo Mortensen, maybe even better looking.

When he finally got around to noticing us, he gave me an appraising look and said, "You two are new here. Although you look a little familiar," he said as he gestured toward McCullough.

"Flint McCullough. Ocean County, Detective First Grade. Yeah, I've been in a couple of times. Not lately though."

"I never forget a face. What's your pleasure, detective. First round is on the house for our brothers in blue. Your friend, too." He paused for a beat, begging my identity.

"Riley King. I used to live up here until a few years back."

"Riley King," the young barkeep said, rolling my name around in his head. "Yeah, I heard of you. You were the guy that nailed the son of a bitch that killed Stevie Perry. I knew her a little, great lady. Hey dude, your money's no good here either."

"Thanks, but I'm on an expense account, so drinks are on me. I'll take a Glenfiddich, if you have it, rocks. Detective McCullough, what are you drinking these days?"

"Heineken works for me."

"Coming right up, gentlemen. My pleasure."

He gave us a swift smile and went about preparing our drinks. His father was on a stool at the far end of the bar, nodding amiably as his son told him about the new minor celebrity arrival. I hadn't had a reception this friendly since I walked into the clubhouse at Harbour Town after a lucky hole-in-one. Then as now, drinks were on me.

THIRTY ONE

"I know you guys protect your own," I said to Flint. "How do you want to play this? I know we talked about it before, but seeing the place and meeting this kid, I wonder if we should change our plan. He seems to think we're hot stuff, maybe this will be easier than we thought."

"Let's play it by ear. By the way, why didn't you tell me that the guy who got rolled was Wally Josephs?"

Good old Flint. Like the Boy Scout that he is, he's always prepared. I had assumed that my little caper was low priority for him --- a pimp who tries to roust a hooker's client is not exactly worthy of the major crimes unit. Yet he'd taken the time to do some research to ID the victim. How? I had no idea, so I asked.

He answered. "I didn't know for sure, but you just confirmed it. I know you and Stone are tight. I know Wally has been AWOL for far longer than he has in the past. Then he pops up today from an undisclosed location. Usually, if a talk show guy is somewhere else, it's because of a sponsor event or a big game. Since he wouldn't say where he was, I put two and two together."

"When did you become such an expert on radio?"

"I'm not. I've just always been a sports fan and I have to admit, the Allie and Wally Show is a guilty pleasure. I mean, the guy is a complete dipshit, but he's so stupid he's funny. Kind of like Jerry Lewis, back in your day."

"And you told me at the diner you hated him. By the way, I'm just a few years older than you, pal."

"It ain't the years, it's the mileage. Although I suppose we both have a lot of miles on the old odometer, don't we?"

"More by the day. Here comes our drinks."

The young man approached gingerly, as if he was about to ask for an autograph. "I was so surprised by you Mr. King, I'm afraid I forgot my manners. I'm John Sullivan. Junior."

"Pleased to meet you."

An awkward pause as I shook his scarred hand, then I said, "I heard about this place from a friend. You probably know him, name of Wally Josephs."

The young vet gave a broad smile. "Mr. Josephs comes in here quite often. Oh, I got it. You're friends with Rick Stone, Mr. King. That was another one of your cases that made headlines. When Stone got shot by that crazy bastard up in Vermont. The perv that aced that woman on LBI."

"Call me Riley. You'd have made a great detective yourself, John. You're spot on, that's how I met Wally."

"That was what I planned to do. I had my life all mapped out. I was going to put in my time as a cop after I got back from the Middle East, then retire and do what I'm doing now. But one of those Taliban fuckers had other ideas," he said, pointing toward his leg.

"I'm sorry. Thank you for your service, though."

Flint spoke up, altering the drift of the conversation. "Wally kind of disappeared for a while on the radio last week. I was hoping I could get my friend

King here to spill the beans on what happened, but he says he's sworn to secrecy."

Sullivan leaned in. "Well, you ask me, it probably had to do with a woman. Dad and me have a running bet going."

I faked a smile. "How so?"

"If I can't be a paid detective like you guys, I can play at it. Wally misses a lot of days on the radio. So, seeing as how you know him well, you know what a cunt hound he is. I'd like to think he comes in here because of the honest pours we serve but it's really to get laid. You wouldn't know it by tonight, but most nights, there are a lot of hot babes in here. Chicks that dig cops."

Flint gave a slow grin. "I'll make a note. But Wally's not a cop."

"But he's a star or the closest any of these girls will get to one. So I got a kind of a system. I rank the lady, one to ten. The higher the number, the more likely Wally will miss work the next day. I been keeping track of it. So far, there's a pretty direct connection."

"Do tell. He was off three days last week. She must have been a doozy," Flint said, looking slyly at me, like he was gathering important information under the radar.

"More than that. I've seen her in here a few times before. Maybe for sale, or maybe just liked the fuzz. Man, she was smoking. Every dick in the joint was hard."

I wondered how Stone had missed this place, or had he? When the name Iron Horse came up, he showed no recognition, maybe because wherever Wally went, Rick headed the opposite way. It said a lot that his dislike for Josephs trumped his libido.

"So what's her story?" I said.

"She didn't hang around long enough for me to find out. Tight top, titties hanging out for the world to see.

Ass to die for. She leaned over Wally to order her drink, practically put one of her boobs in his mouth. Gotta give the dude his credit, he left with her not twenty minutes later."

I said, with false admiration, "Good old Wally. Any idea where they went?"

"His place or the nearest motel be my guess. She broke the scale, far as my little betting system went. Dude was out four days last week. Today he said he was on location, whatever the fuck that means. Located on top of her, I'd say. Although with that rack, I'd think he'd want her on top."

Flint said, "So she came on to Wally? I don't think Wally would mind me saying, he's not exactly Brad Pitt."

"Like I said before, she's probably either a hooker or a star fucker. He must've thought he worked magic with that silver tongue 'cause she was eating out of his hand. Or eating someplace else on him, if you catch my drift."

"How could we not?" I said, pretending to appreciate his keen insight. Jaime would crucify me for tolerating this locker room talk. "Hey, you say you're good with faces. Last time I was in the area, I ran into a guy. We kinda had a lot in common, like he was in my line of work, though he never said that exactly. We shared a few stories, you know the way it is. He said he came here often. I lost his number, figured I'd never see him again but now I'm up for a few days, I thought I might look him up. Maybe you know him?"

"I never forget a face," Sullivan repeated. "What's he look like?"

I pulled out my tablet. "This might help. I use an Ident-i-Kit in my line of work and I did a sketch. Turned out really good. Looks just like him. What do you think?"

I held the device out so he could see the picture. Even though Esposito's camera had captured a better likeness, flashing that would look suspicious given my cover story. McCullough shot me a look. I couldn't tell if he approved of the tactic or not.

Sullivan gave it a quick scan and his smile faded. He tilted his head, and said, "Sorry. Never seen him before. Excuse me, I think my dad needs me. Nice talking with you, fellas."

He limped off to attend to his father, who was in the arms of Morpheus.

THIRTY TWO

A few minutes later, I held up my empty glass and signaled for another round. McCullough and I had trundled off our barstools and made for one of the empty booths lining the left side of the tavern. At the other end of the bar, young Sullivan seemed lost in thought and took his time responding to my request.

I said, "I'm sure you saw the look on Sullivan's face. There's no doubt in my mind that he recognized the picture. I'm a little surprised he isn't dialing the guy up even as we speak."

"Yeah, young Sully isn't much of a poker player."

Sullivan's admiration for me had cooled. He laid the drinks on the bar, making no attempt to deliver them to our table. No more service with a smile. I got up and fetched the booze, slapping two twenties on the slab. Sullivan was already headed in the other direction, uninterested in the cash.

"You know, we're just a couple of dinosaurs, waiting for the meteor to hit," I said, raising my glass to Flint.

"I'm not sure what you mean."

"Just that the end is near for us street guys. We believe in the human touch. It's our first response. Meet the principals. Get a feel for the environment. Try to figure out their motivation. Old fashioned detective work, origins in the nineteenth century."

"God, King, you're much older than you look."

"Someday I'll miss that dry sense of humor of yours. Seriously, I need a name, right? So I journey hundreds of miles, to a ramshackle establishment hard by the sea to converse with an uncooperative Irishman."

"Jeez, now you sound like frigging Dylan Thomas."

"Just the fact we both know who that is dates us." I took a pull of whisky. As Sullivan had promised, it was an honest pour --- eighteen years old, straight from the bottle. "Back to my premise. I need a name. The over/under is ten minutes. I'll take the under. Watch."

I made a couple of swiping gestures at my tablet, tapped a couple of virtual keys while sipping my Glenfiddich. "You ever think of moving South, McCullough?" I asked, while the ones and zeros travelled through the ozone.

"Me? Never. My boys are here. Boys, shit. They're men now. Evan's getting married next summer. I'll be a grandfather soon. I want to be around for that. I could see getting a condo in Florida a few years from now for the winter months, but full time? Nah, I'll never defect to Rebel territory. You seem to like it, but I'd never adapt to it."

"I'm a vagabond, I suppose. Grew up in Virginia, college and feds in DC, a decade at the Jersey shore, Charlotte, maybe Hilton Head full time soon. Ah, an answer. Finally. What took so long? Guy's name is Elvis Crayton. Goes by EC."

"What guy?"

"The man we're after. It'll take a few more minutes to get an address and a dossier. We can hang here for a while if you like. Or find a place a bit livelier and catch Monday Night Football. Maybe tie one on and drool over the waitresses like the couple of old lushes we're becoming."

"Hold on. What did you just do?"

"I sent an email to a guy I know. I call him my Baker Street Irregular, after the Sherlock Holmes street urchins who spied for him. Very obscure literary reference, so I just call him BS for short. He could be seventy, could be twenty five. Could even be a girl or a trained chimp for that matter."

McCullough was staring a hole through me as he said, "How many scotches did you have before you met me here?"

I looked back at him equally hard but he didn't budge.

He said, "You're rambling, King. I'm not letting you get into a car. You want to tell me what the hell is really going on?"

"Yeah, why not? I just did what I should have done before coming up North. I sent the picture I got from Esposito to my computer whiz, and since he was at his desk and not real busy, we had the identity in two minutes. I figured I'd have to come up here anyway to confront the guy. Plus, if I'd done all this from a distance, you and I wouldn't have had this lovely evening bonding over drinks."

"Whatever you've been smoking down in Dixie, keep it away from me. So you're saying you've got a guy with facial recognition software who can tap into government databases?"

"Don't know how he does it. Don't want to know. I only know that he can. And the price is reasonable, even takes major credit cards. I try to use him as a last resort, but more and more I think he should be my first call. The technology isn't there yet, but someday we'll be able to dispatch drones with handcuffs who can corral our perps and bring them in. Then you and I will really be as useless as an eight track player."

McCullough was incredulous. "Forgive me for bringing this up, pal, but you think this shit is legal?"

"Like I say, I don't know who this person really is. He might be a spook, or maybe he works with my old feeb friends in DC. Or maybe he's my guardian angel. I don't know. Could be he just exists in cyberspace. Maybe he's God, I don't know."

"Back here on planet Earth, I have to ask, what's next? You've got your name, you say you'll have an address soon. Then what? And what do you want from me? No report's been made, no charges pressed. I have people I have to answer to, as quaint a notion as you might find that."

"Hold on, more info is coming in. Well, well. Our little field trip here wasn't wasted after all. Seems this Crayton character has a cousin. A fellow who runs a bar in New Jersey. Place called the Iron Horse. Ever hear of it?"

THIRTY THREE

In the twenty minutes that McCullough and I had been at the Horse, the booths had emptied until we were the only customers in the place, except for an older couple who now sat at the far end of bar. They were sipping some fruity concoction. I was surprised a macho joint like this would serve such a beverage or had a ready supply of paper umbrellas to adorn them. I'm sure they were glad no one was around to witness this unforgiveable breach of cop bar etiquette.

I said, "I need to talk to Sullivan. Alone. I'll see if I can get him to meet me in the alley behind this place."

"I can't let you do that." His voice was firm.

"Let me? What do you mean, let me? This guy's cousin was the man who tried to kill Wally Josephs."

"King, you want to talk to Sullivan, that's fine. But I need to be there."

"Why?"

"Much as I like you and get your whole act, you do have a history of taking things into your own hands that are best done through the system."

McCullough and I met under tough circumstances: he was lead detective in the death of Jaime's mom, Paige White. Initially, I was the main suspect --- no great leap since I was discovered unconscious in the room where Paige lay stabbed to death. But I was never arrested or charged. There was the fact that I had received a nasty blow on the head myself while dialing 911, administered by the real killer. On top of that, McCullough couldn't assemble enough corroborating evidence, like motive or a murder weapon.

I knew that in the hands of a less principled detective, some kind of phony proof would magically appear and be used against me. Flint was relieved when we nailed the perp a few months later, given all the heat he'd taken within the department for not pinning everything on Riley King. Although he knows I sometimes employ tactics that he can't, he assumes that they'll be used on the side of the home team.

"So you're saying you still don't trust me, is that it?" I said. "And here I thought we bonded so nicely over scotch."

"All right. Let's cut the shit. I came with you tonight to protect you from yourself. But just so you understand, you do something incriminating and it ever comes down it, I have to tell the truth."

He didn't blink when he said that and I had never any doubt that this would be his attitude. He'd probably grown up watching Jack Webb on *Dragnet* tell people, "Just the facts, ma'am."

I said, "What if I promise not to engage in any rough stuff? I just want to see what he knows about the attack."

"I still can't leave you alone with Sullivan. Even if he tries to go at you first, incidents involving a PI and a decorated veteran could make you look so bad that no state would ever give you a license again. I need to be there."

He was right. If things got hairy, a respected public servant like Flint McCullough would be a great ally. It was time to say yes.

THIRTY FOUR

John Sullivan Junior had yet to collect the two bills I left for him on the bar. Generally, waving money at a bartender will get their attention, but there must have been more pressing issues on his plate. He quickly saw through the little ruse I spun at meeting Crayton. I should have contacted my BS Irregular first, then hit Sullivan with what I knew.

McCullough rose from the booth and walked past the two oldsters sipping their frozen concoctions at the bar. He drew Sullivan aside and quietly made his point. As I read the young barkeep's face, he seemed unconvinced at first, then nodded in reluctant agreement to whatever McCullough proposed. Flint tilted his head toward the exit. He led, I followed.

"He agreed to meet us out there in two minutes. He had to wake up his dad so he could keep the seniors lubricated," he said, when we hit the street.

"What did you say to him?"

"Just that we already had the name. I told him if he tried to contact Elvis before he spoke to us, I'd look at that as obstruction. He got the message. Let me take the lead on this, please. I think I know how to work this guy."

There was a small alleyway adjacent to the tavern. It stank of urine and stale beer, I don't know which was worse. The night had turned cold and we could see our breath. I envied Flint for his lined black leather jacket, scarred and beat up as it was. I hadn't considered the temperature difference between Hilton Head and Bay Head given my hasty departure and was shivering my cajones off.

We didn't have to wait long. Sullivan emerged --- rolled up sleeves, no outerwear covering his muscular arms. He had no doubt endured much colder nights in the mountains of Afghanistan.

Flint said, "John, we know that Elvis Crayton is your cousin. I was serious in there when I said we could get you for obstruction or worst case, as an accessory."

"Dig it, McCullough, you don't scare me. I come from a long line of cops and I know the drill. I ain't done nothing. So let's drop the cheap scare tactics or I'll go back into my place right now and you can stick it up your ass."

I might have reacted to his defiance with a shove, but Flint stayed cool. "You lied to us. You said you'd never seen this guy and it turns out he's your cousin."

"He don't look like the guy in that cartoon. You try to charge me on that and we'll see how far that bullshit goes."

Flint said, "No one wants to charge you with anything. But this Elvis character is a person of interest and we need to locate him."

"I ain't seen him in a week. I got no idea where he is. Okay? We're done here."

He turned and started off but McCullough tapped his shoulder and said, "Be kind of hard to run a tavern without a liquor license. I imagine even those AARP folks at the bar wouldn't appreciate their Pina Coladas much without any rum in 'em."

"I told you, I ain't seen Elvis in a while. I got no idea where he is." He again started to go back inside but thought better of it. "Person of interest for what exactly?"

I enjoyed watching the veteran detective work his man. He had tried a few transparent threats to gauge the resistance level before hitting the man where he lived.

"That blond that Wally Josephs left with that night did take him to a motel. Your instincts were right, John. But then your cousin busted in. Wally got away, but your guy chased him and shots were fired. Now, even if this *was* just a pimp roll and your cousin was using your bar as a place to conduct his business, well, you can see how it looks."

"Look man, I don't know nothing about nothing like that. Elvis comes in once in a while, drinks with some cop friends. That's all. I ain't even that close to him. My dad and Elvis' dad haven't spoken for years. My pop doesn't even like Elvis being in the bar, but it's his sister's kid so he tolerates him. But he always told me that Elvis has more of the husband in him than his sis and says I should stay away."

"What line of work is her husband in?" I said, breaking my vow of silence.

"Waste management. He's Italian, figure it out, gumshoe."

"Gumshoe, eh? And it's not even flashback Thursday," I said.

"Crayton doesn't sound Italian to me," Flint said.

"You think his real name is Elvis, too? The family name is Costello, the first name was Annunzio or some wop shit. He got Elvis from Elvis Costello, I don't know where the fuck Crayton came in. He had it changed legally."

"And how does Elvis make ends meet?"

Sullivan splayed his hands outward. "Look, I don't want to get nobody else in trouble. Let's just say that some of his friends on the job get bonuses from some of the local businesses. For a little extra protection.

Nothing crazy, just an extra drive-by or a word or two that certain places are off-limits. It's possible Elvis picks up them gratuities for his pals, something like that."

"So how does a mobbed up kid get in with the cops?" I said.

Sullivan snorted. "That's why my dad hates his bro-in-law. Dad knew what he was, tried to talk his sister out of marrying the guy, but love conquers all. When Elvis was growing up, he wasn't a real bad kid, had no idea what his dad did. He said he wanted to be a cop, like my pop. Elvis' dad went along with it; my father got the kid into the Academy."

McCullough said, "So why would a mob guy let his kid become a cop?" It took him a nanosecond to answer his own question. "Duh! Then he has an inside pipeline in the department. Knows when busts are coming down. Knows which cops are bent, which ones are straight. But Elvis isn't a cop. What happened?"

"Failed the psych test. That's the official reason."

I said, "But the real reason is that your dad finally realized what the plan was and turned him in, isn't it? Found out that the kid was going to be a plant instead of legit, and let someone know about it."

"You wanna go with that, you go right ahead. I ain't saying, either way."

Flint said, "Okay, we're going to level with you, John, but don't even think about trying to play us. You won't like what happens."

"Ew, I'm shaking in my boots."

I said, "I'm not concerned about that protection business. My job is to keep Wally safe and Wally thinks Elvis was hired to kill him. Does your cousin do wet work, or you think he was just rolling Wally for a quick buck?"

Sullivan looked down and slowly shook his head. "I can't say. This whole thing could have been that ho's idea. Could be she convinced Elvis there was a decent split in it for him. She might be good at persuading, flashing them boobs and all. Far as I know, Elvis never killed nobody, but he *is* crazy."

Sullivan was conflicted and made no effort to conceal his discomfort as he thrashed about on his damaged leg. He said, "God damn it. I like Wally. He comes in like twice a week, throws money around. Lot of times he leaves with some fugly bimbo nobody else wants. He's a funny guy. Good for business, especially when he says on the radio he's going to hit the Horse when he gets off."

Sullivan was starting to come to grips with the idea that losing Wally Josephs as a regular would not be in his tavern's best interest. His mind was flipping back and forth --- between family ties and business. His father had taken the honorable route when he snitched on Elvis to keep him off the force. John junior had sacrificed his career to fight in the Middle East after 9/11. If a blood relative he clearly didn't like was a killer for hire, by his code, blood might only go so far.

McCullough said, "Okay, here's the deal, kid. We need to find Crayton. We'll keep your name out of it. If this was just a minor league rip-off gone bad, King here will make sure Wally knows it's cool to come back to your place and that you had nothing to do with what went down. But if someone hired Elvis to kill Wally, then he needs to deal. We're after the person who hired him. Most likely he skates given his cooperation. Either way --- you help us, we'll keep you clean on both sides."

"I'll ask around, see if my aunt knows where he is. I don't know how much I can help, but I'll do what I can." He wasn't thrilled at the prospect of turning on his cousin, like him or not. "I would have been a good cop, you know."

"Who told you that you couldn't still be? I mean, it's not like you'd need to be walking a beat or anything," McCullough said.

"I was addicted to painkillers. Oxy. I'm good now, but I was hooked for a long time after I got out of the VA hospital. Got 'em off the street. My dad knew and wouldn't let me re-apply until I got straight. Now, he needs my help around the place."

McCullough said, "John, good bartenders are a dime a dozen. Elite cops are more rare. You put those skills of yours to work and who knows? The county force is always looking for a few good men. Just saying."

THIRTY FIVE

There was an all night Dunkin' Donuts shop around the corner from the Iron Horse and we took advantage of the drive-thru to grab a couple of coffees to take the chill off. I was a bad influence on Flint, causing him to drink more caffeine than his doctor recommended. We sipped it without speaking for a minute, savoring the coffee and the silence.

We sat in my new car or more accurately, my maybe new/used car. Or in dealer lingo --- my pre-owned, low mileage, meticulously maintained, one owner luxury vehicle. I started to demonstrate some of its cool features to Flint, who feigned interest but I could see right away he wasn't much of a car guy. Either that or my ability to score such a high-end ride made him uneasy, given the modest compensation he receives for working harder than he figures I do.

"That address you have for Crayton isn't exactly in a gated community," McCullough said. "I expect you'll be paying him a visit."

"Uh, yeah. I didn't fly all the way up here to have a couple of jolts with you at a dive bar."

"When are you planning to drop in on Elvis?"

"In the morning. My guy sent me a big packet of info on the man and I need to get up to speed."

"You packing?"

"Not at the moment. I'm staying at Stone's place in Mantoloking. He's got a couple of pieces there I can use when I visit with Crayton."

McCullough gave a deep sigh as if he was about to belatedly explain the facts of life to his son. "I should come with you. I know what you're going to say, but I can't have you going cowboy on this guy."

There was no dissuading him when he had his mind made up. Do I just specialize in stubborn friends or is all of humanity as pig-headed as those in my circle? Stone and Jaime often listen patiently to me then proceed to ignore everything I lay out.

I said, "I'll call you in the A.M. and we'll take it from there. I really don't need a chaperone though. I worked this county a lot of years without your supervision."

"And how many bodies did you leave in your wake? I can think of three off hand. Ever consider that yours could be the next? Even if Elvis has branched off from his dad's business, that doesn't mean that old Costello will take it kindly if you go after his kid."

"Give me some credit, Flint. The older I get, the more I see violence as the last resort. I prefer the carrot over the stick these days. Wally's got money and so does WJOK. If I told Elvis that I'd double whatever the guy who hired him is paying in exchange for a name, you don't think he'd go for that?"

"Depends on who hired him. You'd have to scare him more than that dude. He'd have to bet on you versus whoever contracted him. If you lose, he loses too. Honor among thieves. Word gets out that Elvis can't be trusted, then his budding career as a hitter goes down the crapper, possibly along with his mortal remains."

"I'll call you in the morning after I do some more homework."

"Do that," he said. He zipped his tattered leather jacket and turned to look me in the eye. "And think about this: why don't you turn this whole thing over to me? I know you told Allie you'd keep us out of it, but you also said she lied to you more than once and you're not sure you trust her. If I haul Crayton in for questioning, I might be able to get us that name for free. Then you could tack the savings onto your fee."

"This isn't a paid gig, copper. I might bill expenses, but I'm doing this for Rick. He hates Wally, but he loves Allie and he thinks that without Josephs, she'll lose her job."

"The White Knight rises. Just be careful and think about what I just said. The story is going to come out when we either catch the bad guy or he succeeds in killing Wally. And like you been saying all along, the publicity probably gives the show a big boost."

"You got it. Get some rest, Flint. Tomorrow could be a long day."

I don't know if I've ever shaken hands with McCullough. No hugs, for sure. We were both too macho for that. But I do respect him and although he won't admit it, he feels the same about me. And I'm starting to think that he actually looks more like that actor on Amazon who plays Harry Bosch than Scott Glenn. He probably would have even less of an idea who Titus Welliver is.

He got out of the car and walked a few paces to his own ride, an aging Chevy Malibu. Like I said, he wasn't a car guy. I waited until he pulled out in case the old rattletrap wouldn't start, but it fired up right away and he was off.

And so was I.

THIRTY SIX

I set no alarm, figuring I'd wake up when my body told me to. I didn't enjoy that luxury. My phone buzzed at six forty five. It was Stone.

"Hey, Riles, did I wake you?"

"Uh, yeah. What time did you say that real estate lady was coming by?"

"The showing is at nine. But she usually gets there a little early to make sure the place looks ship-shape."

"It already does. King's Maid Service may dust and vacuum a bit, but it looks good. Can I go back to sleep now?"

"Uh, that's not why I called. You're not going to like this."

"Let me guess. Instead of that hot blond agent you promised, she's sending an old crone with halitosis."

He cleared his throat, uncomfortable about breaking the news. "No, Jenny is coming herself. Just be gentle with her, is all I ask."

"Uh huh."

He was stalling for time.

"Riley, Wally's gone."

I had all I could do to keep from going into Stone's garage and throwing some of his golf clubs into the ocean. As it was, I exhibited exemplary self control by merely saying, "How the hell could you let that happen?

You couldn't keep an eye on him for even one day, you damn buffoon?"

"What was I supposed to do, sleep with the asshole? He went up to bed at ten, I was up 'til midnight. When I woke up this morning, his car was gone."

"And when you got up this morning, were you alone?"

"What does that have to do with anything?"

"You couldn't abstain for one night, could you? I don't know, could it be that you were so into satisfying your latest flame that you didn't hear his car start?"

He took this as a compliment. "She *was* kind of noisy."

I had to laugh at his crassness. But it was worrisome that I couldn't even count on him to hold the fort for one night until Moses arrived. I'm as horny as the next guy, but sometimes there's work to be done.

I said, "Are you sure he's *gone* gone, Stone? Like, he just didn't go out for doughnuts so he could surprise you with your favorite breakfast?"

"I wish. No, my Comrex and microphone are missing. So I guess he'll be on the air this afternoon, but not from here."

My radio knowledge is limited but I did know that anywhere there was a solid internet connection, Wally could plug in and be on the air instantly. Maybe Rick knew something I didn't that could narrow the search. So I asked, hoping he would pull a rabbit out of the hat.

He said, "I can't think of anything, really. The place would have to be fairly quiet, but not like those soundproof vaults they used to build in the old days. Now, Wally should want a *wired* Ethernet connection, but most decent hotels offer that. Wi-Fi works, but not as well. Although with Allie at the studio, if Wally drops his connection for a second, it wouldn't be the end of the world. No, Riles, he could be anywhere."

"We could narrow it down in terms of time. He's on at two in the afternoon. Do you have any idea when he left?"

"I got up at seven. Bosco was in the room with us. He started whining at five or so, woke me up but I just told him to shut up and go back to sleep. Maybe he heard Wally leaving."

"Great. So if he left at five, let's say he needed to be settled by noon --- so he could grab a bite before going on. That's seven hours. Average sixty miles per. Can't go east, the ocean is there. So he could be anywhere within a four hundred twenty mile semi circle from Virginia to Georgia, the Carolinas, Florida and Tennessee. In other words, forget finding him with anything short of Patton's Third Army."

"I'm sorry, Riles. I really don't think if I was alone last night it would have mattered."

He was probably right but I wasn't about to acknowledge that. His reckless womanizing was going to hurt him someday, but it had precious little to do with Wally's disappearance.

I said, "Did you see any hint that he was planning to split?"

"Not really. I mean, we weren't exactly buddy-buddy. We ordered out. We had the Knicks game on at first. I couldn't argue much with him because they were stinking up the court and I was just as pissed at them as he was. We switched over to the Monday night football game it was a blowout and he went up to bed at halftime. Things were as civil as they could be with him and me."

"We're not going to be able to track him and a lot of it's our own fault. We taught him well. Burner phone. Cash -- no credit cards. No EZ-Pass. Our only hope is if

Allie can talk him into telling her where he is. The only saving grace is that if we can't find him, nobody else can. Just to be sure, I'll have my computer dude check his credit card usage in case he slips up."

"Let's hope he's stupid enough to do that. What's your plan?"

"I got the hitter's name and address last night. I'm going to pay him a visit, maybe with our old pal McCullough."

Stone said, "Oh, the guy who liked me for Stevie Perry's murder last year."

I said, "He never believed you were guilty. He thought McCarver did it, maybe he still does. Look, I'll stop by and see Allie later. Maybe check out this Rasputin, see if he hates Wally enough to have him shot. I could be back as soon as tomorrow night. You want me to call Moses Ginn and tell him not to come?"

"I honestly don't know what help he could be if we don't have any leads on where Wally is."

I said, "I'll talk to him. He's a good man to have around. Just in case."

THIRTY SEVEN

Stone wasn't exaggerating about the charms of the realtor who rang the doorbell at 8:30, just as I was preparing to leave. She bordered on supermodel territory: perfect skin, long legs, great hair and a killer bod. She wore a tight blue skirt, ending just above the knee. A satiny cream-colored top, sleeveless, revealing well toned arms. I am happy to report they were devoid of ink. She was in her mid forties, but guessing her age would be the last thing any sentient male would be concerned about upon meeting this goddess.

I said, "Well, I was just leaving. I think you'll find everything in order. Any bites on the house so far?"

Her voice was pure velvet, sexy, but not artificially so. I don't have a lot of experience with models, but with the few I've come across, the minute they open their mouth, my interest fades faster than a pair of cheap jeans. But this lady had the whole package going on from the get-go.

She said, "There's been a lot of interest. It could take a while though. Sandy blew away a lot of the smaller houses on the ocean and after the insurance pays up, a lot of the owners are selling the raw land. Rick's place is too nice to be a knock down, but not big and lavish enough for the top end buyer. Someone who can afford oceanfront with the new insurance rates wants something really spectacular. Even though this house is nice, other than the view, it doesn't have that 'wow' factor the one per centers are looking for."

If it wasn't for Jaime, I'd be making a strong bid myself. A gorgeous woman who was making big bucks. Now that I knew her name, I recalled seeing it on numerous 'for sale' signs up and down Ocean Avenue. The sellers' commissions alone would easily hit six figures, maybe seven in a good year.

I suppressed taking my little fantasy any further. "Well, seriously, I've got to get going. Good luck with the buyers and I *will* call you, one way or another."

I hopped into my new ride, maneuvering around her Mercedes C300 in Stone's narrow driveway.

Stone's arsenal in Mantoloking was not large but adequate for my purposes: I had selected a small .22 Beretta amongst the half dozen available. I took the peashooter, not anticipating any real difficulty.

Elvis Crayton's ground floor condo wasn't in a luxurious gated community, but it wasn't in a crime-infested ghetto either. It was in a tightly spaced quadrangle of row houses, similar to what you might find in an affluent area of a major city. It was intended to resemble one of the nicer streets in Brooklyn, the Inner Harbor of Baltimore or Georgetown. The difference was that those neighborhoods had been around for centuries and this one had sprung up within the last twenty years. The facades were well maintained, and although the materials used were modern, they honored the appearance of traditional features like clapboard and shake siding, shutters, stone faced stoops and brick clad foundations. The river, just blocks away, could be seen from the upper floors in the winter.

Ever cautious, I parked the Audi just outside the main entrance, in case some neighbor had prying eyes. From there, no one could see the dealer tags.

"Nothing to see here," I said to myself. "Elvis has left the building."

There was no sign that anyone had been there recently. I could look into the master bedroom from the rear of the house --- the queen size bed was unoccupied and neatly made up. No clothes strewn about. There were no dirty dishes in the drain board, no stray pizza boxes littering the counters. Baking ingredients were in neat little ceramic containers resting next to the double oven.

It made me think that this place was only for show. It looked like it was staged by a realtor, preparing for a sale. It didn't look lived in, especially by a bachelor who rolled johns, was a courier for crooked cops and maybe was willing to up the ante to paid assassin. Elvis Crayton lived elsewhere, perhaps with a girlfriend. Maybe the hooker from the Iron Horse.

THIRTY EIGHT

Crayton's place was only a few minutes away, just over the causeway linking Bay Head and Mantoloking with the mainland. I had decided not to call McCullough. From what I was able to glean from BS's research, Elvis didn't seem to be such a tough customer. He was forty, younger than I, but gave away five inches and thirty pounds. He looked soft and slow. He was on the books as a principal in his dad's waste management business, but although it provided him with a modest income, John Sullivan suggested that he made more by moonlighting with his crooked cop buddies. From what I could gather, he struck me more as Fredo than Sonny.

Even though the place seemed deserted, I rang Elvis' bell. No answer. A couple of moves with a credit card and I was in. I gave the place a quick once over. I didn't expect to find a receipt from whoever hired Crayton to kill Wally, but I hoped to stumble on something that would give me a hint. The second bedroom was tasked as an office with a sofa bed, bookcase and a small oak desk. No laptop. A drawer containing bills and other household documents yielded nothing. I again was struck by how tidy everything was. Nothing lying around on the countertops or furniture. A magazine rack beside the sofa in the main room held but a few neatly stacked magazines. Out of curiosity, I pulled a couple out, thinking that maybe one of his hobbies or interests could give me some insight.

Sports Illustrated. Entertainment Weekly. General Aviation Monthly, Flight Journal, and PC Pilot. Did Elvis own a plane and a pilot's license? BS could find out --- maybe he already had, since I'd only skimmed the research he sent for obvious keys.

Although I didn't see any silent alarms, I didn't want to stay in the place any longer than I had to, so I slipped out the back door not more than ten minutes after entering. I strode casually out of the complex, trying to blend in with the surroundings. My next step would be to contact BS and see if he could trace Crayton's credit card use. That might give me an indication if he was still in the state, or if somehow he'd managed to trace Wally south.

I was lost in thought as I rounded the corner to where the Audi was parked. After less than a day, I was still getting used to looking for a pearlescent white S5 as opposed to the black A5 beauty I'd been driving for the past six years. I grinned in anticipation of seeing my new love.

The smile dropped at my first glimpse of the car, or rather who stood in front it.

"Breaking and entering. I could run you in for that," said Flint McCullough.

THIRTY NINE

"Your lack of faith disturbs me." I sounded like Darth Vader.

McCullough said, "You're blaming me? You said you'd call. Not a peep, so I figured you were coming here on your own. And what if Elvis was home? Were you planning to beat it out of him and didn't want me around to stop you?"

I had succumbed to that temptation in the past, years ago, but I am a kinder, gentler man now. But it's also true that the type of cases I have attracted of late don't call for any such persuasion. Although just because the situation hasn't called for it in recent days, doesn't mean that it isn't still in the old repertoire.

I said. "Have a little faith. I told you that type of thing is strictly the last resort. I now start with logic, a rational argument, some gentle persuasion, even money."

"You stopped before you got to the water boarding part. I told you last night, I couldn't care less about what happens to Elvis Crayton, but for some strange reason, I want to protect you. Far as I know, you've never lied to me. Been less than revealing mostly, but never out and out lied. I got nothing big going at the moment. Let me help."

If it was anyone other than McCullough, I would have suspected ulterior motives. The most obvious would be basking in the glory of busting the attempted killer of a prominent radio celebrity. But I took Flint at his word that he didn't want further conversations with me to be monitored by prison authorities through two-way mirrors.

"You want to visit this Rasputin character with me then?" I said.

"He's really a suspect?"

"No idea. Hey, I'm here, eight hundred miles from home. I might as well exhaust all the possibilities before heading back. Unless you think I should visit Elvis' dad next."

"To what end? To get him to give up his kid? That ain't happening."

"Exactly. I want to catch Allie around lunchtime; you're welcome to join me then. Maybe now that you're single, hooking up with a radio babe might be appealing."

I'd never seen him whiten before through his perpetual tan.

"Strictly business these days, King, strictly business. But sure, I'd love to join you for lunch. Does Allie know the Starlight?"

"No offense, but she's a bit higher maintenance than that. Will they call out the National Guard if you aren't at your favorite booth on time?"

That brought a real smile to his craggy face. "No, because I'll call first. Just don't take me to some chic-ass French place. Eating mostly salad's bad enough but I do need some sustenance."

"Meanwhile, I'll visit Rasputin on my own. I promise to leave the torture devices in the car."

He laughed. "Okay, sport. I'll give you credit for enough smarts not to beat up a media guy. You pick on folks who buy ink by the gallon, they have a way of fighting back."

FORTY

Rasputin, a.k.a. Chuckie Schwartz, lives with his parents in one of the toniest parts of Toms River, on a peninsula called Silver Bay. The house is perched on a narrow spit of land extending out to Barnegat Bay where a quarter acre is considered a large lot. Chuckie's parents had accumulated enough wealth with their medical practices to stitch together several parcels to accommodate their substantial contemporary home. The barrier island containing Seaside Heights and the Island Beach State Park stands just across the bay, but the MTV *Jersey Shore* mentality is light years away from this setting, which is more reflective of the Hamptons than the boardwalk in Asbury Park.

The building was elevated on pilings but on ground level, there was a large section which served as Rasputin's private lair. There was a private entrance so that its occupant can come and go without notice. Stone had told me that Rasputin was a nocturnal creature who generally did not arise until late morning.

Since I wasn't expected, Rasputin opened the door with caution, fearing a stalking fan or maybe a disgruntled reader.

"Perhaps you didn't see the sign on the way into our street that no solicitors are allowed. Please leave," was his friendly welcome.

"I'm only soliciting information," I said. "You and I have a common interest and I'd like to talk to you about him."

"I don't know who you think you're talking to. I have no enemies."

"Are you saying that your attacks on Wally Josephs aren't for real? If so, I'm barking up the wrong tree. I thought I'd found an ally instead of an opportunist."

The young scribe was barefoot, clad in bicycle shorts and a tee shirt. The all-black get-up could have been sleeping apparel or his everyday work outfit.

He said, "Ah, a Rasputin follower. But call me Chuckie, Mr....?"

"King. Can we talk inside? I think you'll find that our interests coincide when it comes to the despicable Mr. Josephs."

I hoped I wasn't overplaying contempt for Wally. It was an easy role to slip into.

Chuckie Schwartz stepped aside and gestured me in. His straight hair was fine and jet black, waist length. He had a silky black goatee and an equally dark brow, which further underscored the Satanic caricature he affected in tribute to his Russian namesake-de-plume.

"Nice digs," I said, meaning it in an ultimate man cave sort of way. The open office space was dominated by an eighty inch LED display unit, flanked by several smaller screens, servers and gaming consoles. Seven floor-standing Altec-Lansing speakers stood tall, strategically situated for optimum audio. The display monitors were illuminated with programming ranging from CNBC's stock ticker to music videos and reality shows.

"What's your interest in Josephs?" Schwartz said, inviting me to sit.

"I'm trying to dig up dirt on the bastard. I figured there was material you had on him that you couldn't or wouldn't print. Or maybe point me toward someone who does."

His voice was high pitched and nasal. "Why? I repeat, what's your interest?"

"I'm a private investigator. I have a client with a pretty serious beef with Wally Josephs."

"And the nature of this *beef*, as you so quaintly put it?"

I said, "I can't give you specifics but let's just say that a person dear to my client was harmed by one of his rants."

"That narrows it down to several thousand, I'd imagine."

He was giving me nothing so far. I had underestimated Rasputin as a journalist. I'd written him off as an amusing hack but he was deeper than that. He was more interested in drawing information from me than pursuing an agenda against Wally. For now, anyway.

I said, "I understand you have to protect your sources but I was hoping you could point me toward some people who might have gripes with Wally. Some who might need a champion."

He said, "I'd like to think that I'm that champion. But King, as much as I don't like Josephs, he does give me regular fodder for my column."

I picked up a strong flowery scent, like honeysuckle musk or jasmine. The man clearly indulged in a bit of weed and was using artificial means to cover the distinctive bouquet. He didn't seem high at the moment, but I doubt something so minor as the time of day would place any restrictions on his use.

I said, "So I take it you aren't into helping me get rid of Josephs' poison tongue?"

"Look man, I personally find the dude repulsive. He physically attacked me at one point and I was all set to press charges. But the boss man talked me out of it. So in answer to your question, I'd like to see him mortally wounded, but not dead."

I'd try one more tack then give in to the inevitable. There was synergy between Josephs and Schwartz. As adversarial as the relationship was, they fed off each other.

I said, "I'm not out to do him physical harm, just his career. I guess I need to find someone who really has something on him, not just someone who's using him to advance his readership."

He knew I spoke the truth. "Let's understand one thing. I don't write one word about Josephs or anyone else that I don't believe. The man's a sleazebag. He appeals to his listeners' baser instincts. He tortures his partner mercilessly. The poor woman comes off as a martyr."

"You think so? I think she uses him just like you do. Feigns offense but secretly, she loves it."

"Okay, I shouldn't be telling you this, but she complains to me all the time. I used to feel sorry for her. I thought if some of the things he does to the poor woman came to light via my column, maybe he'd stop. But now, I tend to agree with you --- she's in bed with him. The more outrageous and wrong he is, the better Alison comes off to anyone with a modicum of intelligence. She seems like the sensible one. As bad as she says he treats her, she knows where it's at. She's a publicity whore like the rest of them."

He might have said like the rest of *us*, including himself in the mix. There was no way Schwartz would hire anyone to kill Wally. They were symbiotic creatures, feasting off one another without remorse. This twenty eight year old kid living with his parents was wise to the trashy motivations of modern media. No wonder he had rarely written about Stone: nothing Rick did generated much controversy.

I said, "So you can't help me with anyone who has serious dirt on Wally?"

"If I did, I wouldn't tell you. I hate Wally and all that he stands for, but in the end, the general population aren't sheep. He only says publicly what simpletons like Trump supporters already believe. Intelligent people don't buy into his bullshit. If do they listen, it's to hear her put him down."

He paused to reconsider his stance. "The biggest thing he does that I think is really dangerous is his queer bashing. I'm afraid that he gives courage to the assholes who might act on it. Some drunken creeps might ride up to Asbury Park and beat on some gays."

It was a cheap trick on my part, but maybe it would spur Rasputin to offer more help. "Well, you couldn't have known it, but you've just stumbled on why my client wants him out. In terms of who he injured."

"I want him out too, but not the same way you do. I'm convinced that Wally is gay, in the closet, to use an expression from back in your day. He's in denial and he fights it by bashing the rest of us. Some day he'll realize it and stop living the lie. But for now, he covers it up by bedding every woman in sight. I bet he takes no pleasure in it. That's why he tried to beat me up that time. Because I called him on it."

FORTY ONE

Despite McCullough's distaste for the cuisine of our Gallic brethren, I met Alison at L'Ètoile de Mer, the restaurant of her choosing. Rather than call, I texted Flint to meet us there, hoping to avoid his annoyance. The chic French seafood joint was on Main Street in a converted Victorian, a few blocks south of WJOK's studios. The main room could accommodate less than fifty diners, but like Yogi Berra famously said, *nobody goes there anymore, it's too crowded.*

Alison Middleton was a regular and had no problem securing a last minute reservation. She was already seated and sipping white wine when I arrived, followed closely by McCullough. Had I not been friends with Stone, I might have been shocked by the idea that she was consuming alcohol this close to airtime, but boozing is an occupational hazard in the radio biz. Once upon a time, radio trade publications advertised job openings with the caveat, *no drunks or floaters.*

"Alison, meet detective Flint McCullough. Flint, Alison Middleton," I said, expecting the dirty look she gave us both. "I know you said to keep the police out of this, but I trust Flint implicitly and we need his help."

They both grunted simultaneously in strange harmony, his tenor to her alto.

"No offense detective, but I didn't want to drag the authorities into a private matter," she said, no conciliation evident in her tone. "King obviously doesn't listen to me or anyone else. I hoped we could handle this quietly."

Flint and I sat and she made no attempt to dissuade us from doing so. The table was small and simply adorned, white linen tablecloth with a single red rose in a glass vase.

McCullough said, "Quietly? You're talking attempted murder. Much as I hate to admit it, King here is pretty competent. But this is above his pay grade and he knows it. If it's real, of course."

Alison said, "What are you insinuating?" She set her wine glass back on the table, not gently.

"I'm thinking this is one big publicity stunt. I'm thinking that you and Wally and someone else at the station cooked all this up to boost your ratings, which have been down lately," he said.

Her voice took on an edge foreign to the reasoned approach of her radio persona. "This is the kind of dunderheaded thinking that made me avoid the police in the first place. I told King to keep this quiet. Not to bring in the authorities. The opposite of a publicity stunt, wouldn't you say?"

She gathered up her purse, preparing to walk out in a huff.

"Stay right there, Ms. Middleton," McCullough said. "You might take your listeners for a bunch of fools, but you're in the big leagues now. The first trick of a con artist is to make the mark think that everything is their idea and that the shill is only going along reluctantly. Madoff was great at this. Made the poor victims think they were being allowed into an exclusive club that he didn't really want them to join."

"You're comparing me to a man who swindled billions," she said. "That's rich. Where did you get the idea our ratings are down? We're the highest rated show on the station."

"You think you're the only person I have contact with in your business?"

I was amused by this by-play. McCullough was doing the bad cop bit, a role he'd taken with me a number of times. Since we hadn't discussed strategy on the way in, he was either counting on my silence, or my assistance in playing the more sympathetic inquisitor. For now, I was content to listen.

Alison said, "So you told a competitor about what happened to Wally. Great. King, this is a man you trust implicitly. I never thought you were a gullible asshole, but I see I was wrong to place any faith in you."

McCullough came to my defense. "I didn't tell anyone what *allegedly* happened. I just gathered some background from an objective source, not a competitor. Your station's in trouble. Net revenue down dramatically. It's true your ratings haven't dropped as fast as the rest of the day, but you're off 20 percent in the last two quarters. I congratulate you, though. You've played it masterfully. First, Wally's MIA for a few days. Papers are writing stories like *where is the bad boy of WJOK and why isn't he on the air?* You put out easily disproved releases about how this was a scheduled vacation."

Alison's anger was boiling to the point where I expected her to slap us both and turn over the table on her way out.

McCullough went on. "Then he's suddenly back, but from an undisclosed location. Mysterious, leading to more speculation and curiosity tune-ins. Now King tells me that he's gone missing again, but he's taken the remote equipment with him. What's the plan for today? AWOL again or broadcasting from a new hidey-hole?"

I hadn't told Allie that Wally had abandoned our little safe enclave. She was surprised.

She said, "What do you mean, he's missing again? King, what's he talking about?"

I said, "He slipped out this morning before Rick was up. Took the Comrex and microphone with him. No note, nothing. He could be anywhere."

A waiter approached and she waved him away with a curt gesture. "Why would he do that? You said that Stone would watch him and that you had another bodyguard coming to help."

I said, "Rick didn't handcuff him to the bedpost. This came out of the blue."

"Do you agree with what your cop friend is saying?" she asked, as though McCullough wasn't sitting at the table.

"I don't know what to think, Alison. I can't be responsible for someone who won't let me protect him. I came all the way up here on my own dime to help and your boy bolts at the first opportunity. How can I protect someone like that?"

She said, "He's scared. He doesn't trust Rick. He's trying to stay invisible. If you can't find him, then how can anyone else?"

I could waste more of my time tracking down Elvis Crayton and risking the revenge of his mobbed up father. I have too many problems of my own to keep killing daylight to save someone who I don't even like. Moreover, someone who wouldn't listen to my advice.

I said, "Alison, I'll assume your heart's in the right place. It's entirely possible that Wally or the station's people duped you and you have no knowledge of what they're trying to pull."

McCullough softened his tone and tried to appear more conciliatory. "Whatever the case may be, I'll promise you this. I'll track down this blond lady Wally claims picked him up at the bar. We have a witness who corroborates that much. But no guarantees. If another case with more substance comes up, this gets put on the back burner, maybe for good."

Alison took a long sip of her wine.

I said, "Allie, that's a good offer. And I'll tell you what I'll do. You talk to Wally off air if he does the show today. If you can convince him to come back to Hilton Head, I'll keep him under wraps. I'll take care of it personally this time. And if Flint can locate the blond or get something more to go on, we'll pick it up again here. Otherwise, I'm headed back South."

She slapped a bill on the table. "Thanks for nothing, you two."

She stood and walked out, as if jilted by a lover and too proud to let anyone see that it affected her. Neither of us made an attempt to stop her.

When she was gone, I said to McCullough, "Did you mean it about the blond? You'll look for her?"

"I'll check it out. I can't spend a lot of time on some bullshit story that we can't confirm. I should be able to find her. Most hookers have been arrested at one time or another. Even if she's not for hire, she sounds like she makes a strong impression. Someone will know who she is, maybe even a bar hopping cop."

"That's all I can ask. Keep in touch if you find out anything and I'll do the same."

McCullough nodded. "Deal."

"And I could see a little spark between you and Alison. Despite her being pissed off at the situation, I could see she likes you, you animal."

"No comment. You hungry?"

"Yeah, but this isn't my kind of place either."

He smiled. "Thought so. I knew I couldn't digest the shit on the menu here and that these piddling portions certainly wouldn't get me through the day, so I called the Starlight and told them I'd be a little late but to save my spot. There's room for you in my booth, Sherlock."

FORTY TWO

After lunch with Flint, I called Jaime and she told me she had to stay in New Jersey for the time being. A big time novelist had just quit her previous representation and the courtship process was gearing up. Whereas Jaime's agency was doing very nicely, a writer of this magnitude could catapult them even higher. So there would be the requisite wining and dining, a bit of negotiating and then some legal work if she decided to come aboard. It could take days or weeks, depending on how arduous the seduction played out.

She couldn't neglect her business. When she agreed to try doing her work from the Carolinas, she made it clear that a lot of the job required hands-on contact and that she would have to be away one or two weeks a month. But it was turning out to be more than that, and combined with work that called me away, we had been together maybe ten days every four weeks. I didn't see it getting any better since her agency was growing and taking on new business by the truckload.

After talking with Jaime, I came to the conclusion that this wasn't the time to buy an expensive toy to fill the void in my heart she was leaving. I dropped the car back at Esposito's and drove the economy rental to Newark, where I grabbed a flight home.

The Last Resort

As I got settled in at Hilton Head and gave Bosco some quality time, my phone buzzed. It was Rick, calling from some bar.

"Hey, bud, how's it going?" he said. He sounded a little high, as if he wasn't quite sure if I'd forgiven him for bungling the one simple task I had assigned him.

I told Rick that I had essentially put the case on hold, opting to turn matters over to McCullough.

"I knew that," he said. "Alison called after your lunch, ticked off like I've never heard her. Said you betrayed her. Couldn't understand how I could be friends with a shit heel like you. Questioned my judgment recommending you. Need I go on?"

"No, I get the gist. It's not like she was worried about hurting my feelings when she stormed out of the restaurant."

He cleared his throat. "Where are you now?"

"Back home on the island."

"Don't expect me home tonight then. I was going to come back for Bosco, but since you've got that covered, I've got plans. Lady I met yesterday is here for one more night and she's staying at a great hotel. Hotel sex! Not that I don't miss you, but she has it going on."

"So much for you learning a lesson from what happened to Wally. I hope she's at least within ten years of your age."

"Didn't check her passport. She's British. Liverpool, home of the Beatles. Have you ever had a Brit? All that reserve melts away in the throes of passion, my friend. And that cool accent. Oh, by the way, there's one other thing I thought you should know. I can't find my gun. In addition to making off with my remote equipment, Wally stole my piece, too."

"Great. Do you want me to check your sock drawer in case he took all of those and your undies as well? God, I am so done with this guy. Maybe you too, if you can't learn to curb your appetites."

"I'm sorry. I need this tonight. I'll explain when I see you."

He let that hang for a moment. Something else was bothering him that he wasn't ready to share just yet. *Here we go again.* All he said was, "With Wally, I guess I underestimated the little shit. But Riles, it's not like you to quit anything. I don't have to tell you how many cases you've been on where you could have let things run their course and instead you kept at it. I mean, just the other day, you were saying how you shouldn't have left that Serpente thing hanging."

This *was* a bit out of character for me, but in a good way, I think. I have a friend who's into Buddhism and he has always advocated that I should learn to let things go. Holding grudges is generally counterproductive. Forcing your ideas onto people who don't want your help may result in short term victories, but in the end, wind up causing more pain when they renege. I wasn't going to get into any deep philosophical discussions with Stone now.

I said, "I heard Wally on the air today. It's like nothing ever happened; you'd never know he wasn't in the studio with her. Look, the man fought us from the beginning. We offered him protection at no cost to him or benefit to us and he bolts the first chance he gets. He obviously doesn't trust us, or Alison for that matter. So frankly my dear, I don't give a damn. My only interest in this would be getting your remote equipment back."

"Gable is turning in his grave. Would you be pissed if *I* followed up?"

"Hey, you're free to do whatever you want. The guy hates you and you have no love for him. But if you want to keep beating your head against the wall instead of working on your golf, it's your call."

"Will you help if I need you to?"

Now this was really out of character. A Marine asking for help in advance. Stone's default position has always been that he can handle anything, even when he's in way over his head. The only motivation I could come up with is that he feels he let Alison down. He made a promise to her and he intends to honor it, come hell or high water. Sounds like me a week ago, before enlightenment. In-a-Gadda-da-Vida, or whatever the hell they say.

I said, "Look Rick, McCullough will investigate the woman and this Crayton character and report back. He's got a dog in this fight now because there might be some cops in bed with Crayton and Flint hates dirty cops. Wally is safe for now. If we can't find him, there's no way Elvis or whoever is after him can. You might stay on Alison and try to get her to convince Wally to come back to us, but failing that, we're at a dead end as far as what we can do on our own."

"I'm sorry. Was that a yes?"

"That was a *qualified* yes, idiot. By the way, what happened with Moses? I decided not to call him off. Did he show up yesterday?"

"The big man *was* here. He's gone now. Long story that I'll tell you about when I see you."

"Did you at least treat him to a round at Harbour Town? I bet he gave you a tougher time than I do. He breaks eighty from the tips at the Nat or so he told me."

"Yeah, we played. I'll tell you about it later."

From his tone, I could tell that he didn't want to talk about golf. That could only mean one thing. Ginn had beaten the pants off him. Now wasn't the time to rub it in, but I would later.

I said, "And Bosco did okay?"

"Didn't seem to care if you and Jaime were here or not, Riles. I walked him on the beach and he's been eating well. He's good company, but I can't say I like picking up his shit."

"Well, save it up in case you run into your friend Campbell again. Oh, something I didn't tell you. I got the impression that real estate lady, Jenny Lightower really digs you. And she is the whole package, my friend."

"Yeah, well, we've had a few dates. No action. She didn't give it up for me, that's for sure. Felt like I was back in high school. Good night kiss was all I got."

I said, "When you get back, we'll have to talk about that. Things of lasting value aren't easily obtained."

"What Hallmark card did you get that off of?"

FORTY THREE

I had a dinner at a local restaurant in Shelter Cove and followed it up with a fitful night's sleep. Stone was right in that I didn't like to leave loose ends, and when I knew there was unfinished business, it had a way of intruding on my slumber. Even though I had told all concerned that I had written Wally off, that wasn't how I operated.

The phone rang at six thirty.

"King. Got some news for you."

It was McCullough.

I said, "It couldn't wait until regular business hours?"

"No such thing in our line of work, buster. Sorry to wake you at this outrageous time of day, old man. I spent most of yesterday afternoon chasing down your shit. You wanna hear it or go back to your much needed beauty sleep?"

"Okay. Sorry. What's up?"

"Your faithful liege did what he said he would. I found the girl and hauled her in for questioning."

I sat up. Rubbed Bosco's ears, which brought a contented sigh. If only humans were so easily pleased.

"So Flint, are you just going to keep me in suspense? Do you have any news or do you just miss me?"

"Keep playing the wiseass, King and you can read about it in the papers."

"Okay, Detective McCullough, please share your bounty with me, sir."

"That's better. Showing proper respect for the legal authorities. Bottom line, I think Crayton is running girls, or should I say, a girl. I'm thinking this isn't the first time he pulled a pimp roll."

"So you located him?"

"Not yet. But I corralled the blond. She wasn't hard to track down. I got her name, Darla Diamond. Typical story, wanted to be an actress, wound up cutting hair. We picked her up once for solicitation, no conviction. One of her johns came forward and told us how it worked although he later refused to press charges. The way I see it, she and Crayton target wealthy guys. She pretends she's a cop working undercover. Of course, the vic is scared and tries to talk his way out of it. She lets on she'd be willing to let everything slide for a small gratuity. Of course, she denied everything yesterday and swore she had no idea who Wally Josephs is."

"So the girl gets paid off and doesn't even have to surrender her virtue, such as it is."

"Bingo. She keeps her day job as a stylist. This is a nice supplement. And as long as they pick the marks carefully, she stays clean. She just made this one boo-boo and even that didn't stick. Only reason I know is I'm friends with the cop who busted her."

"Got it. So how does Crayton fit in with shooting Wally?"

"I can't tie that together yet."

I thought about it for a moment and said, "Let's say someone hired Crayton to kill Wally and he used her to set it up. Maybe even stick her with the rap if they got busted. She might not even have known it was supposed

THE LAST RESORT

to be a hit. She might have just thought he was turning her on to an easy mark."

"Could be. She gave me nothing. I couldn't even budge her when I said that witnesses saw her leave the Iron Horse with Wally. She said she recalled some goofy guy hitting on her there but she dumped him when he got fresh. I couldn't prove otherwise."

"Only trouble is, Wally doesn't really fit the profile, does he? I mean, he gets caught with a hooker, it only makes him cooler with his listeners."

"That's a fact. He was a poor choice for blackmail, even though he does have bucks. This is strictly amateur hour with these two. I'd need Josephs to come in and press charges, ID the both of them and you say he won't do that."

"Hold on a sec."

My dog was nudging me, sticking his snout under my arm, attempting to pry the phone away from my ear. He wanted his breakfast ---now! I got out of bed, carrying the phone with me.

Bosco looked at me in puzzlement, if that expression really was in his repertoire. Or maybe I just assign his Johnny Carson-like blank looks into what I imagine him to be thinking. Whatever was going through his mind didn't stop him from attacking his kibble with vigor.

I was punishing Flint for waking me so early by feeding Bosco and keeping him on hold while doing so. I finally said, "So what do you do now? What about the girl going forward?"

"I'll wager she's done with Crayton and Wally. I'd like to think I put the fear of God in her. She may tell Elvis that the cops questioned her and she told them nothing but it scared the shit out of her and she's pulling out, maybe she even dissolves the partnership."

"What about Crayton? Doesn't this put her in a bad spot if he figures that she did talk?"

"She's a big girl. If she's in over her head and can't talk her way out, there's nothing I can do. I told her if she'd fess up I'd protect her, but she wasn't interested. If she was scared, she didn't let it show. She's either a great actress or a real tough cookie."

I've run similar games, both with the feds and in private practice. My fear was that Crayton might be so ruthless that he decides to eliminate both Wally and the girl to cover his tracks.

I said, "The girl might be a high class hooker and a small time blackmailer, but paying for her sins with her life is just a bit excessive. The thing with Wally's car bothers me. Crayton tracked the Porsche to Esposito's lot. If he was just trying to scam Wally, why bother to track the car?"

"My guess is he was trying to retrieve his tracking device. Again, amateur hour. If they were really pro killers, they could have just waited until he came back to the motel to fetch the car and blow him away then."

"Who knows? Like you say, this could be a one or two man show and they need to sleep sometime."

Flint said, "Well, if this was a publicity stunt, it's served its purpose and there would be no use pursuing it further."

"There are better and easier ways to boost the ratings. I can't buy this was a game. Too many variables that could blow up in their face."

"Okay then, if it was for real, Crayton will get the message from Darla that he's on my radar now and he'd be my first stop if anything happens to Josephs. That may deter him from pursuing this, unless he thinks he can out maneuver me."

"I wouldn't want Flint McCullough on my tail for any length of time if I were him. Been there, done that."

"I'll take that as flattery from the likes of you. I'm thinking my main interest in this should be the dirty cops Sullivan hipped us to. With all the shit going down in this country, that's something we can't afford to tolerate."

"You got that right. Thanks, Flint. Talk soon."

FORTY FOUR

Stone stumbled in early that evening, and I do mean stumbled. He was heavily hung over, making grunting noises at the slightest exertion as he lumbered toward the kitchen. He ignored Bosco, even though my dog greeted him with his characteristic canine enthusiasm.

Keen observer that I am, I said, "Rough day? Rule Britannia or did she rule you?"

"Ah no, she took off. London Calling."

"Thanks for not trying to sing it like the Clash."

Stone gave me a sour look and a bitter note infected his smooth FM voice. "Ha, ha. Got me there, jerk-off."

We're sarcastic with each other all the time, but in jest. This time, it was real. I wasn't sure how I inspired it, unless it was delayed payback for the tongue-lashing I gave him for losing track of Wally.

"Look Rick, I'm sorry if I gave you shit about Wally taking your gun and remote equipment. Even if I was there, he might have pulled the same stunt. But you have to admit, you got me into this and I trusted you to keep an eye on him and he split right under your nose. Is that what's bothering you?"

"It's on the list. Let's add Allie not speaking to me. Like I told you, she usually stays pissed at me for a few hours and then she's cool. She's been ducking my calls."

He opened the refrigerator and extracted a half gallon jug of skim milk, guzzled most of it down straight from the bottle, then carried it to the breakfast bar to polish off the rest.

I said, "Maybe you like her a little more than you admit?"

He rolled his eyes. "No, I was just trying to get her to talk to that asshole Josephs and get my stuff back. I told you, she's like a sister. Nothing physical going on, especially since you said she screwed Campbell."

I told him about my talk with McCullough. He listened with half an ear, while fiddling with his smart phone.

I said, "Something else is going on with you. Come on, tell me what the problem is."

He took a big gulp of milk again and wiped his mouth on his sleeve. He wasn't talking.

I kept at it. "So let me guess. You couldn't perform with the limey. A little too much to drink? Brewer's droop?"

"Never been a problem. No little yellow pills for this guy. And if it ever does become a factor in ten years, I'll just steal one of yours."

"Congratulations. We've risen up to seventh grade insults now. Come on, Rick, it's me. What's really bothering you?"

He ran his fingers through his hair. Although it had started to thin, he was still far from Sy Sperling territory. He was very self conscious about it but his current state had to be more than that perpetually nagging concern.

Finally, he opened up and said, "It was Ginn."

"You two didn't get along? Hey, if you don't like him, there's no reason your paths ever have to cross again."

"No, it wasn't that. He's a great guy. I really did like him. It was his game."

"He cheats?"

Again, the milk. I'd have to rummage around to find something else for my coffee in the morning because he drained it to the dregs.

Stone looked up at me, his eyes bloodshot. "He shot 75. I had a 77."

"That's not bad. So he beat you by two. Big deal."

"But I played from the blues, he played from the tips and he still was way past me on every hole. I played great, as well as I possibly can. He said he was off his game, hadn't played much lately. Riles, it was like a man playing against a boy. He beat the shit out of me and that was with him conceding me four foot putts. Senior Tour? Not happening for Rick Stone, that much became crystal clear."

This was as down as I'd seen him since his depression over Lisa Tillman. His dream girl had dumped him. Now he believed his fantasy career was out of reach. Added to getting canned at WJOK, life had dealt him a couple body blows recently.

"Rick, you've been out of work a month. Sure, you've played a lot in that time, but you can't expect to right away challenge guys who've done this all their lives. Takes time. You don't have a coach. You haven't taken any instruction that I can see."

"Damn it Riles, this is reality staring me in the face. Ginn must be close to seventy years old. He dusted me. And he's just a pretty good amateur, not even a scratch player. He's light years ahead of me. There's no way I can make up that kind of ground, no matter how long I work at it."

He was probably right. His new mission was daunting: playing golf against seasoned pros, however past their prime they may be. Even escapades with hot Liverpudlian women couldn't paper over the pain.

I gave blind optimism another shot. "You lectured me yesterday about quitting. You said it wasn't in my DNA. You were right. I do want to see this Wally business through and I will."

This felt like trying to drag Bosco along when he plants his feet and refuses to budge. "You want my two cents, I think you're giving up way too early on golf. You're a Marine. You think the Senior Tour is tougher than that? Didn't you see men in basic training that could beat you in every way when you first started? How many could do that in the end?"

I was proud of my Knute Rockne pep talk. But it didn't move the needle.

Stone shook his head in resignation. "Nice try, Riles. I appreciate it, but the writing's on the wall. I knew in college I'd never be a major league pitcher. Just didn't have the talent. It feels the same now. God willing, I've got thirty years left on the planet. I need to figure out what to do with them."

FORTY FIVE

I'm not Rick's keeper or even his biological brother, but I owe him. He stepped in front of a bullet for me. But I couldn't think of anything I could do to help except to try to stay positive and encourage him to keep trying. Or maybe find something more urgent to occupy his time.

If Alison continued to avoid taking Rick's calls, there was no way she'd answer mine. I thought about sending Stone up to Toms River to confront her in person, which could give Rick some purpose in life. But returning to the scene of his old job might send him spiraling in the opposite direction.

I really wanted to tie a bow on the Wally "situation" and move on to other things. I wasn't quite sure what those other things were, but when there might be filet mignon in your future, you shove aside the veggies to make room.

I called McCullough at noon the next day. I hoped to catch him chowing down at the Starlight. Sure enough, when he clicked on, the clanking dishes and hum of conversation in the background told me I had timed it correctly.

"Hey Flint, how's that kale tasting today?"

"You know King, they had a new waitress here the other day who kept asking me the same question. I almost pulled a Jack Nicholson and told her to stick it between her legs. But if you really want to know, I cheat one day a week and go back to my omelet. Can I eat it in peace or do you have another assignment?"

"I'm not a high school teacher giving you assignments detective, but I'd like to ask a favor."

"Only if you say pretty please. Okay, what?"

"We really ticked off Alison Middleton the other day. She won't even take Stone's calls, she's so mad at him. I was thinking you might be able to catch her on her way into work and tell her what you told me about Wally and the pimp."

"Sounds like an Elton John song, *Wally and the Pimps*." Stone had snuck up on me and overheard. He sang the chorus of *Benny and the Jets* incorporating his new lyrics. As annoying as the habit was, it showed him to be in a slightly better mood than last night.

"I heard that," McCullough said. "Tell Stone he sounds like your hound in heat."

"I've told him that many times, but I hate to insult the dog. So, can you do the thing with Allie today?"

"What makes you think she'll talk to me if she won't talk to you or Justin Beiber there?"

"Your badge. And your rugged-Scott Glenn-looking mug."

"For someone asking a favor, you're hitting a lot of sour notes. Even worse than Stone's singing."

I waved Stone out of my office and he headed for the kitchen, presumably to scrounge up some lunch. "I was thinking of sending Rick, but why send a messenger when she can hear it firsthand. Maybe she'll trust you enough to at least listen and convey the news to Josephs."

"Of course I'll do it. I was only stringing you along. I think I could arrange to bump into her today. You know King, despite getting off on the wrong foot with her at that frog joint, she's a damned fine looking lady. Makes a good buck too. And I like her style on the radio. Just saying."

So old Flint wasn't carved out of granite after all. A grizzled cop could do a lot worse.

I said, "Go get her, Flint. Let me know how it goes. I'd really like to put this Wally affair to bed."

The double entendre flew harmlessly over his head.

He said, "We'll see. At some point, I may need to hit him up to testify about Crayton. Like we talked, it could be leverage for the other stuff about the dirty cops. But for now, I'll keep it on the down low."

"Okay. Appreciate it. See ya later."

Mission one accomplished. I dialed Jaime.

"Hey Jaim, am I calling too close to lunch?"

She sounded a bit harried. "I've got to be out in ten minutes. I think we're about to get down to specifics with our lady writer."

Stone was in the other room so I wasn't in danger of being serenaded with a Dire Straits refrain. I closed the office door so he couldn't overhear, since part of what I wanted to talk about was his situation. I told her about the golf and how down my friend sounded.

When I was finished she said, "Are you afraid he'll do something to hurt himself?"

"Rick? No way. He's a Marine."

"Ex-Marine."

"He'll tell you there's no such thing as an ex-Marine. You're in the corps for life. I don't see him sinking to that level yet. He took losing the gig at WJOK pretty well."

"Yes, but that was getting stale anyway and he had the golf as a backup plan. Now you're telling me that's in the wind. He's got nowhere to turn."

"He's smart. He's helped me work cases. He's tough. I could use him sometimes."

"Riley, come on. You aren't really looking to expand your business. If anything, you're scaling back. I'm actually a little worried about *you* keeping busy."

"You could keep me busy by greeting me at the door the way you did last time you were here."

"Your turn, big guy. If you don't want to go the Full Monty, a Speedo would do."

"Not my style, but I'll come up with something for you." Even I had to groan at my weak attempt at witty sex repartee. I like to think I'm more a man of action in that arena.

I said, "When are you coming back?"

"I'm afraid I saved the big news for last. Our writer friend wants her books made into movies. She wants to meet our rep on the coast who helps me set up video deals. And maybe hook her up with a few big execs in the film industry to prove we have clout. If this lunch goes well, we may hop a flight out west as soon as tomorrow."

"Oh."

"Don't sound so disappointed. This could be huge for the agency. Oh, and some good news for you, too. In addition to H, they've signed two of your heroes to supporting roles. You might even want to fly out and meet them on the set after we start shooting."

"How did you manage to resurrect Bogie and Robert Mitchum?"

"Silly. I'm talking about Bill Shatner and Don Johnson. Captain Kirk and Sonny Crockett. Two of your faves."

I wasn't sure I wanted to meet those guys. I've always enjoyed the roles they play, but when you really love a character, the flesh and blood actor usually falls short. Sometimes they turn out to be narcissistic assholes which ruins the illusion for you in the future.

And sometimes, it's just plain awkward. Jaime had introduced me to Harrison Ford, or *H* as she now calls him. He was very nice, shook my hand and all but I had no idea what to say to him. After a couple of mumbled compliments on what a gem Jaime was, he had little to add and I couldn't come up with anything other than how much I enjoyed him as Jack Ryan, Indiana Jones, Richard Kimble and about ten others. He must hear variations on that fifty times a day.

I went away feeling let down by my inability to find common ground. We live in different worlds, Jaime being our only link. He probably wouldn't be too receptive to my idea about how Han Solo should have been cloned before he perished in the last Star Wars flick. Then he could be brought back in the next installment to battle that bastard son of his. Works for me.

I said, "You know I love those guys. Please don't tell me if they're jerks in real life."

"Promise. Hey, I just thought of something for Stone. I won't tell you now in case I can't make it happen but I have an idea."

"How about a hint?"

"Nope. I'm gonna be late for lunch. If my idea works, I'll know pretty soon, maybe even today. I'll call you later. Love you."

FORTY SIX

I streamed the live feed of WJOK to see if I could detect anything in Alison's tone that reflected an encounter with Flint. I wasn't naïve enough to think she'd refer to it directly on air, but maybe she'd let something slip that indicated a change of attitude. After their opening, I sensed that nothing had changed. I'd keep it on in the background, but rather than sit around all afternoon and wait for McCullough and Jaime to call me back, I decided to follow up on a lead I should have pursued earlier.

Stone poked his head into the office before I could act. "Going out to the range to hit some balls. Even if I can't play like a pro, I still love the game."

"Again, don't let one bad day affect your whole outlook. Maybe you should hire a swing coach, try a little different approach. Might make a difference."

"We'll see. Hey, turn that up a little."

I wasn't sure what he was talking about until he pointed toward the two Bose speakers flanking my monitor. I hiked the volume up a couple of notches, and the not-so-glorious sound of the Allie and Wally show flooded the room.

"Wow. You hear that?" Stone said.

"Haven't been paying that much attention. Just wanted to hear if Allie seemed different after talking with Flint. He hasn't called in yet so maybe he missed her."

"That's not what I mean. Listen closely to Wally."

"Must I?"

"Not to what he's saying. He's full of shit as usual. Listen to his voice."

No one has ever accused Wally Josephs of having great pipes for radio. Back in the day, his shrill tone never would have passed muster on air. He'd either be a behind the scenes producer or a provocative columnist if he could write a little. But standards have been lowered, or perhaps more fairly, shifted, from style to substance. Broadcasters with lousy voices have found their way onto the airwaves if they have something compelling to say.

After listening to him joust with Alison for a minute I said, "Sounds the same to me. You think he has a cold or something? And how could you tell?"

"I guess my ears are more attuned than yours, shankasaurus. The room is what I'm talking about. Assuming he's still using my mic, listen to the acoustics of the room. Definitely more hot sounding, more echo-y than yesterday. He's not in the same place."

"Interesting. That could be good or bad for us. If he's on the move, he might make a mistake. Use an ATM for cash or buy gas on credit. On the other hand, he might be harder to trace as a moving target."

"What about those audio analysts who pick up background sounds and can locate someone based on that?"

"That works great on NCIS, but we don't have Abby and their fiction writers. He's likely in a hotel room and one hotel room sounds pretty much like any other."

"Well, it was a thought," Stone said.

"Creative thinking, nothing wrong with that. But our real problem is that this expands the territory. He could be driving further west, north, south, every day. Our original four hundred mile radius might be eight or twelve

RICHARD NEER   177

hundred miles now. He could be in Texas for all we know."

"Sorry. So much for my amateur ideas. I'll be back in a couple hours."

"Hey, it might be important. You never know. Every little bit of info helps. Go hit 'em straight." I tried to buck his spirits up as he left for the driving range. I hoped that Jaime's idea to keep him stimulated would blossom, whatever it was.

I contacted BS. He is a techno-nerd par excellence, but in some ways he's a traditionalist. I use AIM to contact him. I opened his private chat handle and he was there.

RK: Need some info.

BS: What can I help you with?

RK: Need to track down Ted McCarver. Man you helped me with last year.

BS: Require current location?

RK: If possible.

BS: Trust issues with you. Five minute answer.

RK: Thanks, Yoda. I'll be waiting.

Someday, I needed to meet this fellow, or lady or whatever I was talking to. It could be some bot for all I know. But whatever it was, it was damn good. In under five minutes, I received an email, another outmoded form of communication amongst the cognoscenti. Easily hacked, even with high governmental security measures as recent political campaigns have detailed. But there was nothing in the BS report that threatened the national interest, so I didn't sweat it.

Ted McCarver was in Hilton Head. In addition to the house that he gifted Stone and me, there was a condo he had kept for friends and business associates in Sea Pines. BS noted that he had paid for lunch at Truffles Café within the last hour, a fashionable eatery less than a mile from the condo. Additionally, his local dining-out charges had resumed several days ago, so I assumed Ted had been in town since then.

McCarver had discovered Wally Josephs at a small station in Pennsylvania and brought him to the big time at WJOK. He had nurtured the kid's career through numerous rough patches. He had Wally's back and in return, his loyalty. If anyone might persuade Wally to come in from the cold, it might be Ted.

I planned to ambush him to find out.

FORTY SEVEN

I hadn't laid eyes on Ted McCarver in over a year. The last time we saw each other was in a cell at the Ocean County lockup. He was wrongly accused of killing his fiancée, a charge I cleared him of, with an assist from Stone. He didn't look good back then, although other than in those 'feel-good' prison movies, who does look good in an orange jumpsuit?

Ted is seventy. Before his incarceration, he cut a debonair figure. Dressed in bespoke suits fitted to his sleek frame, he could have been a Ralph Lauren model. But after six months in a monastery and six months god-knows-where, I had no idea what to expect: an emaciated facsimile of the stylish gent I once knew or a bloated version of Friar Tuck.

Sea Pines is at the southern tip of Hilton Head. It's probably the most touristy area on the island, which is not necessarily a bad thing. The yacht basin adjacent to the famous red and white striped lighthouse harbors some of the largest privately owned vessels in existence. There are dozens of condominium buildings amidst this affluence, none rising higher than four stories. The most elite have commanding views of the basin, Calibogue Sound and the eighteenth fairway of the lush Harbour Town links. Of course, the most exclusive building contained McCarver's little crash pad.

THE LAST RESORT

This was a perfect Indian Summer day: not a cloud in the Carolina blue sky, low seventies and no humidity. I parked in a gravel lot near the basin and walked over to Ted's building.

McCarver's unit was on the top floor, a corner layout where the sightlines were optimal. I knocked on the rough hewn cypress door, and he answered promptly, as if expecting someone. His jaw dropped when he saw me, but McCarver recovered quickly and invited me in.

"I must say, an unexpected pleasure," he said. "Not that I didn't figure that we'd meet while I was on the island, but I expected it to be a time and place of my choosing. Please sit down. Can I offer you a drink?"

Always the perfect host. Ted wasn't wearing a suit but was turned out stylishly nonetheless. He wore chocolate brown corduroy slacks, a cream colored boiled wool sweater with elbow patches, woven leather moccasins on his feet. His face was tanned, and he had grown a beard. It was neatly trimmed and he now loosely resembled the actor who played 'the most interesting man in the world' on those beer commercials. Given Ted's cosmopolitan background, the character could have been modeled after him.

I said, "You know what I like. A single malt, rocks if you have it."

"Of course. Coming right up."

The view was as I had imagined and the expansive wall of tall windows showcased it to the best possible advantage. There was a light chop on Calibogue Sound and the multi-colored flags on the yacht masts were standing stiff in the breeze.

Ted said, "So I might ask what brings you here but I think we both know so let's dispense with the preliminaries."

"Let's not. Unless you have a pressing engagement later, let's do the prelims. Like where the hell have you been and why didn't you let us know you split from the monkery?"

He went about preparing our drinks. He was abstaining for now, just club soda. It was a little early in the day for Glen (fiddich or livet) but a small jolt might be in order given the surprise revelations that have accompanied my meetings with Ted over the years.

I said, "So catch me up. Rick says you left the monastery six months ago. The austere, celibate life not to your liking?"

"It was what I needed at the time. Quiet contemplation. Penance. Not that I'm a true believer, but I owed the world something after what happened to Stevie."

Stevie Perry was the love of his life. She was one of the three women who he felt he had wronged in his younger days. He believed that if he could clear his conscience with them, he might be able to find love again. The first woman on his list not only refused the apology and the money, but she shot Stevie and would have put a bullet in Ted had he been with her at the time. She was currently residing in a New Jersey mental facility.

He said, "I'll never be able to make up for it. But I'm trying to do the best I can. I gave a good size donation to a foundation for abused women. And of course, I can never express my thanks enough to you and Rick."

He was understating the extent of his gratitude. He'd given Rick and me the oceanfront house on the island. For my services in finding the three women, he wired an overly generous sum directly into my account

"Ted, the house still has all your furnishings and we haven't done a thing to it other than routine maintenance. If you'd like it back, Rick and I have no problem with that."

"No, I want you guys to have it. And anticipating your next question, I *am* seeing Doctor Mills again. She's doing what she can to help me. I have good days and not so good ones."

Mills was the therapist who had gone along with his plan to find the women. If it were me, I'd seek counsel elsewhere. "So you've been here for a while then?"

"I go back and forth. I still have the plane, so I get up North when I need to. The airport here is very convenient."

He sipped his club soda. I would have expected the stress of the past year to have aged him, but he looked better than ever. The beard suited him and the robust tan was just what he needed to complete the GQ look. His grey eyes were clear as ever, and he hadn't put on an ounce that I could see.

I said, "Okay, let's catch up some more later. You and me and Rick should do dinner soon. But I guess you know I'm here about Wally Josephs."

He said, "Of course. My wild protégé gone rogue."

"The very one."

"Wally was my boy. The best raw radio talent I'd come across since Rick, but in a very different way. I hired him to do weekends at WJOK, paid him way more than the other part-timers. Guided him along and made him a star. Right before I sold the place, I gave him a contract like no other in the business. Guaranteed for ten years. No out clauses for morals or anything slippery. I knew about his predilections. I didn't want some bible thumping exec at Cirrus cutting him like CBS did with Imus."

"So you're responsible for the crap that comes out of his mouth on a daily basis?"

"Coarsely put, but yes, it's all on my plate. You know I sold the station not long after signing that deal with him. I hoped that the security would smooth some of his rough edges. I'm afraid it only made them worse. I wasn't around to rein him in when he went off the reservation, and the new management let him run wild."

"That's an understatement."

"Yes, but it did work at first. The first two years, his numbers skyrocketed. Although honestly, I was glad to be out of it because it's not the kind of radio I want my name on."

"I'm relieved to hear that," I said. "It surprised me that you took that asshole under your wing."

McCarver said, "Had I stayed at WJOK, I'd like to think he'd be a different broadcaster today. What's happened to the industry is appalling to an old fogey like me. They live quarter to quarter. They've piled up so much debt that they'll never get out from under it. Frankly, the money they paid me is three times what the place is worth now."

"You always had good timing. Although by covering your own butt, you left a lot of good people hanging."

"It's like an avalanche. You can stand your ground and get snowed under, or retreat. The former may be more courageous, but only in memoriam. I chose to survive."

Ted's voice had a classic radio timbre. Crisp enunciation, deep baritone, no trace of any regional accent. His choice of words is somewhat stilted. He was born a couple of decades late. Back in the days of great national networks, he'd be a star booth announcer, giving Don Pardo competition. I've mused with Rick that Ted could be spouting the most outrageous bullshit and it would sound logical because of his mellifluous tones and command of the language."

I said, "So back to Wally, I take it you're aware that he thinks someone tried to kill him?"

"Of course I am. Where do you think he did his show until today?"

FORTY EIGHT

Once again, I was gobsmacked by Ted McCarver. I was angry. At Ted, Wally and the whole situation.

I said, "Did Wally tell you that we agreed to protect him and actually hired another bodyguard to help? To thank us, he ran out in the middle of the night and stole Rick's remote equipment and gun."

"Calm down, Riley. He ran out on me, too. We argued after his show yesterday and he picked up his toys and left."

"So where is he now? In hell, as far as I'm concerned."

"Look, the kid has problems. Wally called me right after he was attacked. He insisted I not tell anyone at Cirrus. He made me swear to keep everything between the two of us. He was really scared and it was hard to talk sense to him."

"So how did he know you still have a place down here?"

"Let me refresh your drink. And I think I'll go for something harder too." Ted rose from the sofa and walked over to the liquor cabinet. He came back with a fresh bottle of Glenfiddich and two ice filled glasses. He poured a generous portion into the new glass, even though I hadn't finished the first.

He said, "He called me again Saturday, right after he first talked to you. I told him that he couldn't find anyone better to investigate the shooting and keep him safe. It took some persuading because he was wary of your relationship with Stone, but I convinced him to come down. I was up in Vermont when he called but I said that I'd fly down to the island the next day if he needed more support."

"So Tuesday, he left our house before sunrise and hooked up with you?"

"He called me that morning and asked if I could put him up for a while and could he do his show from my place? What could I say? I wanted to know why he left your protection and he said he'd tell me once he got here."

I said. "I've never had a client fight me harder when all I was trying to do was help. What the hell do I have to gain from working with Wally Josephs? You or Cirrus gonna give me a gold star or something?"

"King, at the root of all this is Wally doesn't trust Stone. He said they came to blows the first day he arrived. Even said you threw him up against the wall."

"After he tried to kick Bosco."

"He neglected to mention that. Wally didn't feel comfortable or safe in that house. That's why he left and sought asylum with me."

"So why did he leave *you*? Bed wasn't soft enough?"

Ted played with his scotch, swirling it around the glass but not partaking. "No. I hadn't heard his show in quite some time and I was upset at how low he had sunk. The dog whistle racist stuff. The gay slurs. I don't think he really believes any of it, mind you. But I guess he thinks that kind of pandering to the unwashed masses makes them relate to him better. When he got off the air yesterday, I confronted him about it and he didn't take it well. He said that he had trusted me. He thought I really understood him and now even I had betrayed him. In case you hadn't noticed, he's pretty paranoid and doesn't respond well to criticism."

"And if he won't listen to you, who will he listen to? He doesn't even trust Alison. She flew all the way down here the other night to ask for our help."

"Well. I have to agree with him there. I wouldn't trust that back stabbing wench from here to the lighthouse."

I had never heard Ted speak about a woman in such harsh terms. Despite his difficulties with one on one relationships, he was quite the feminist in the abstract.

I said, "Why do you say that, Ted? I thought you were the one who put Wally and Allie together."

"My original idea was to team Wally with Stone. Do our own version of Mike and the Mad Dog. I convinced the brass at Cirrus that it would be a winning combination. But I sold the place before I put the show together and with new management in place, she poisoned Stone against Wally. Made up awful things out of whole cloth. They were fine with each other until she started agitating. Rick eventually said he could never work with Wally, even though they said they offered him more money. From afar, I tried to tell Rick that Wally wasn't such a bad guy, but her scheming worked out perfectly to her benefit."

"Why didn't you tell the Cirrus people what was going on?"

"I didn't know it then. She covered her tracks well. I only found out months later. BJ Campbell told me the whole story. I just thought Alison was a sweetheart who got along with everybody. Campbell gave me chapter and verse about her machinations."

"She does handle Wally's bullshit pretty well. She rebuts most of the stupid stuff he says."

Ted was exasperated, like Victor Frankenstein trying to defend the monster he had created. "My idea for pairing Wally with Stone was not to make him a clown, but the voice of the average fan. You know, the ones who are wrong most of the time, but appeal to our more primal instincts. Then Rick could balance that out as a voice of reason and the dynamic would play well on both sides of the aisle. I suppose that's her role now."

This time he really did take a long pull of Glenfiddich, instead of just gaze at it as it swirled around the glass. "But what do I know? That warped chemistry they developed has him playing the role of a know-nothing bigot. That's not really him. Although like a method actor, he's so deep into the role he doesn't know who he really is. That was far from the way I would have drawn it up. And silly me, I gave the kid a virtually bulletproof contract."

"Like you said, he was your boy."

"I also was foolish enough to think that a company like Cirrus would care about those foul diatribes. They encouraged him to take it further. And initially for their bottom line, it was a success. It made the Allie and Wally show the highest billing program on WJOK."

FORTY NINE

Ted promised to contact Wally after his show concluded and encourage him to come in. We agreed to meet at Ted's restaurant on New Orleans Road the following night and I headed for home.

No word from Flint yet but Jaime called just as I was pulling into our garage. Stone's red Mustang was nowhere in sight.

"So how did it go with the lady writer?" I said.

"I don't want to jinx it, but I think we're going to get her. She does want to meet our west coast people so I'm afraid I'll have to fly out there with her tomorrow."

"You gotta do what you gotta do."

"I'm sorry. But I can combine it with some early shooting on the new Spicer film, so that should impress her and maybe save me another trip out there later. And I do have something good on the Rick Stone front."

I said to Jaime, "Great. Okay honey, Rick's not home and I've got to give Bosco his dinner. I'll call you right back on the landline."

I entered the house and laid my junk on the kitchen counter, Bosco trailing behind, panting with excitement at seeing his dad after a long day away. Or maybe he knew it was dinnertime and he hoped his faithful server would be punctual. I ladled two cups of kibble into his dish and refilled his water bowl.

I was always putting down the phone in the middle of conversations to feed my friend. Bosco understood my priorities and took advantage.

I called Jaime back on the hard line, which always sounded better than the cell. I said, "Sorry for the delay. Bosco's nose is deep into his dinner. Whatcha got?"

"I told you Don Johnson is going to be in the next Spicer flick. Well, Don's longtime stand-in just retired. So as one of the executive producers, I used a little influence. I sent the casting folks some pictures of Rick and they agreed to have him double for Johnson, and maybe do a little light stunt work. Nothing too difficult, like long shots in scenes where he's chasing bad guys. Times when a guy pushing seventy like Sonny Crockett would rather cool his heels in an air conditioned trailer."

"That sounds great. I'm not sure how Rick will see it, but if I tell him there'll be a lot of young available starlets on the set, I'm sure he'll jump at the chance."

Jaime laughed. "Don't make me feel like a pimp, Riles. Rick mentioned over dinner once he did some acting in high school. He still looks good. This could open some doors for him. At the very least, it gives him something to do rather than sit around and feel sorry for himself. I'm sure my dad could hook him up for a few rounds at Riviera while he's out here."

"Of course, the downside for me is that you'll both be three thousand miles away."

"Why don't you come out with him? We start shooting Johnson's scenes in a couple of days. Why not take a break?"

Okay, I'm a pig. The first thought that crossed my mind was hotel sex with Jaime. Unless we stayed at her father's Holmby Hills manor, located within walking distance of the Playboy Mansion. I guess Stone and I have more in common than I care to admit. There are worse places to hang out while your girlfriend is working.

I told her about my meeting with McCarver. "So basically, if I can wrap this up in the next day or so, I might be free. I just have to arrange for Bosco the Wonder Dog, but I think Ted's old housekeeper Anna might be willing to handle that while we're gone. She still has the combination to the house."

"So call her and put her on hold. I wish you could bring the pooch, but he's not a great air traveler. Too bad my dad sold his plane to that Saudi prince."

It really wasn't *too bad*. The last time I flew with her father on the stick, the old man was confused as to which airport he was cleared to land. He almost overshot the runway after clipping some trees on the descent. I'd love to have Bosco with me in California, but my attachment to him fades when it comes flying with an inept pilot.

Jaime said, "I've gotta go. Talk to Rick and let me know. That stand-in gig won't wait. If he can't do it, I've got to let them know to get somebody else."

"Will do. Call ya later."

Now I had even more incentive to close the Josephs file. I didn't want to go to Hollywood with this still hanging, but why should I soldier on? Wally had spurned me by vanishing. And Alison Middleton was sinking even further on my list, after hearing the tale Ted had spun about how she plotted to steal Rick's job.

I don't feel I owe either of them anything. But as Rick observed, it's not in my DNA to quit something I've committed considerable time and energy to. I can't abide unresolved outcomes. They have a way of coming back to haunt you.

FIFTY

"Riviera Country Club? The Playboy mansion down the street? Hot young starlets --- bronzed, oiled and ready for action? Lock and load, brother. Where do I sign?" Stone was excited.

I had anticipated a tougher job convincing him to hop a flight to Los Angeles at a moment's notice. Clearly, I had underestimated the lure of Jaime's offer. She knew the right buttons to push and that among many other talents made her a great agent.

I said, "Whoa there, bucco. Don't you even want to know about the pay?"

"I knew there was a catch. It sounded too good to be true." He sighed and hung his head as if preparing for disappointing news. "Okay, how much do they want me to pay for all of this?"

His droll delivery had me going for a second.

He said, "Come on, Riles. You know I'm not hurting for dough. I don't know that there's a career in this for me, but a chance to live large with topless beauties sunning themselves around your dad-in-law's pool. I'm there."

"Okay sport, a few of things you need to get straight on. You have to talk to Jaime about specifics so don't assume you'll be staying at the house in Holmby Hills. Second, he's not my dad-in-law. We're not even engaged. And last but not least, Mr. Johansen is a seventy five year old man, so I doubt he's running a bunny farm like the guy down the street."

"The guy down the street who's like ninety, that one? The one who practically invented sex? Seriously, why wouldn't I do this? What have I got to lose? And if you're coming, too, that's the only downside, far as I can see."

Trash talk. It was gratifying to see him in such good spirits after the despair he'd sunk into from playing golf with Ginn. He's generally a happy-go-lucky guy. He'd experienced a couple of major setbacks, personally and professionally. He dealt with them by wining and whoring, not exactly an uncommon remedy amongst normal males.

"I may not be coming right away." I told him about my meeting with Ted and how I wanted to resolve the Josephs case before heading west.

"The hell with him, Riles. I'm halfway inclined to file a police report about the stuff he stole from me. And Ted McCarver is not my favorite person right now, either. He's been on the island on and off for what? Six months and nary a peep? After all we did for him?"

I said, "He did throw a ton of money my way, not to mention this oceanfront house he gave us both. Boy have you done a one eighty. You were practically begging me to keep working for Wally, now you're done with him. And you're willing to toss your thirty years with Ted aside because he didn't call you while he was in town?"

Ted had called me and said that he'd tried Wally and gotten no response but that he'd keep calling. Wally-boy was operating with a series of burners, so the phone Ted had dialed might well be at the bottom of the Port Royal Sound now. The one time Wally actually followed my instructions was an impediment not only to his safety but to me moving forward.

Stone shrugged. "Whatever. I'll call Jaime and get the details. You do what you think best, but I'm just saying, if you're passing up a chance to have fun in the sun with the lovely Ms. Johansen and me, I think you're a complete fool."

I couldn't argue with that assessment. Unfortunately, the events of the next forty eight hours proved that my instincts were correct. I wish they weren't.

FIFTY ONE

I was propped up in bed in an awkward position, watching an old Inspector Lewis episode. I had been dozing on and off and the byzantine plotline wasn't making much sense since I had missed so many key scenes. Bosco was snoring next to me, every so often rolling over onto my legs and nudging me semi-conscious.

Stone was out for one last night on the island before embarking on his Hollywood adventure. He'd worked everything out with Jaime and the production company. The money wasn't great, but the studio was picking up first class airline tickets and a limo from LAX. Not bad for a stand-in.

McCullough called and woke me for good.

"Flint. It's after ten. Do you ever sleep?"

"The law never sleeps, King. If you're too drowsy to take my call, I can get back to you in the morning. Say at 5:30 or so, old man?"

I said, "It's not that severe yet. But early to bed, early to rise is becoming more the rule than the exception with me. So, did you see Alison?"

"We had dinner. I just got home."

"Dinner? I'm curious as to what she found enticing on the menu at the Starlight Diner."

"Only the best for my uh, persons of uh, interest? Dinner with a woman who's not my wife is new territory for me, King. Maybe you can give me some tips."

I said, "Maybe later. So what did you find out?"

"She promised to tell him before the next show that I think he's in the clear. That's the only time they talk off air, after the remote equipment is hooked up to test the line. He still doesn't trust her. Fact is, this cat is paranoid and doesn't trust anybody so I wouldn't take it personally that he left your place without notice."

I told him about McCarver and how Wally had done his show from Ted's condo the day before. I didn't mention how Alison had manipulated Rick. I could tell from their meeting the other day, even though it was contentious, that there was a mutual attraction. I needed to clue him in that this lady isn't everything she appears to be, although Flint's bullshit detector is pretty effective.

I said, "I have no idea where he did the show today after he left Ted's place, but I'm thinking he stayed close, maybe even still on the island. I just wish Ted had let us know when Josephs contacted him initially. Do you trust Alison to tell Wally?"

That was my not-so-subtle way of letting Flint know that he couldn't just accept her at her word. I wanted to see if her native magnetism had mesmerized the lonely old cop, or if his veteran detective instincts superseded his vulnerability.

He asked, "Why wouldn't she?"

"I don't know. You think he doesn't trust her for a reason or is he just paranoid?"

"I think the guy is crazy scared. Civilians aren't used to being shot at."

"Or this is one big conspiracy launched by Cirrus to improve the ratings."

Flint laughed. "I only floated that to get a rise out of her. I don't believe it now that I've gotten to know her a little. But you with conspiracy theories? I suppose you know who killed Kennedy, too."

"Yeah, it was Ted Cruz's daddy. Look, McCarver told me that Cirrus is desperate. They're deep in debt and they'd do just about anything to raise their quarterly numbers."

"Well, forget Allie being part of that. Fact is, she invited me to join her at the station before the show so that if need be, I can talk directly to Josephs. If he won't listen to reason then, I'm inclined to just drop the whole thing with him and concentrate on busting Crayton and his merry band of crooked cops."

FIFTY TWO

I gave Stone a ride to the airport, even though he could have expensed a limo to the studio. Bosco hopped into the back seat, sensing that Rick would be away for a while. Maybe it was seeing him pack a suitcase or he just picks up a sign that flies under human radar. He whined as Stone got out of the old Audi and removed his bag from the trunk. I lowered the rear window so Rick could say goodbye properly. He gave Bosco a kiss on the snout that was more loving than I'd ever seen him display with any of his overnight guests.

Driving back, I cruised a couple of hotel parking lots. Esposito had given me the tag number and a description of the car he had rented to Wally, so I took a chance that I might come across it if Josephs had stayed close by. The yellow Jersey plates would stand out against the native tags and the smattering of states and Canadian provinces. It was a long shot --- no luck.

McCarver called and said that he'd still been unsuccessful in his attempts to reach Wally. I told him about Stone's good fortune and he promised to keep trying to find his other wayward protégé.

I played golf alone that afternoon. Played well. McCullough called while I was driving home and told me that Wally had refused to talk to Allie off the air. When she told him that she had enlisted Flint's help, Josephs cut the connection and only reinstated it seconds before airtime.

That clinched it. I was done. This back and forth with Wally, *should I stay or should I go*, was wearing on me.

I went home, cooked up some pasta and finished watching the Inspector Lewis episode that I had started the night before. The sun and golf had tired me out, so by ten o'clock this super sleuth was out cold.

I was awakened at seven by the police, and this time it wasn't by a phone call from up north. A uniformed cop was at the door and there was a black and white cruiser parked on the cobblestone circular drive. Another officer stayed in the car, watching me.

"Sorry to bother you so early, sir. Are you Rick Stone?" The man was under thirty, not tall but muscular. His black hair was clipped as short as his speech. Deep set brown eyes and hard features reflected a Latin heritage. He was no-nonsense efficient, like a young McCullough might have been. The name above his badge was Epifanio Cabrera.

"No, I'm not Rick Stone." I knew better than to volunteer anything else.

"We have this listed as his island address. Is he on the premises?"

"I'm afraid not."

"Do you expect him to return soon?"

"Hold on, officer. I'm a licensed private investigator. I'm reaching for my I.D." His hand slid down to his sidearm and his colleague opened the car door.

He took the wallet from me and studied my credentials and drivers' license. "All right, sir, it appears you are who you say you are. Your name is listed on the deed to this place as co-owner with Stone. Can you tell me where he is?"

I tried to imagine why the local cops would be interested in Stone. The only thing I could think of was that his escapades with barely-legals had caught up with him. I'd warned him a number of times to make sure that his partner was not only willing, but verifiably of age. This was the last thing he needed now, given his setbacks of late.

"I don't know exactly where he is at the moment," I said. No point in lying, they'd be able to find out on their own soon enough. "He left for Los Angeles yesterday on an early morning flight. Can I ask what this is about?"

"You are certain he was in California at two a.m. this morning?"

"I assume he was. I'm sure he'll cooperate with whatever you're looking into. I can save you a lot of legwork if you tell me what it is."

The young cop glanced over at his partner, a middle aged white guy with a big belly who had come out of the squad car when I pulled my identification. The older man nodded.

Officer Cabrera said, "A gun registered in his name was involved in a murder on the beach behind the Sonesta. Tests haven't come back yet, but we're pretty certain it was the murder weapon."

FIFTY THREE

"**C**an you tell me who the victim was?" I said.

My fear was that a hit man from up north had dispatched Wally with Rick's gun, somehow wresting it away from Josephs. Rather than use his own gun, this scenario would provide the added dividend of diverting suspicion toward whoever actually owned the other firearm, in this case, one Richard Stone.

Cabrera again looked to his partner for counsel. The older man spoke for the first time. "We can't release that information to someone who may be a person of interest."

I expected as much. "I spent ten years with the FBI so I know what *person of interest* means. Let me save you some time. Tell me exactly why you think I fit the bill."

I'd ruffled feathers. Cabrera started to respond, but the other cop cut him off. "We ask, you answer. You're not a fed now and even if you were, that doesn't change the way we do things here."

I wasn't eager to get into a pissing contest with the locals. "All right, we can be stubborn and work at cross purposes, or we can share information and try to get to the bottom of this. Just give me some credit, considering my background. If I really did kill this person, do you think that you would have ever been able to find the gun and trace it back to me or Rick?"

This whole confrontation felt like *In the Heat of the Night*, like I was Sidney Poitier trying to avoid coming off as condescending to the country bumpkin sheriff played by Rod Steiger. *They call me Mr. Tibbs*, indeed.

The name tag above the older man's badge read Eugene Walker. I've seen countless pairings like this. A young cop, often a minority, does all the legwork, especially the dangerous stuff. The veteran partner might either be a wise old guru, or just a lazy schlub cruising toward a pension. His legacy would be passing on bad habits to his acolyte --- like jumping to easy conclusions that could be effortlessly knocked aside by a skillful attorney.

But the dynamic between these two didn't fit precisely into my preconceived notions. Cabrera raised a stop signal toward his colleague and to my surprise, the older man deferred.

Cabrera said, "The reason we have questions is that you share this house with Stone, so you probably have access to his weapons. We know that he has others registered in another jurisdiction that may be on the premises. Do you see the point now?"

As we spoke on the front porch, there was a scratching sound behind us. I turned and saw Bosco pawing at the glass door, trying to join the conversation. I motioned for him to sit and amazingly, he did as I ordered. Jaime's work, paying off again.

I said, "I'd like to help you, really I would. As I said, Stone is in California. I can't say anything for sure about the whereabouts of his other guns. But, if you tell me who the victim is, I might be able to give you some background that could help. It'll be in the papers or online soon anyway, you know that."

In a slight southern drawl Walker said, "We can't do that because we haven't confirmed the identity yet. She's mid thirties, white."

"Whoa, whoa, whoa. She's? The victim was a woman?"

Cabrera said, "Yes, sir. Well built, almost six foot tall. Blond hair. One tattoo in a very private spot. Put together like a beach volley ball player, actually. That's all we got. No wallet or ID on the body."

I needed time to process this. I had assumed that Wally had used the gun to fend off an attack and been killed in the process. A female hitter? Hollywood would love it, but it had to be a rarity in real life. I'd certainly never encountered such a being.

I said, "Okay, let's get down to it. I know the drill. Your boss sent you guys out to chase down leads. Give me his name and I'll be in touch."

Walker was offended. "You're afraid to share anything with us peons? You Yankees are all alike, think you're smarter than us grunts, is that it?"

They had extended an olive branch by giving me the vic's description and now I was clearly planning to go over their head. But his partner, weary of dealing with me, supplied the name.

"I appreciate the cooperation. If I do have any contact with your boss, I'll put in a good word as to your professionalism and thoroughness. Now if you have nothing further, I have some business to attend to."

I didn't linger for a reply. I went in and closed the door behind me. They didn't have a search warrant and they had no probable cause to arrest me, however much they may have wanted to. They just stood on the porch for a moment, then retreated to their black and white, unsure what to make of this mouthy Yankee PI.

FIFTY FOUR

The logical conclusion was that Wally Josephs had killed this unknown female with Rick's gun. Self-defense? Romantic liaison gone bad? Senseless act borne of paranoia?

Well built blond. Tall. Could it be Darla Diamond? And if so, how did she track Wally all the way down here?

I had to prioritize. Rick hadn't reported the gun stolen. That could be explained away. Stone didn't walk around armed, no reason to. So he could say he didn't even realize it was missing. It could have been taken months ago.

In giving the officers at the door short shrift, I had neglected to ask a critical question: where exactly had they found the gun? Had Wally made a clumsy attempt to discard the weapon in a nearby dumpster? That was unlikely since it had been discovered so quickly. That led me to conclude that he had left it near the body, either out of panic or to deliberately point the finger toward Rick, given his knowledge of Stone's history with women.

Implicating Stone didn't make a lot of sense since Rick would say that Wally had stolen his gun along with the remote equipment. I was just taking shots in the dark now and running down trails that led nowhere. I needed more information and I didn't think that the locals would be eager to share it with a civilian.

I could only think of one way to make that happen quickly, so I called my FBI buddy Dan Logan.

He was wise to my habits and answered in a bored monotone. "You only call when you want something."

"Gee, good morning to you too, Loges. I figure that you're usually too busy just to chew the fat, so I only call when it's important."

"Important to you. That's the way it's been lately. Important to me, like tickets to Giants-Panthers in Charlotte this season? Never happen."

"I might be able to score you a couple. Is that the price of this call?"

He laughed. Logan was a longtime friend, dating back to my days as a fed. He'd risen to agent in charge of the New York office, whereas I had washed out in less than a decade. We keep in touch frequently on the phone or digitally; in person, maybe once a year. The big guy is into Broadway shows and sports, a unique combination that few men share. I often send him gossip about his favorite players in both endeavors, or pithy headlines involving strange cases that might pique his interest. He usually sends back the latest ribald joke he'd heard around the water cooler.

He'd saved my bacon on numerous occasions, including the recent McCarver debacle which I may not have survived without his intervention. I think of him as a guardian angel, knowing I can never fully return the favors.

"I'm only funning ya, lad," he said, mocking my current residency. "What's the problem? Revenuers cutting out your supply of moonshine?"

"Keep it up. The fewer Northerners who know about paradise down here, the more room there'll be for us."

I told him about Wally's situation and the murder at the Sonesta beach involving Stone's gun.

When I was finished he said, "Guns involved in a crime that crosses state lines makes it federal in the strictest sense. I hate to inform you Johnny Rebs, but we do have a few more important things on our agenda. I could muscle in if need be, but I sense that's not why you called."

"We're on the same page, Javert. I wasn't looking for you guys to take over. I just thought you might put in a call to the detective running the case here and coax him into reading me in. I assume they're pretty territorial but the specter of FBI involvement might shake them up."

"Territorial? South Carolina? Perish the thought. How far did you say you are from Fort Sumter?"

"Well, it might be a test for your political skills, Mr. Lincoln. What do you say?"

"I have a few minutes. I must admit the possibility of a female hit man is intriguing. Especially if she looks like Angelina Jolie in *Salt* or *Mr. and Mrs. Smith*. I'll get back to you. By the way, that stadium in Charlotte looks like it has a nice shady side and a really hot sunny sideline. You know how us redheads are sensitive to too much sun."

"That is, if there's any red hair left on that balding head of yours that hasn't turned grey. I'll keep that in mind. Thanks, Dan."

I would be shocked if my FBI buddy didn't have my little problem solved before lunch. The man took care of business. My next call was to Stone. It was barely six a.m. on the coast, but this couldn't wait.

FIFTY FIVE

I expected voicemail or a sleep-addled Stone, but I was greeted with his perky "Good Morning, you're-on-the-air" radio voice.

"Hey, Ricky, didn't think you'd be up and at 'em this early."

"I'm still on eastern time, pal. I'm already at the pool, drinking coffee. Hard to find a Dunkin' Donuts in Holmby Hills, all the way out in Culver City was the closest. Just had a morning dip, au naturel. Getting ready for my close up, Mr. DeMille."

He was exchanging classic rock references for movie quotes now, a sure sign he'd already gone Hollywood. Once in a while, an original line of dialogue from him would be nice. "If Jaime caught a glimpse of you in your birthday suit, you might wind up like William Holden, floating face down in that pool," I said.

"If she did, you'd be in trouble, once she saw what a real man is built like. But no worries on that score, amigo. She stayed at the hotel last night with that lady writer."

He had blown the opportunity to use a *Dire Straits* line from *Lady Writer*. Maybe my fear is groundless that his sources for inane quotations have doubled.

"Well, listen up. We have some serious stuff to talk about." I filled him in.

He said, "So are they coming after me out here? Am I going to be arrested on the set? Don't they understand they'll have to get past Sonny Crockett?"

"Glad to see you're finding humor in it. Do you have an alibi for around eleven, your time, last night?"

"Jaime's dad and I were doing brandy and cigars until the wee hours. Turned in just short of midnight. Unless he's hiding some dementia that nobody has picked up on so far, he'll vouch for me. I take it that's the time of death."

"Their best guess. You're five hours away by air. They may come out to ask you some questions but you're covered on the shooting. I'm just struggling with what to tell them about the gun without pointing them at Wally right away."

He thought for a moment. I'd already considered several possibilities which did not involve outright lying, a losing strategy. But I didn't want to volunteer anything either.

"Well Riles, much as I'm sure that Wally stole the gun, I didn't *see* him take it. It was in a drawer in the upstairs hallway. If I was alone, I guess I would have just put it on the night stand, but I didn't want to spook my friend. You know, a loaded gun next to the bed ain't the most romantic thing for most chicks, although I've been with a few who would dig it. Mea culpa, man."

So his unchecked libido did factor into this after all. Hopefully he realized the result of his fecklessness.

I said, "Anyway, speaking of women, does the description of the victim ring a bell? I know mid-thirties is a little old for you, but a finely toned beach volleyballer? Encounter any of those in your travels on the island?"

"In my dreams. Most of them are dykes, no?"

"I'm not so sure I want to save your sorry ass. So the answer is no?"

"Afraid so. Are we sure she's even from the island? Is it possible she was imported? Like that chick that pimp-rolled him in Jersey."

He was arriving at the same conclusions I was, but we still had no firm basis. I said, "Back to the gun. Other than your floozy, was there anyone else in the house who could have taken it?"

"No. And I had her occupied the whole time she was here. Ginn was in the house for a bit before golf, but that was after Wally had split and the gun was already missing. Nope, it had to be Josephs."

"Okay. Logan's trying to get me access to the investigation, hopefully soon. I'll call you when I know more."

"Should I tell Jaime what's going on when I see her on the set?"

"No. All it would accomplish is to make her worry and she doesn't need distractions now. She's already got a lot to deal with and there's nothing she can do to help from California. Just firm up your alibi with her dad without letting on why. Hopefully, if the cops are coming to see you, I can give you a heads-up and I'll tell her then. Otherwise, just give my regards to Sonny Crockett and Captain Kirk."

FIFTY SIX

"What is it with cops and diners?" I said.

The woman sitting across from me was around forty. She was solidly built, all muscle, no loose flesh. Medium height. Short blondish hair, world-wise brown eyes that see everything. Attired in a charcoal pantsuit, tailored appropriately for her line of business: Detective First Grade, Hilton Head PD.

Detective Alexandra Tomey said, "Service is quick. Food is okay. They appreciate having us around in case anyone skips out on a check or gets funny ideas about the register. And they serve donuts if that's your next quip."

A sense of humor about cop stereotypes. I like that.

She said, "Well, Mr. King, this is unprecedented. You must have some pretty strong connections, because my boss has never allowed me to share information on a case we're just starting to develop. Especially with someone we initially thought was a person of interest."

"Well, I'd imagine you've never come across a stud muffin PI like me before, either."

She sniffed and drank some coffee, which she'd ordered black, no sweeteners. "Ho-hum, how much of this byplay do I have to put up with before we get down to business?"

THE LAST RESORT

She shoved a manila envelope across the table to me. "You'll find all I can give you in there. If you have any further questions, here's my card."

"Wait just a second, detective."

"I'm very busy. You are an unnecessary distraction. I follow orders from the top, but they didn't include repartee over coffee. The deal was to provide you with information, the same stuff we're going to be handing out to the media at some point, so you have a head start. In return, your FBI pals will facilitate the VICAP search on the fingerprints so we can at least identify the victim."

She didn't get up to leave. A minor victory.

I said, "Look, believe it or not, we want the same thing here. Stone's gun was stolen. I might be able to figure out who took it and help you find that person."

"Oh, please. We've accepted that your friend Stone was in California at the time, but that doesn't mean he didn't contract this out and give the killer his gun."

"Detective Tomey, don't insult me and I won't insult you. If Stone wanted this woman dead, you really think he'd hire someone who doesn't own a weapon? I can hear it now, '*Oh, then take my gun. And leave it at the scene. It's registered to me but the dumb cops on Hilton Head won't figure that out*'. I think we both can do better than that."

She smiled for the first time. I wouldn't call her pretty, but she was nice around the eyes. She certainly didn't look like any of the glamour-puss female cops you see in the movies. She presented herself like a buttoned-up business woman who knew her stuff. I hoped we'd get along if our paths crossed again, but that was up to her.

She said, "All right, King. I'll stipulate that dog won't hunt. You have any better ideas?"

"I might when I go over the evidence you've put together so far."

There was nothing to be gained by detaining her further. "Okay Detective Tomey, I don't want to waste any more of your time. I'll call you later if I find out anything. Matter of fact, I'll call you either way. You know, I'm not a bad guy to work with. I was with the FBI for almost ten years and I haven't completely gone over to the dark side. I'll get the check. You take care of business."

She got up and almost extended her hand but decided against it. Good call. I might still be the enemy, looking to protect whoever did this. I waited until she was out the door before opening the envelope.

The victim was as previously described by the gentlemen who came to my door earlier, but this report contained details. Five-ten, a hundred thirty five pounds. Clad in dark jeans and an Iron Maiden tee shirt. Running shoes, no socks. Body discovered by a young couple walking their dog at three in the morning.

Two gunshot wounds to the chest. Instantly fatal they assumed, pending autopsy. TOD around two a.m., on the beach behind the Sonesta. Desk clerks had no recollection of the victim registering to stay at the hotel. Uniforms would canvass rental cars in the lot to see if any belonged to her once they had positive identification. In addition to the report, there were a few decent shots of the crime scene and the vic, probably just a greatest hits package since they take dozens from every imaginable angle.

On my tablet, I summoned up the picture that Stone had drawn from Wally's description of the hooker from Toms River. They could be twins. Or the same person. Darla Diamond?

THE LAST RESORT

The Sonesta Resort is located inside the Shipyard Plantation. The victim or perp didn't necessarily have to be a guest there. They might have rented or owned a house in the plantation. Or not. The Atlantic Beach stretches for twelve miles along the easternmost end of Hilton Head, so either one could have entered from almost anywhere.

The Shipyard Plantation is just across 278 from the diner. After I gathered up the file and paid the check, I drove over there to nose around. There was a guard stationed at the entrance --- a flash of my PI license satisfied his curiosity and he went back to his Maxim.

The resort hotel parking lot is typical Hilton Head: double rows of finely crushed gravel mixed with shells, separated by miniature palm trees planted on small berms. There were very few signs indicating where guests are allowed to park or how they should get in or out. You might drive in circles for ten minutes trying to find an exit.

I parked the Audi and checked each row on foot. In the fifth lane, there was a grey Camry with New Jersey plates. It matched the tag number Esposito had given me. I finally had a lead on where Wally had stayed. It also linked him to the murder scene.

I walked over to the hotel. It had been renovated recently and was trés chic. Limestone floors, soaring ceilings with wooden beams, plenty of stainless steel trim. A fountain illuminated with multi-colored LEDs. The entry lobby was a vast open space, extending to a bar and dining area, which were barely hidden behind potted palms. An expansive pool with a Tiki bar was visible outside through tall glass windows. The ocean was shielded from the ground floor by the dunes but guest rooms from the second story upwards had extraordinary Atlantic views.

The twenty-something girl at the desk looked preoccupied. Time to turn on the charm. I hoped it would work better than it had with Ms. Tomey.

"Excuse me, miss. I'm a little embarrassed to tell you this but I had a bit of an accident in your parking lot. I'm afraid I backed into one of your guest's cars. Not much damage. Fact is, it's an old beater and I don't even think they'd notice, but I'd like to make it right."

I gave her the plate number. "Can you tell me what room they're staying in. I'd rather just take care of this without troubling the police or the insurance companies."

She tapped a few keys on her computer. "That would be the gentleman in Room 212. But he checked out this morning."

"That's odd. His car is still in the lot. Do you have an address for him or a phone number where he can be reached?"

"Well, I'm not supposed to give out information on our guests. You could leave your number and address with me and I'll try to contact him and explain the situation. Then he can call you if he chooses."

"Okay, I wouldn't want to get you in trouble," I said. She handed me a pen and notepad and I gave her my address on the island along with my cell number.

She took the pad back and her eyes widened.

"Is there a problem?" I asked.

"Look mister, I don't know what you're trying to do here. You're not Mr. Stone."

"Of course not. Why would you think so?"

Stone? He was in California, or was he?

"Because the address and phone number he gave us when he registered is the same one you just gave me. His name was Rick Stone."

FIFTY SEVEN

As I stood in the parking lot of the Sonesta, my mind was reeling. As much as Wally Josephs and I had almost nothing in common, I tried to put myself in his place and anticipate where he would turn next.

I've just killed a woman with Stone's gun. I've never killed anyone before. The gun repulses me. I throw it into the sand and run.

What to do next?

I can't stay at the hotel. It's too close to the crime scene. They have my car on record. When I filled out the registration they took my plate number so the police will be on the lookout for that car.

I used the identification I stole from Stone. Paid cash for the room, so they'll have to track Stone down. That might buy me a little time. I'm short of money now and I can't go to an ATM.

Who can I trust to lend me cash and hide me until I can figure out my next move?

There was only one answer.
Ted McCarver.

FIFTY EIGHT

I entered Alexandra Tomey's number into my speed dial before heading to Ted's place, just in case. I didn't know Tomey nearly well enough to trust her but I had a good initial read. She seemed to have a priggish adherence to the letter of the law, although she might prove to be a flexible ally down the road. So far, she had only shown me her "by the book" side.

That's not me. Both with the bureau and in private practice, I have seen enough miscarriages of justice to convince me that although the system generally works, there are too many exceptions to follow it on faith alone. I need to make my own calls, especially in cases like this one.

Ted was home when I knocked. He didn't look surprised to see me this time, but he was clearly uncomfortable. There was something he knew that he didn't want me to know. Or was he wrestling with how to handle this, same as I was?

"I assumed our lunch plans were awaiting confirmation," he said, the door open only slightly.

"I'm not here to eat, Ted. We need to talk. About Wally."

His eyes darted about. His condo is spacious: the open living area flows into a high end kitchen and generous dining space. Three bedrooms were down a short corridor, and the doors to all of them were closed.

"I'm not sure what more I can tell you, other than what we spoke of the other day."

"Can I come all the way in?"

He opened the door with an exaggerated sweeping gesture. His eyes flitted around again, as if he was expecting someone to emerge from one of the bedrooms. That someone could only be Wally.

"Hey, Ted, it's a beautiful day. Let's talk out on your balcony. I love the view here."

He shifted for a moment before saying, "Good idea. Can I offer you coffee? It's a bit early for our usual adult refreshments."

"Nope. Let's just sit outside and enjoy the view."

The balcony was a large stamped concrete affair, textured to look like tumbled marble and decked out with a powder coated table surrounded by cushioned chairs. On the opposite side were a couple of chaise lounges, folded into a reclining position. Heavy hurricane-rated glass doors separated the balcony from the living area. Ted left them open, I pulled them closed behind us.

"I don't want anyone inside to hear us," I said. "I know Wally's in there."

Ted whispered. "I wanted to leave the door open in case he tries to leave."

"Just a crack then. Let's stand where we can see in, but he can't hear us."

We found a spot that served both purposes.

I said, "He killed a woman, Ted. He used Rick's gun. Luckily Rick's in L.A. so he's not at the top of the list of suspects at the moment. But Wally can't hide forever and you can't be party to helping him."

"So what are you saying? We turn him in? That would be a betrayal of the highest order. He turned to me for help."

"Those few days you spent in jail after Stevie died not enough for you? You want to go back? Because that's where this is headed if you shelter him."

Ted stared out at the water. I thought for a moment that he might leap over the railing and plunge three stories to the ground. But Ted wasn't suicidal, just conflicted.

"Riley, the kid is scared out of his wits. The woman he shot was the same woman who led him into that motel room back in New Jersey. He said she tried to kill him."

That came as no surprise. McCullough had told me that the initial incident with Wally and Crayton had scared her straight, but the pictures matched and Ted had just confirmed it. She obviously hadn't scared easily, but given what had just happened, she should have.

I said, "If that's true, someone *is* out to get him. The safest place for him is in custody down here. Trust me Ted, it's the best way to go. I'm calling in the troops."

Ted was ashen faced, not sure whether he wanted to protest or just go with my instincts. He stood silent as I called and gave Tomey the address. I told her I had found the man who pulled the trigger and that she should bring backup.

"Now let's go inside and talk to Wally," I said after I finished with her. "We'll have a few minutes before they get here and I need the truth from him. Once I get his story, I can call my cop friend in Jersey to trace down this woman he shot."

We went back into the condo. Standing there with a .38 pointed at us, was Wally Josephs.

FIFTY NINE

"And I trusted you bastards," Wally said. "It's every man for himself, I see."

Ted moved slowly toward Josephs. "Put the gun down. We only have a few minutes. King needs to talk to you."

"You called the cops, didn't you? I'm outta here."

"Wally, please," Ted said.

I said, "No, it's okay, Ted. If Wally wants to die, suicide by cop isn't the worst way to go. At least it'll be quick."

That got his attention. Josephs was inexpertly waving the gun back and forth at me and Ted. As an inexperienced shooter, there was no way he could take us both out; the other would have time to tackle him in the confined space.

But there was no need for any pseudo-gallant sacrifice. I said, "Wally, there's a way out for you. But you need to put the gun down and talk to me. I know you feel betrayed, but the police would have found you soon enough on their own. This way, you go in peacefully and Stone and I will back up your story. But you make a run for it and some rookie yahoo trying to make a name for himself might shoot first and skip the question part."

"I guess since I'm not black, nobody will care."

He was making it hard for me to want to help him. But a semi-famous white guy accused of gunning down a woman? The presumption of innocence would end right there as far as the authorities and media were concerned.

"This isn't the time for politics You tell me the truth now and I'll do everything I can to help you," I said.

"How? My career's over. I killed that woman. There's no getting around that." He saw his world crumbling around him.

Ted walked up to him, hands outstretched. "Wally, listen to him. The police in Jersey were happy to blame me for killing my fiancée until King proved otherwise. Do what he says. You're running out of time."

Wally lowered the gun and McCarver took it by the barrel. He turned to me, his eyes asking what to do with the weapon. I gestured for him to lay it on the kitchen counter. Ted then embraced Wally like a repentant father who realized that his son had gone astray and that he had failed in his attempts at parenting.

He whispered something in Wally's ear that I couldn't hear.

I said, "Okay, we don't have much time. First thing, where did you get that gun?"

"I took it from Stone when I left your house. I figured that if somehow those sons of bitches found me, I might need it. I was right about that, wasn't I?"

If Wally still had *Stone's* gun, how did the police trace it back? I carefully picked up the one on the counter and quickly ascertained that it wasn't Rick's. It *was* a Smith and Wesson 642 Enhanced Action like his, but Rick had carved a notch into the handle, commemorating the foolish/heroic act that saved Jaime and me. The notch was a shallow slit that an uninformed eye would not notice.

I decided to save that for later, since time was short. "Tell me how you came to be out on that beach at two a.m. and what happened with that woman."

Wally, head in hands, sunk into one of Ted's side chairs. His eyes were vacant when he looked up. "I did my show from the hotel. Stayed in and ordered room service. I couldn't sleep. There was a full moon so I figured I might grab a quick drink at that Tiki bar by the pool and take a walk on the beach. But the bar was closed so I just headed for the water." He smacked his lips. "I'm so dry. Can I get something to drink?"

"Ted, get him some water, please. All right, you're walking on the beach. Then what?"

"I just got this feeling there was someone behind me. I don't know, like a sixth sense. Or maybe I heard something. Anyway, I turned real quick and there she was, the woman who set me up with that pimp. I was clutching the gun the whole time under my jacket, and soon as I saw who it was, I pulled it. I figured maybe I could get her to talk, tell me who was after me. I don't know how she found me."

Ted brought him the water and he took a big gulp. "But she wasn't looking to talk. She was real surprised I was packing. She went for her gun and I pulled the trigger. Twice. I never shot no one before. I was scared. I threw the gun down and started to run. Then I figured she might not be dead and maybe I could get her to tell me who sent her. That's what went through my mind anyway."

I said, "You hit her square in the heart. Beginner's luck. She might have been dead before she hit the ground."

"She was dead, far as I could tell. I didn't know what to do. There was nobody around. I looked up at the hotel and there was no lights on in any of the windows. I figured I'd just grab my shit and check out. I picked up the gun out of the sand, in case she wasn't the only one after me. I was afraid about the car. I thought maybe that was how she found me, so I stole a bicycle and pedaled here. I didn't know where else to turn."

That explained the gun. He had taken *her* gun, thinking it was Rick's. That was the only coincidence, but it was a critical one. Otherwise, Wally's plan might have succeeded, at least short term. There would be nothing to tie him to the shooter. If they had found her gun in the sand, it would have taken a while before ballistics proved that they had the wrong .38. By that time, Wally could be anywhere and if he was smart enough to toss Stone's piece, even the FBI would have a hard time proving his involvement. But they did have Rick's gun and it didn't take genius detective work to trace it back to Wally.

I said, "Wally, do you swear that what you just told me is a hundred per cent true? If you're caught in a lie, even a small one, they'll twist it around and you'll dig yourself in deeper."

"I swear that's what happened. You think I should have called the cops from the beach, don't you? I was just thinking I could get away without them knowing anything." He threw up his hands in frustration. "Why did you have to call them?"

Ted had remained silent since disarming his friend, taking everything in with that analytical computer brain of his. I could tell he had reservations, but his trust in me had been rewarded when his life was on the line last year. So despite his qualms, he extended the benefit of the doubt in my direction.

There was a hard knock on the door. Looking through the peephole is a good way to get shot in the eye, so I just opened the door slowly, hands empty and in plain sight. Detective Alexandra Tomey and her crew, guns at the ready, awaited on the other side.

SIXTY

We were in the stairwell down the hall from Ted's condo, every so often glancing around to avoid being overheard.

"Let's see, I could run you in for obstruction. Felony accessory. Unlawful possession of a firearm. Let me count the ways."

Tomey was enjoying this too much. I hoped my keen wit and boyish charm had won her over at the diner, but apparently she was immune.

"Gee whiz detective, if you want to spend more time together, I can think of more interesting ways."

"Keep pushing, King, and this won't end well for you. We're talking about murder here."

Her friends in uniform had ushered Wally away. I believed it was in everyone's best interest to place Wally in custody for the time being. They could hold him for two days before preferring formal charges. I had that much time to make a strong case for self defense. Hell, even the sports radio audience would benefit by a holiday from his inane football predictions.

I said, "Let's get real for a moment, Detective Tomey. How do you charge someone with obstruction when they contact you after convincing your suspect to turn himself in? And unlawful possession of a weapon? Is that because I happen to be in the same room as a gun that

I turned over to you voluntarily? If anything, I think a gold medal and a parade are in order here."

She looked as if she had just run over a dead skunk on her bicycle. "You really need to check out Open Mic night. They do one Tuesdays at Shelter Cove. Then you'd see by the audience reaction how unfunny you really are."

"Tell you what, Ms. Tomey. I'm going to stop jousting with you, much as I enjoy trying to match your superior wit. If Wally Josephs shot the woman in question, it was a clear case of self defense. I advised him to surrender and after he speaks with an attorney as he has a right to do, I said he should explain what happened. He has nothing to hide, nor do I. In fact, I'll be happy to visit you at your headquarters later and make a statement."

"Why later? Since you're so public spirited, why not join us now, Mr. King?"

"*Mister* King. I like that. Shows respect. I need to make a couple of calls. I do have a business to run," I lied. "I'll see you later. Can I bring anything? Coffee? Danish?"

She flashed an Elvis sneer and walked away with purposeful strides. Either she was angry or she had to pee. I went back to McCarver's place, where Ted stood in the kitchen, holding a drink that looked and smelled suspiciously like a vodka tonic.

I said, "Thanks for holding your tongue there, amigo. I could tell you wanted to jump in a couple of times. Now that the boys in blue are gone, you have permission to speak freely. At ease."

He smiled at the military jargon. "I'm just not sure I understand your strategy here. Why give Wally over to these yokels?"

"He's safer in their care than anyplace I could stash him. And the longer he stayed on the lam, the more guilty he looks. They can trace that other gun and maybe Logan's people will help. Meanwhile, McCullough can attest that she was the woman he questioned about the attack on Wally in Jersey. That alone makes a good self defense argument. And Tomey is no fool, despite how uptight she comes across. She knows the false arrest of a minor celeb wouldn't look good on her resumé. I asked her to keep his name under wraps to the press for forty eight hours and she agreed. She'll get plenty of joy nailing him later if we're wrong about your boy."

Ted tilted his drink my way. "Can I offer you something? It's early but we both could use a jolt, I suppose."

I shook him off.

He said, "What about confidentiality, Riley? Aren't you violating that by cooperating with the police?"

"Wally isn't my client. We never signed papers. No money was exchanged. I only offered to help through Alison, and he refused it by bolting. So I could tell his whole story with a clear conscience. Not that I will, but I could. Now let me call my attorney friend Jack Furlong in Jersey and get him to hook us up with a colleague down here."

"While you do that, do you mind if I look through that evidence packet Tomey gave you? A fresh set of eyes and all."

"Go ahead. Just warning you, the pictures of the body may not be pleasant. There's wildlife on that beach."

I handed him the manila envelope that Tomey had given me at the diner. I called Furlong and he came through, as always. It seems that he frequently vacations on Hilton Head and has established contacts in some top law firms here. He said he'd get the best criminal attorney on the island down to headquarters as soon as humanly possible.

I thanked him and called Stone. Voicemail. I was about to try Jaime when I heard a loud gasp from Ted, who had spread the contents of the envelope on his dining room table.

He said, "You won't believe this. I know this woman."

"What woman? The victim?"

"Yes. She's a prostitute."

"And you know this how?"

"I've been with her. More than a few times."

SIXTY ONE

"And her name is?" I asked, already knowing the answer.

Drum roll please.

"Darla Diamond was the one she used. Double D. Initials proudly displayed on personal items and her business card. I don't know if it was her real name or a marketing gimmick based on her cup size, which was substantial. Artificially augmented, but impressive."

Ted and hookers. I had hoped that chapter had closed after last year, given the events that changed the trajectory of his life.

For over twenty years, McCarver had been unable to form meaningful relationships with respectable women. For his carnal needs, he turned to expensive escorts. After he retired and moved to Hilton Head, he started dabbling in psychotherapy. He became convinced that his troubles stemmed from his past abusive treatment toward those three females. Things could scarcely have ended worse. I should have just bought him a dog.

I said, "Tell me everything you know about this Double D woman. And don't be shy with the gory details."

"I only know what she told me about her past, so I can't say whether it's true or not. I didn't usually run a background check on my consorts."

I said, "Just start at the beginning. How did you first hook up with her?"

"She cut my hair. She was working at a small boutique salon in Bayville, in a converted bungalow off Route 9. I became aware of the place from some Cirrus execs who were sniffing around about buying the station a year or so before they actually made a bid. Anyway, it was very convenient, sort of a concierge service. Darla would come to the office if I needed a quick trim, even on short notice. I got comfortable with the convenience of that set-up and started just to use her privately instead of going to the shop."

"So how did she transition from barber to concubine?"

He showed no shame as he said, "One day while she was cutting my hair at the office, I invited her to a charity function the station was sponsoring. She asked me point blank what I was *really* after. She said she'd be happy to come along as my escort, but that her services came at a price."

"You told me last year that you'd used working girls because you didn't trust yourself with women who could be taken seriously."

"I guess that's where the double D comes in. This woman was a tonsorial goddess. I can't say I was disappointed when she told me that all it would cost was money to sample her wares."

Ted has a unique way of describing things that sometimes sounds like dialogue in a Harold Robbins novel. But it seemed like the same approach Diamond used with Wally in the bar. Rub her boobs in his face and make it clear they were his for the asking. For a price.

"You said you saw her more than once. Did she have a pimp that you knew of? And when and why did you stop seeing her?

"She turned out to be a little rough for my taste. Handcuffs, whips, bondage, that sort of thing. I mean, I'm not adverse to a little role playing, but she took it to extremes. As far as a pimp, I got the feeling she was an independent contractor."

"Final thing. Anything unusual, other than the S and M? Did she ever try to rip you off in any way?"

"No, she had no need to. I never quibbled when she put out her rate. It was good value as far as I was concerned. She was very good at her sideline profession. At first, it was a perfect storm for me: great arm candy, fine haircut and sexually, whatever I wanted, whenever I wanted it. It just gave me pause when she shifted into dominatrix mode, and I retreated. Not my cup of tea."

"A veddy, veddy civilized way to put it. Did you ever tell her that straight out?"

"No. At the time I made the decision to end our assignations, I was in the process of selling the station and leaving the area. She was owed no explanation. It was strictly a business association and our interests no longer coincided."

That was the most bloodless description of the end of a relationship I'd ever heard but then again, did this constitute a relationship? I've never paid for sex so it's hard for me to put myself in that position. Someone you sleep with more than once should create *some* sort of bond, even if it is only for money.

Ted still has female problems, that's for sure.

Right now, I couldn't feel too empathetic with Darla Diamond. She was cold meat on a slab nearby, where her considerable physical assets would do her no good. Darla Diamond was a mercenary, sexual primarily, but it looked as though her business had expanded.

SIXTY TWO

"Another dead woman? What are you trying to set a record?"

McCullough's sarcasm was duly noted.

"Oh no, Flintster, this one's on you. I never met the lady. You interviewed her and let her go."

He breathed hard into the receiver. "Yeah, it's really not funny is it? I don't suppose the world will miss one less hooker, but I'm sure she has a mom and dad who will grieve, same as if she were a ballerina."

There was that.

I said, "So Darla Diamond is the name she gave to you?"

"Have her business card right here. Double D. She sure knew how to make an impression that maximized her strengths."

"I just wonder why Crayton sent her instead of doing this himself. I take it you haven't talked to him yet."

"Afraid not. He doesn't answer his phone. I stopped by his place, a few times at different times of day and he's never in. Now that there's a dead body, I can officially bump this up and get some help."

"Well, at least we know one thing. This was more than a pimp roll. Darla doesn't fly all the way to Hilton Head in pursuit of Wally because he scooted away without paying to see her boobs the other night. Question I have is how she found him."

The weather and setting couldn't have been nicer, at odds with the gruesome nature of the calls I needed to make. I was drinking a beer at an outdoor café overlooking the yachts in the Sea Pines marina. Off season, the place wasn't crowded after lunch hour. I imagine most of the high rollers on the boats had personal chefs at their beck and call in their own galley.

"Good question," McCullough said. "Who knew where he was? You and Stone didn't even know he was still on your little island until yesterday. Seems to me that your pal McCarver was the only one privy to that."

"Yeah, I thought of that. But after Josephs stormed out of his condo, Ted says he didn't know where he went. It's a small island but there's a lot of hotels and that's not even counting Bluffton. And why would Ted want Wally dead?"

"Can't help you there, Sherlock. You said they quarreled the night Josephs ran out of his place."

"Unless Ted totally lost his mind in that monastery, which I'll admit is a possibility. A little spat over talk radio etiquette is hardly a reason to kill. Besides, the same girl was part of that original attack on Wally up in your neck of the woods. There's one other possibility. You won't like it, though."

McCullough said, "Since when do you give a shit what I like? Who?"

I was my turn to take a deep breath. "Your new girl friend. Alison Middleton."

"How would she know? And by the way, she's not my girlfriend. I'm taking it slow so keep your trap shut about it."

I had touched a nerve. I didn't think McCullough had any sensitive areas, but throughout our quasi-friend/partnership, we never really talked much of personal matters.

I said, "But think about it. Maybe Wally let something slip when he was in a break. Didn't realize his mic was live and she overheard something. Maybe Wally was talking to Ted while the commercials were on and she recognized Ted's voice. And she was pissed Wally called her an old dyke on the air. Could be she never let that go."

"I'm seeing her tonight. I'll see what I can find out."

"Undercover work under the covers."

"Not funny, King."

"Just don't forget to call Tomey and tell her that Diamond was part of the motel scam on Wally. I doubt they'll spring him on your word alone, but it'll deflect their case. And I actually want them to hold him for as long as they can, so we at least know where he is. And Crayton probably doesn't have the stones to storm a police station."

"I'll get around to it when I can."

"Come on, detective. You can't take a little teasing? Big tough guy like you?"

"You know, King, I'm not a bon vivant PI like you with lots of ladies in my wake. Nadine was my high school sweetheart. Ever since I met her, we only had eyes for each other. Now she's out there, probably dating. Who knows, she looks great these days, maybe she's even sleeping with somebody. It's hard to let that go after over thirty years. I'm just taking baby steps with Allie. I haven't even kissed her cheek yet. So lay off. Please."

Flint McCullough was as hard bitten as they come. He was one of those foxhole guys, the kind of man who you want protecting your back in a tight spot. He never whines or complains about anything and I imagine over the years, he has accumulated plenty of legitimate gripes, even some against me. But he always works everything out on his own terms, and just gets it done. No questions asked, no apologies.

I said, "I'm sorry, detective. Just a word of warning. I was pretty deep into a relationship last year with a country singer who had a lot more going on than I ever could have imagined. You're smart to go slow. Keep your eyes wide open. Show biz folks, male and female, have mighty big egos and a lot of secrets. They don't get to where they are without breaking a lot of hearts."

SIXTY THREE

De plane, boss. De plane.

Sometimes the mind takes wicked twists. If you have your wits about you, those thoughts stay inside your head. However, if the tongue is loosened by drink, a mind altering substance or simply lack of sleep, you may just blurt it out.

(Didn't I read somewhere that it's bad English to say that people blurt things out?)

What I'm trying to get to in a semi-sensitive fashion is that even though I've spent hours trying to figure out who is after Wally Josephs, a bit of dumb luck coupled with free association proved pivotal.

I had just hung up with McCullough. I tried Stone and got voice mail again. As I was preparing to leave the little café, a vertically challenged busboy who reminded me of Hervé Villechaize came by to refill my water glass.

De plane, boss. De plane.

I imagined he'd endured that insipid insult from bullies throughout his childhood and adolescent years. It probably still stung. Was I an awful man for thinking it, even if I didn't give it voice?

My Catholic upbringing was rearing its head. *Lust in your heart* is a sin. Not as bad as acting on it, but a sin nonetheless. So I was taught by the nuns. Now I think you deserve a merit badge for not giving in to your baser impulses when you *really really* want to. While I was pondering my guilt at reducing this kid to an obvious stereotype, it hit me.

The plane!

Elvis Crayton kept a number of aviation magazines in his condo. He had a pilot's license and owned a small plane. BS had provided me with the tail number of his Cessna Skyhawk 172, and I had dirty access to private airport flight logs. I referenced Lakewood N12 on my tablet and there it was.

Crayton had flown out of there two days ago. Destination --- HXD, Hilton Head Island. I scrolled to the island log. It noted that he had taken off three hours ago, headed back to Lakewood, New Jersey. Since the Cessna would need refueling, it would stop over at VG03, CEC, Chesapeake, Virginia. All in all, about a seven hour flight.

I redialed McCullough.

His voice was more clipped than usual, which is saying something.

He said, "Okay, if you're calling to say you're sorry again, King, it's not necessary. I shouldn't have cried on your shoulder about Nadine. You just caught me at a weak moment. It won't happen again."

He was apologizing for giving me a glimpse into his human side. I was tempted to go all touchy-feely with him and tell him how I felt honored that he'd trust me with his inner feelings. But that's not me and that didn't seem to be what he needed just now anyway.

"That's not why I called. Crayton is due to land his plane at Lakewood soon. Can you get up there and grab him?"

"On what charge?"

"He flew his Cessna down here two days ago which coincides with the timing of the attack on Wally. I can't prove it yet, but I think Diamond was with him. I bet someone at Lakewood noticed he was accompanied by a buxom blond. She was kind of hard to miss."

"What does that prove? They were friends, going on a romantic vacation together. If I were him, I wouldn't say a thing."

"Do you have to answer everything like a defense attorney? Open your eyes. Can't you just tail him until I get up there?"

"Why? Are you thinking of pulling some kind of torture to get him to talk?"

"Not my style. But you said Elvis isn't the sharpest knife in the drawer. Maybe I can convince him into telling me who sent him. Especially since Darla is dead. That might have scared him."

I could hear the inner conflict in his voice. "Okay. I'll personally head out to Lakewood. I don't have enough to bring him in but I could tip you off where he is. But I'm telling you straight out now, if anything bad happens to him, I'm coming after you. Just because we've shared a few stories over the years doesn't give you blanket immunity."

"I'd expect nothing less. I promise I won't harm a hair on his chinny-chin-chin."

He said, "And if my little warning doesn't deter you, don't forget he *is* the son of a minor crime boss here. Whatever their relationship is, I doubt his father would approve of you roughing up the kid, no matter how much it's justified."

"Understood."

"So what's your plan?"

"When I come up with one, you'll be the first to know."

SIXTY FOUR

I called Ted McCarver. "How fast is your plane?"

"That depends. I generally feel comfortable cruising at 300 knots. Why?"

"Range?"

"Maybe 1700 nautical. Why?"

"How far is it to Lakewood?"

"700 miles give or take. Two and a half hours. But that's a short grass runway. If I'm going to New Jersey, I usually fly into MJC, the Monmouth Jet Center. 7300 foot paved runway. Why are you asking?"

"How old is your crate and what's it worth?"

"It's a 2009 Socata TBM 850. I bought it three years ago. Got a bargain. Two mil."

"Busy later today?"

"Nothing I can't re-schedule."

"Feel like a trip to New Jersey?"

"I'm always up for flying. I'll call the airfield now and have them top it up. Pick me up in fifteen minutes."

SIXTY FIVE

I finally reached Jaime while I was on the way to pick up Ted. She had been on the set with Rick for a short time to help him get acclimated, although he and Don Johnson hit it off immediately. She had to pry him away from the old actor and remind him that there was work to be done. I got the feeling that club-hopping might be in the boys' future, since they seemed to share the same vices, Miami or otherwise.

I told her about the murder as gently as I could and about my trip to Jersey. "Any chance you'll be back east soon?" I asked.

"Not soon, I'm afraid. The good news is that we've got our lady writer locked in. Breakfast with Rob Reiner clinched the deal. The bad news is that Cheryl Connors, our film rep out here, is leaving to work for James Cameron. He made her a great offer. I couldn't ask her to turn it down and there was no way I could match it. So I'm going to have to run things from here until I can find a replacement."

"How long will that take?"

"I can't say for sure. She was pretty much a one woman show. She had some girls working with her but nobody near ready to take over. This could be a while. I can't rush it because we're really hot now. A bunch of our authors have options entering the script phase. It's getting to be more lucrative than our publishing stuff in New York."

"Well, that's great," I said, not really meaning it. I knew what was coming next. However long it took to stabilize things in L.A., knowing Jaime, she'd then want to spend time in New Jersey to ride herd on her literary agency, which until now had been her bread and butter. She wouldn't be in the Carolinas anytime soon.

She said, "How about you coming out here? Any chance of that happening?"

"Not likely. It's a murder case now. I think I can clear Josephs of that, but whoever sent this woman out to kill him is still out there. It may be Crayton, but I'm thinking that I'm just peeling layers off the onion. There's got to be someone above him calling the shots."

"Be careful, sweetie. That tie with organized crime scares me. Sounds like Josephs is better off in jail in Hilton Head than going back to the old Garden State."

"For now. Tomey has been great so far at keeping him under wraps without divulging his stage name. But he can't stay in custody forever. What I can't figure is how anyone up north knew where he was."

"Seems obvious, doesn't it? Ted. He admitted he knew the woman. He could have engineered the whole thing, right from the start."

"McCullough said the same thing. I don't know. Ted had to be pretty messed up after what happened with Stevie. But it's been over a year and he had a lot of time in that monastery to get his head on straight."

"But you always said, he never was very emotionally available. Always a hard man to get a bead on. Again, maybe I've been working on so many of my dad's books over the years, I see conspiracies that aren't there in real life."

"Yeah well, I came to the same impasse with McCullough. Ted really loves Wally. Sees him as the son he never had. He shepherded his career from a nobody in rural PA to a star in the New York metro area. And just last week, when Wally had nowhere to go, Ted took him in."

"Devil's Advocate? His prodigal son has gone astray. You said that Ted didn't want his name on that kind of radio. Maybe he doesn't want to take responsibility for what Wally has become. You know what he tried to do with the three women. He wanted to erase his past mistakes."

"But in a positive way. He wanted to help those women. I think he wants to help Josephs, too. Although if there's a murder rap hanging over Wally, who knows if he has a career left?"

"Any pub is good pub. You clear him and he'll be bigger than ever. Take that to the bank. Look, honey, I have a conference call now. Gotta go. I miss you."

"Yeah. Me, too."

I was just about to pull in to Ted's complex. What was it about him that women didn't trust? My ex Charlene hated him from the start. The fact I was working for him was one of the main reasons for our break up. I saw a chastened older man trying to do the right thing and make restitution for his past sins. She saw a rapist, a stalker and a wife beater who was beyond redemption. She couldn't understand how I could associate with, much less work for, such a fiend. Fortunately, Jaime was a bit more nuanced about Ted --- suspecting him but not condemning outright.

At this point, I wasn't a hundred per cent sure who was right. I might be flying to New Jersey with a killer at the stick.

SIXTY SIX

I'd never flown with Ted before. It hadn't crossed my mind as to whether he was a decent pilot until we were accelerating down the runway. I accepted on faith that his navigational and piloting skills were commensurate with everything else he undertook: first rate, no detail overlooked. I wasn't disappointed.

Two negative images did occur to me as we gracefully climbed to the 30,000 foot altitude that the Socata found favorable for cruising. The first was my frightening experience with Jaime's dad, who since had given up flying, or more likely had failed his re-certification testing. Clipping trees and almost landing at the wrong airport is a hard picture to erase when you're in a small private plane.

The other had to do with the story Ted's psychotherapist revealed last year. Ted had given Dr. Mills permission to speak freely to me about their sessions trying to resolve his "mommy issues". His mother was a relentless nag and his father, while as calm as Ted externally, had reached his boiling point internally. His dad had deliberately crashed their small aircraft into the side of Whiteface Mountain, killing both himself and his wife. McCarver only discovered this ten years after the fact.

If Ted had hired Darla Diamond to kill Wally, would he consider crashing us into the ocean? As much as

I tried to push the thought to the back of my mind, it surfaced whenever there was a lull in the conversation.

To that end, I tried to keep up idle chatter. I was sitting up front with Ted in the co-pilot's seat, not that I'd be able to do anything if McCarver cackled with evil intent, twirled his mustache and suddenly parachuted out. The cockpit was tight but fairly quiet, given the huge jet engine driving us forward.

I said, "So Ted, what does it cost to fly this thing? Just out of curiosity."

"It costs nothing out of curiosity but in the physical world, about four hundred fifty bucks an hour."

By his standards, that was hilarious. He and McCullough would make a lively pair if they didn't intensely dislike each other.

"Before I called you I checked out airfares on line. Last minute, it would have been seven hundred bucks round trip and taken a lot longer. Hilton Head to a layover in Charlotte, then on to Newark. Direct from Savannah to JFK only two hours or so but then a couple more down to Toms River. I really appreciate the lift."

"Is that the reason you chose me? To chauffeur you to New Jersey at no cost?"

"I'll pay you if that's a problem." I had thought that Ted understood I was working gratis. A couple of grand wouldn't be a problem, but I'd be shocked if he didn't spend that much on dinners every week.

"I'm sorry if it appeared I was asking for recompense. I know many are put off at the way I express myself. I try to be precise but perhaps it sounds overly formal. No, what I meant was that I hoped could help you with your investigation.

"You've already helped. Just understand, the man I need to get to is the son of an organized crime boss. He probably was hired to kill Wally. It could be dangerous."

"I understand that. But you're not actually going to shoot anybody, are you? I assume there's a gun in that duffel bag."

"Two actually. I never plan on shooting anyone, but you never know. I was thinking I'd just rent a car at the airstrip. If you need to get back right away, I'll fly home commercial."

"Not necessary. They keep a car for me at the Monmouth Jet Center. It's not very new, a ten year old BMW, but it suffices. Why don't you let me drive you? At the worst, I can remain in the car and stay vigilant."

"A getaway driver? Oh, goody, just what I need. Let's see how this shakes out. I don't want to put you in any danger."

Ted was stoked. "I admit, this is exciting. I'm actually doing something first hand as opposed to hiring others as I've done for most of my life."

That gave me an opening to broach a subject that had been nagging at me. If I had thought about it ahead of time, I would have waited until my feet were on terra firma, but I was in "blurt out" mode, I guess, regardless of how ungrammatical that is.

"Ted, I need to bring this up because it may come up later. Believe me, I'm uncomfortable asking it. How do you think Darla Diamond knew that Wally was on Hilton Head? The only one who knew his whereabouts was you."

He turned to me. "So you're asking if I hired the late Ms. Diamond to murder my young friend? Is that what you want to know?"

"I told you this would be uncomfortable. But unless we find someone else who knew, the police are going to ask you the same thing."

"Is that really it? You're protecting me from the authorities? When Stevie was killed, you believed I was

THE LAST RESORT

guilty right off the bat. You didn't trust me. When you
found that I was telling the truth all along, I hoped that
would have affirmed in your mind that I have been an
honest man all my life. Not perfect, as you also
discovered last year. But hiring a killer? That's not in my
playbook, to use one of the sports metaphors you and
Stone toss around."

I said, "Ted, I wasn't accusing you. I was asking
how anyone could have known where Wally was. Help
me, because I can't figure it out."

"Nor can I. I told you when he and I argued and he
left in a huff, I had no idea where he would go next. I
might have guessed a nearby hotel, but he had a vehicle.
He could have gone to some obscure village in Georgia
for all I knew."

He was sticking to his story. "All right then. When
Wally did his show from your place, do you recall any
time you spoke to him when he was on a break? We were
thinking that maybe his mic picked up your voice and
someone on the other end recognized it."

"Let me think. No, Wally was ensconced in the
room I use as an office with the door closed the whole
time. I never went in. During those long commercial
breaks, he occasionally came out for refreshment or to use
the facilities. I was listening on my internet radio, but
after a while, I was becoming annoyed at a lot of the
things I was hearing so I went out onto the balcony with
an adult beverage and a book. Made a couple of phone
calls. We talked outside during a couple of breaks but no,
I never spoke to him in that room."

"That eliminates Allie then. We were thinking she
might have picked up on your voice."

"I wouldn't eliminate her based on that. How do
you know Wally didn't tell her? I'm sure she'll swear he
didn't but can you trust her?"

RICHARD NEER   245

"You obviously don't. But it goes to motive. She thinks they'd fire her if Wally was gone."

"Pardon my French, but that is horse shit. I know the business. There's no logical successor working at WJOK currently. And sure, there may be some obscure act out in the hinterlands I don't know of, but sports talk is local. You need in-depth knowledge of the teams in the market. I'm sure they'd keep her on as a solo act. They use the Mike and the Mad Dog paradigm here, where Mike by himself does just as well if not better than the team ever did. I'm not revealing any secrets that you couldn't discover on your own, but she's making less than a tenth of what he is. They leak phony numbers on him, partially to make her feel better, but he's making a lot more than they let on. And if she found out they'd been lying all along, she'd be angry. And you know what they say about a woman scorned."

SIXTY SEVEN

"She came from Providence. The one in Rhode Island, Riley, not the hundred others."

I had called Flint from inside a hangar at the Monmouth Jet Center. Ted had landed the Socata smoother than twenty one year old Glenfiddich. He was attending to the business of berthing and refueling the plane, while I waited for his Beemer to be delivered.

I said, "Was she in any trouble up there? Was she looking for a place to hide?"

"Nope. Just brought her dreams of making it with her acting. She was twenty nine although she looked older. I won't bore you with her high school grades or anything, but she was a model student. Drama club. Sports. Seems she gave up pretty quick on being an actress. Tried modeling for a spell. Her birth name was Darlene Diamente."

"And no arrest record in the Garden State?"

"Just that time I told you about when no charges were pressed. She'd been cutting hair for seven years or so. We searched her apartment. Nice little complex in Point Pleasant. There were signs a man was shacked up with her there; my guess would be Crayton, that's why we never caught him at home. There was a laptop but our IT guys haven't gone through it yet. I saw she used TurboTax but these hairdressers don't declare half their tip money, so I don't know if that will tell us much."

Flint had accomplished all of this while I was in the air. Impressive, but I expected no less.

I said, "I doubt she'd declare her hooker income either. Did you call Tomey down in Hilton Head?"

"Yep. At first she was a little put off when I told her I'd gotten her cell number from you, but she eased up after I gave her the dope we had on Diamond. They're still holding your boy, but it sounds like I've stayed in worse hotels than his accommodations in their holding pen. No wonder they call it paradise."

"Don't call it paradise to your Yankee friends or we can kiss it goodbye. Has Crayton landed?"

"I'm there now. Elvis hasn't hit the runway. Apparently stopped longer for re-fueling in Virginia than he originally figured. Bad news is that no one at the landing strip in Lakewood noticed a big blond with him when he left a couple of days ago. So it's gonna be hard to tie him in to anything to do with her down your way."

"I guess we could make a call to Chesapeake. If they re-fueled there on the way, maybe someone saw her."

"Already got a call in. Wrong shift. They said the guys who were manning the tower that day are off until tomorrow."

"I'm probably ten minutes away from Lakewood. So you don't plan to pick Crayton up?"

"Like I told you, we really have nothing that'll stick. Even if you can prove he flew down to the island with Diamond, where does that get us?"

McCullough and I had done this dance before. He was very cautious about making arrests on flimsy evidence. My cop buddy Pete Shabielski had told me stories about how he and his colleagues on the force in central Jersey weren't above roughing up suspects to get them to talk, but that was twenty years ago. I am sure that it still goes on, but with body cams and zealous activists, it's not the Wild West show it once was. And despite his colorful cowboy name, Flint McCullough would never tolerate such extracurricular activity from his charges.

I said, "You know Flint, I hate the idea that the taxpayers are footing the bill for you in Lakewood when you have nothing on Crayton. Seems like a waste of county resources to me. Sometimes the private sector can provide more efficient answers."

"True. But they're still governed by the same laws. Just remember that."

"I will. But sometimes, these calls aren't black and white. Public-private partnerships can be pretty effective."

He caught on without further prompting. "Hey, it's the quarterback's job to make a smooth hand-off but after that, breaking tackles falls to the ball carrier. Happy hunting."

SIXTY EIGHT

Ted and I sat in his old Beemer outside of Villa Vittoria, a pretty restaurant on Old Hooper in Brick, just north of Toms River. A couple of blocks inland, it doesn't attract tourists seeking a water view, just local foodies who appreciate the authentic Italian cuisine. What Elvis Crayton was doing there is anybody's guess.

We had followed Crayton from the time he landed his Beechcraft in Lakewood. McCullough and McCarver shot each other dirty looks as the cars passed --- ours on the way in, his on the way out. There was no place to confront Elvis at the open airfield, so I decided to wait until I could corner him in a setting where I could do what needed to be done.

Ted's presence and observations made the stakeout more tolerable. I had to be careful not to expose him to anything that could come back to haunt either one of us, but he was someone to talk to during what is normally a lonely vigil.

McCarver said, "You and I should clear the air, King. We spoke on the plane, but we never had that dinner with Rick to get *everything* out in the open."

"I'm not sure this is the time or place. Try the confessional if you're still in your mea culpa mode."

He started to protest, then backed off. After a moment he said, "While I was in the monastery, I had a lot of time to think. No distractions. The monks were meditating about God or some other unanswerable questions. I was more pragmatic. I was acting like my own shrink, I suppose. Asking myself questions and calling myself out when the answers weren't honest. I actually verbalized all this. If anyone saw me, they would have thought I was insane. Maybe I was, temporarily. But it led me to some realizations that ultimately will make me better."

I had all I could do to keep from rolling my eyes. Ted's voyage of self discovery might be fascinating in other situations, but I really wasn't interested now.

I said, "So write a self help book, Ted. You could make millions. Call it, *Lean Out* or something. Ted, I appreciate the ride up here. We didn't have time to get me a separate car, but I need to handle this on my own. No offense."

"King, we can sit here and drink coffee and you can play with your smart phone, or we can talk like human beings. If Crayton is here to dine, I can tell you it's not fast food. He'll be at least ninety minutes. I have some things I want to tell you about myself. If you're not receptive, I'll just shut up. Or call a cab and get to a hotel. You keep the car."

He said this with no anger or reproach. We were going to be here for awhile. His idea of calling a cab was cleaner, but another set of eyes might be useful.

He said, "What I'm leading up to is that I learned I do have a rather large ego. When I sold the station and moved to Hilton Head, I had no plan other than to find a good woman and live quietly and well. That's why I started going to Doctor Mills. I wanted to remove the impediments I'd accumulated over the years that kept me from forming a relationship. I thought that Stevie would be my salvation, that I'd finally arrived at a good place.

But when she was killed, all that went away and I had to start from square one."

The delectable smell of highly seasoned Italian food permeated the air. It reminded me I hadn't eaten since breakfast. An order of calamari to go? Then I could intimidate Crayton with my breath.

I suppressed the hunger pangs and said, "So you went to the monastery."

"Yes. At the time, I thought I could live in seclusion, doing good deeds and taking no credit for them. But that wasn't me. I thought I could leave radio behind but I grew restless. I realized I had to do something I could sink my teeth into. Something that made me attack the day with purpose, not just thinking about where I wanted to have lunch."

I could relate. As I get older, I wonder what I'll do when my physical presence doesn't intimidate and my mental acuity doesn't compensate. Could I turn into Elton Spicer, John Peterson's creation? A man in his seventies fighting crime and busting baddies a half century younger? It works in fiction. In real life, not so much.

McCarver said, "I started helping the foundation on the island. Good work, but not my bailiwick. I don't want to be one of those cranky old men complaining that things aren't like they used to be in the good old days."

"Rick and I used to talk about how great progressive radio was, how the greedy corporations ruined it."

"But try talking a big company into experimenting with that idea again. They'll laugh in your face. No one has the courage to try something different."

I took a sip of my now cold coffee. I had a great idea. A heating coil you could plug into a cigarette lighter to heat your coffee on stakeouts. I'd check Amazon to see if someone had already invented it. Of course, thermos bottles work. I think I still have my original Star Trek model, complete with matching lunchbox. But what about if you forget to carry those clunky things?

Bottom line is, I was bored by Ted's navel gazing.

I said, "So what do you do? Stone feels sorry for those rock bands that become oldies groups, playing their greatest hits over and over, back to when they actually meant something. Even their old fans don't want to hear new material, even if it is any good, which it usually isn't."

I had no answers to Ted's dilemma, one that could be mine someday. "Ted, you have to come to grips with the fact that you can't re-invent yourself and expect anyone to care. You've had your day in the sun. Be thankful you had those highs that most people never could even dream of."

"I get that. Sure, I feel guilty that I wallow in self pity as I drive my BMW to my luxury condo after enjoying a two hundred dollar dinner with a gorgeous lady of the night. Yet just giving a big piece of it away didn't make me feel any better."

I've known Ted McCarver for twenty years. I worked for him last year, when he revealed his dark side. He provided files detailing his abuse of the three women he wanted me to locate for him. But in a way, I'd learned more about what makes him tick in the last ten minutes. He'd always built walls around his heart. He shared his considerable intellect freely to anyone who would listen; his heart, never.

Ted said, "In any case King, I'm grateful you let me tag along with you. I'm doing something. Something that could show tangible results. Hands on, as opposed to writing a check and leaving the dirty work to others."

"Ted, get this into your head. If I decide to let you stick around, you need to follow my lead and do exactly what I tell you. Otherwise, we'll call you a cab right now."

"So stipulated. What I meant was, I have a simple mission now. To help a kid who has lost his way. When Wally Josephs comes out of this, I'll be there for him, like the son I never had. Make him into a positive force instead of what he is now. Maybe he can be my legacy."

First Stevie Perry, now Wally. Ted was still seeking deliverance from outside. I might have said that he should pick a more worthy candidate for his largesse than Wally. But where's the satisfaction doing mere cosmetic work on an already nice house, as opposed to taking a shambles and restoring it to greatness above its original station?

My observations would have to wait. Leaving Villa Vittoria and heading toward his car, was Elvis Crayton.

SIXTY NINE

I've always been fascinated by football coaches who script the first fifteen plays of a game. Bill Walsh was famous for it. But how can you predict with certainty which plays will work? What about penalties? If play number three calls for a run off-tackle but you're faced with a third and twenty, do you go off script or stick with what is obviously an ineffective call?

I had a plan for confronting Crayton, but it was flexible enough to allow for improvisation. Ideally, I envisioned waiting for him at his home, sitting in the dark, Beretta in hand. But what if he didn't intend to go home after his meal at Villa Vittoria? He might head straight to Darla's. I could wait at his place for days, and I wasn't even sure he had HBO.

The restaurant parking lot is surrounded by trees and there are numerous areas that the light fails to reach. Crayton's Mercedes was parked in one of those darkened spots. I dialed McCarver on my cell, even though he was sitting right next to me.

"Ted, pick up and listen, don't talk. I may need you to corroborate my story if I can get Crayton to tell me something."

"I wish I could record it somehow. But I'll listen and take notes."

"Right." Like he'd really take notes. Ted with shorthand? He'd say that's why God invented secretaries.

As Elvis emerged, I ran over to his car, hidden by darkness. I crouched behind it on the passenger side. When he reached the Mercedes, the doors unlocked. He got in, wriggled into the perforated leather seat and pulled on his seatbelt. What a law abiding fellow.

Before he could touch the ignition button, I was sitting next to him with my gun leveled at his head.

"What the hell?"

I said, "Hands on the wheel and shut up, Crayton. I'm here just to talk. Don't make this go any further than that."

"Who the fuck are you? Do you know who I am?"

"Since I addressed you by name, you could assume that. Elvis Crayton, nee Costello."

Crayton was a few inches short of six feet. Looked to be fit, but not overly muscular. Casually dressed in chinos and a black cotton sweater. Short dark hair, unremarkable face, save for a wispy mustache, Errol Flynn style.

His voice quavering, he said, "Just telling you, asshole, if you think you can take some cash off me, think again. Even if you do get away now, you're a dead man."

"I said talk, not rob. I'm looking for one little piece of information from you. Easy-peasy."

"You gonna shoot me if I don't tell you what you want to hear? You got the balls to do that?"

"Past performance is no guarantee of future results." My wit was lost on him but I decided to keep this formal. "Violence is not my first choice. But things sometimes escalate."

"What the fuck you talking about?"

"I know that you flew the late Darla Diamond to Hilton Head where she tried to kill Walter Josephs. Sadly for her, she got the raw end of that deal."

"I don't know any Darla whatever her name is."

"Elvis, Elvis. I'm not the most patient man in the world. You're wasting our time by lying to me. What I need is the name of the man or woman who hired you to kill Wally. That's it. One name and our interaction comes to a merciful and permanent conclusion."

"I'm getting out of the car now. Shoot me if you want to. Otherwise, get the fuck out of here."

He'd called my bluff. I'm not Jack Bauer on 24. I won't shoot somebody in the thigh if they don't cooperate. But I *am* good at menacing verbal threats.

"Before you do that, consider this," I said. "I have a lot of evidence I can turn over to the police. Or not. Pictures of you at a car dealer, checking out Wally's car. Testimony from the late Ms. Diamond, implicating you in a pimp roll involving Wally. Flight records. Adds up to attempted murder, conspiracy to commit murder, even some creative federal charges that the FBI can cook up. So before you get out of the car, think about what you're exposing yourself to."

"Who are you anyway? A cop? Undercover? A fed? Who are you?"

"I'm either your guardian angel or the anti-Christ, take your pick. Names aren't important."

"Shit, I *know* you. Just came to me. You're King, ain't you. Slick P.I. who fucks up and gets people killed. That right?"

"The *gets people killed* part is the one you should be concerned about."

"I'll take my chances with that. I got some friends in the restaurant. Be healthier for you if you're not in the car when I get back. But don't worry. I'll find your ass later. Count on it."

With that he unbuckled his seat belt and popped the door handle. I was tempted to go all Bauer on him and shoot him in the leg. But while he recovered, he'd likely recruit his father's goons to come after me. I may have unleashed that demon already.

He slid out of the driver's seat and opened the door. I was stunned by what happened a split second later. Elvis screamed as the door slammed closed, crushing the fingers of his left hand.

Standing outside the car with a macabre grin on his face was Ted McCarver.

SEVENTY

I motioned for McCarver to get the hell out of there and he complied, running back to his car which was parked sixty feet away. Crayton was too focused on his mangled fingers to notice his assailant.

Sometimes you are presented an opportunity. Time to play hard ass.

"I'm sorry we couldn't work this out amiably, Elvis," I said, trying to sound unfazed by the wanton act of violence. "I don't think you're gonna be able to drive with that hand. I'd be happy to drop you at the Ocean Medical Center where they can try to save your fingers. Sooner the better or you might lose a couple. Your call."

"You son of a bitch." He grimaced in pain, his voice guttural through clenched teeth. "You're a dead man. You hear me?"

I shoved the gun into his ribs as a reminder. "Much as I'd like to make this about me, I think your problems are a bit more urgent. All I ask is a name."

"I don't have a fucking name, all right? Darla set this all up. Now get me to the hospital."

"I'm going to need more details, my friend. Be quick, now."

His hand was a mess, fingers spread akimbo like a veteran baseball catcher's. He'd never play guitar again.

"Darla came to me for help on a job. That's it. We were supposed to roust this Wally guy at the motel. She didn't say nothing about killing him. Just roll him for money, like we did with a few others."

"Wait a minute. You're saying you were working for her? She was running these scams?"

"Damn straight. She set these rich guys up, I was just along for the ride if things got hairy. Now get me to a doc."

We switched seats. I was wearing nitrile gloves so I wasn't worried about prints, although there was no way Crayton would involve the law. I shoved him into the passenger seat and plunked myself down on the driver's side. I hit the ignition button and since he had still the key fob in his pocket, the Mercedes roared to life.

As we pulled out, I said, "Wally says you chased him and fired a gun at him. You flew Darla down to Hilton Head. That wasn't a scam to steal money. You had to know she had a contract out on him."

There wasn't a lot of blood coming from the damaged hand, but there was enough to ruin the upholstery. He held his wrecked paw up with the other, pressing on the palm.

"*She* did that. I ran after him, *she* shot at him. Look, she was crazy. I mean yeah, I stayed at her pad sometimes and she was a great fuck, but that's all it was. She didn't tell me till afterwards she'd been hired to off this dude and make it look like a hooker deal gone south. I wouldn't have agreed to go along if I knew that. Killing's not my thing." He said all this through clenched teeth, then he screamed, "God damn, this hurts."

We drove up Route 70 toward the medical center. I glanced in the rear view and sure enough, McCarver was following in the Beemer. I hadn't instructed him to follow, but his instincts were correct.

I said, "Sorry. All this could have been avoided if you just told me the truth straightaway."

"The motel job was just supposed to be a quick roll of a guy with some serious cash. We'd done it before. She was the mastermind. She had connections to sell wallet stuff to hackers, Russians maybe, to max out the take. Don't ask me how."

"So when you found out she was dead you just flew back on your own from Hilton Head? No pay, nothing? Why weren't you backing her up on the beach?"

"I'm not a killer, man. She told me she done shit like this before. After this one went down, I was ready to dump her sweet little ass. But she got word where this Wally dude was holed up and she said she had to get there fast before he moved again. She asked me to fly her down direct. I was just transport. A few bucks and free blow jobs for life. That's it."

"And you have no idea who she was working for?"

"Swear to God, no clue. Maybe the Russians, I don't know. This whole deal had gone way bad, but I learned the hard way Darla was someone you didn't fuck with."

We were almost at the hospital. Lucky for him, Villa Vittoria was less than three miles away and the lights were in our favor.

"Elvis, tell you what. The Ocean County cops are all over this. But you're small potatoes if your story checks out. I might be able to talk to some people and keep you clear. But you send someone after me, they'll nail your ass for every charge in the book."

"Fuck you, King. I told you, you're dead meat."

"I hope for your sake, you'll reconsider that. It'll save you a world of hurt."

I parked the car in a dark spot not far from the entrance and he got out. Even though nothing had happened to his legs, he hobbled toward the emergency room door, not looking back to see if I was following.

I got out of the car and ran a rag over the drivers' side door to obliterate any prints Ted may have left. So in the end, I'd managed to put myself into Crayton's crosshairs, and I was no closer to discovering who had paid for the hit on Wally. Russians? Really? Another botch job by Riley King that only made things worse.

I was about to call McCullough when I remembered that I'd been dialed in to Ted the whole time.

I said, "Ted, you there?"

Silence on the other end. Disconnected. Where was he?

My question was answered a moment later. As Crayton limped toward the entry, a dark figure emerged with a baseball bat. The first blow caught Elvis on the back of the neck, causing him to crumble to the sidewalk. Before I could reach him, several more hard shots to the head had landed.

SEVENTY ONE

I'd seen Ted's temper once before, when it was unleashed on me over what I considered a trivial matter. It took the form of angry obscenities, a far cry from the savage beating he'd inflicted on Crayton.

I grabbed McCarver from behind before he could do any more damage. "Damn it, man, have you lost your mind? What are you doing?"

"Protecting you," he said, as calmly as if he were explaining a hedge move that threatened my portfolio. "I heard what he said. He was about to unleash his father's soldiers on you."

I was stunned by his ability to defend this violence in such measured, almost professorial tones. He hadn't acted out of blind rage. His logical brain had come to the conclusion that if Crayton were allowed to live, he'd start a war that we were unlikely to win.

McCarver was right in that if Crayton were to bleed out on the pavement, the senior Costello would be hard pressed to discover our role in his demise. But something human in me couldn't allow a man to die within steps of an emergency room, however repugnant I found him.

"Ted, get in the car. Get rid of that bat. Throw it as far into the bay as you can or better yet, burn it. Make sure you don't get any blood on the car. Get rid of all your clothes. Shoes, underwear, everything. Take a long hot shower."

"What about you?"

"Get the hell out before I change my mind."

For once, he followed my orders.

I wish I could say that everything I did next was rational. I was smart enough to avoid security cameras, shielding my face with a pulled down ball cap and upraised hands. I hustled to the ER entrance and grabbed the first medically garbed person I encountered. I told the young women that there was a man on the sidewalk, obviously badly hurt and they needed to get him in as quickly as they could.

Then I walked away.

I headed for Route 70 on foot. There was a nearby motel on that well traveled highway where I could gather myself and think.

My immediate concern was the police. The young nurse/doctor/assistant I had accosted wouldn't be a reliable witness. I altered my voice when I spoke to her. If questioned, she could only give a very general description that wouldn't hold up, even in a lineup.

McCullough knew I'd been tailing Crayton. It would be elementary for him to surmise that I was responsible for Elvis' condition. I just had to hope that in both our interests, Flint would look the other way, ignoring our role in meting out street justice.

Of course, there was Crayton himself. If he recovered, I'd be the first item on the agenda. As soon as he was able to speak, he'd point whatever weapons he had at his disposal directly at me.

I was in a deep hole. All because I agreed to help a shock jock I didn't even like, much less trust.

SEVENTY TWO

Ted met me at the Brick Motor Inn a few hours later. The place wasn't fancy, but the room seemed clean enough to suit my short term purpose, which was to pop McCarver in the kisser for his stupidity.

He tried to defuse some of my anger as he walked through the door. "King, I realize what I did is going to cause repercussions. I just want you to know that if this gets out of hand, I'll step up and take the blame. I deserve it and whatever else you deem appropriate."

"Damn right you do. What the hell were you thinking?"

"The way I saw it was that I was willing to do what had to be done and you weren't. This Crayton character threatened to kill you, in no uncertain terms. I couldn't let that stand. You have a good life ahead of you. I don't want you to jeopardize that for me or Wally or anybody else. If you think I should turn myself in, I'm willing to do that. Just say the word."

I said, "Did you do what I asked --- ditch the clothes, the bat, any evidence that could tie you to this?"

"I did. Tied the bat to a rock and tossed it off a jetty. Incinerated the clothes. Went over the car with a fine toothed comb. Jesus, I hated to throw that bat away. I kept it in the Beemer's trunk. The jocks at WJOK made it up for me as a going away present. A Ted McCarver autographed model."

"Tough shit. The problem is, McCullough knows we were tailing Crayton. To protect you, I'd have to lie to him. I could say he came out of Villa Vittoria with some mob guy and we decided to let him go and catch up with him later when he was alone. But if Flint finds out I'm lying to him, he'll never trust me again and knowing him, he'll run us both in without a second thought."

Ted bit his lip. "So what should I do? Should I surrender?"

"As they say, the truth will set you free. In a few minutes, we're going to put that to the test."

We didn't have to wait that long. Seconds later, there was a knock on the motel room door.

It was Ocean County Detective First Grade Flint McCullough and he didn't look happy.

SEVENTY THREE

I didn't expect McCarver and McCullough to shake hands so it was no surprise that they eyed each other as if they each had festering leprosy sores. Bro-hugs and a chorus of Kumbaya were off the table as well.

The room was too cramped to accommodate three grown men. There was only one small rickety chair in the tiny room. I didn't see us all sitting on the bed, so with palpable unease, we stood in our separate corners, like boxers anticipating a bloody match.

"Flint, I called you here to tell you exactly what happened a few hours ago," I said, and proceeded to do just that.

When I was finished, McCullough clucked his tongue against his teeth. "Well, gentlemen," he said, not bothering to hide his facetiousness. "You've put me in an impossible situation. I was just at the Med Center. Elvis Crayton is expected to survive, but that's about it. Traumatic brain damage. He'll be what we call a vegetable. Sorry to be so anti-PC, but I don't know another way to put it."

I exhaled. "I feel rotten for saying it but the man was a POS who tried to kill Wally, stole from a bunch of johns and corrupted some of your fellow cops. The next thing on his agenda was to kill me, so I can't feel too bad for him."

McCarver said, "Detective McCullough, if you need to make an arrest, take me in now. King had nothing to do with my actions. He was willing to let Crayton walk regardless of the danger to himself. I couldn't let that happen."

"Shut the fuck up." McCullough was pissed at the position we'd put him in. I'd never heard him raise his voice until now. He was like an old DOS computer, given contradictory instructions that caused the hard drive to go haywire.

He had warned me about taking things into my own hands to punish Crayton. I had heeded his advice, but I was lax in assuming that Ted could be trusted.

I said, "Let's try to think rationally about what we want to happen next. Step by step. Outside of this room, no one knows how Crayton got hurt. Right?"

McCullough winced. "Far as I know. But make no mistake, I'll be a target on this one. If it's not me, whoever they assign to the case will know that I was interested in Crayton and they'll be asking questions."

I said, "But that's where your part ended. There's no way anyone can tie you in to anything that happened tonight. You have an alibi in case it comes down to that? Where did you go after the Lakewood airstrip?"

"I was at headquarters, doing some paperwork. When the call came in that Crayton was at the Med Center, I went over there, being that he was a person of interest in a case I was looking into."

"So you might still catch the case?"

"Unless someone higher-up sees it as a conflict, yeah, I'd say it's likely."

We took turns looking at each other, waiting for someone to state the obvious. I drew the short straw.

"Well, detective, you have a decision to make. You throw Ted in jail for this, he's dead. Costello senior will make sure of that. Same goes for me. If old man Costello wants vengeance, we'll all be in the line of fire."

McCullough hated to have his hand forced like this. He was the one who usually did the forcing. "You don't leave me much choice, do you?"

"That's your call. I screwed this whole thing up. I was hoping to use the threat of you arresting Elvis on accessory charges to shut him up, but I let things get out of hand."

I turned to Ted. "I never should have let you near the stake out. I'm supposed to be the professional here, so if the heat comes down, it's on me."

McCullough spoke in such a quiet voice we had to strain to hear him. "I have to go through the motions. I'll ask a bunch of questions at Villa Vittoria. A few at the Med Center. They'll all be dead ends, of course. Forensics won't find anything in Crayton's car, will they?"

"Just his blood. I was careful. So was Ted."

McCullough sat down on the edge of the bed in a daze. "I'll meet with Costello senior. Assure him we're doing everything we can. Try to talk him out of acting on his own, but good luck with that. The public won't give a crap. Same with my bosses. They'll see it as one less mobster and chalk it up to a dispute within the family."

He extended his palms upward in a helpless gesture. "I guess this means that trying to find whoever tried to have Josephs killed is over, too. We'll never find out who instigated this hot mess."

SEVENTY FOUR

Flint did catch this case and followed procedure to the letter. He churned up a lot of paperwork and interviewed people with ties to Crayton. Anyone reviewing his work on paper would find little to criticize. He touched all the bases, however lightly.

A more dogged investigation by an outside party might ask for Flint's phone records relating to the case. They would notice the unusual number of calls made to me and Allie. But since there was no report filed on the original assault on Josephs, connecting those to Crayton would be difficult. Forensics should lead nowhere if we had been as thorough as I believed we had.

Surveillance cameras, while not as prevalent as they are in England, are still functioning in unlikely areas and if one happened to catch me driving Elvis' car with him bleeding in the passenger seat, I'd have some explaining to do. And there could be an unnoticed witness: a waiter who happened to be taking a cigarette break or a patron gazing out the restaurant window.

But checking through all these sources requires time, manpower and persistence, which the cops on TV have in abundance. In real life, these are scarce assets. Certain cases are assigned priority status and are pursued vigorously. These catch the eye of the media and the citizenry assumes that every such infraction receives equal attention.

But others go unnoticed and quietly fade by the next news cycle, if they even reach that level of public interest. Ask anyone who's had a break-in where under ten grand is missing. File a report for insurance purposes, and then move on to the next case.

Flint contacted boss Costello, and played the role of a dedicated cop who would relentlessly seek justice, regardless of the victim's worthiness. Under other circumstances, it wouldn't require any acting skill on his part. That's who he was.

I hoped that he could be that idealistic crusader again at some point, but I feared that this situation had compromised him to the point where there was no turning back. Like any big lie, it tends to spawn others until the subject loses any contact with the truth.

McCarver and I stayed ensconced at Rick's unsold home in Mantoloking for the duration. I didn't have much to say to Ted; things between us were pretty tense. He'd put me and a good cop in an untenable position.

The only bright spot was provided by Miss Jenny Lightower, who brought a potential buyer to survey the place and came back for a drink afterwards. I told her about Rick's Hollywood journey and we had a couple of laughs.

Her visit was therapeutic for me, relieving some of the tension that had built up over the last hours. And in an odd bit of free association, a couple of pleasant hours with this blond goddess got me thinking about another --- Darla Diamond. Angry as I still was at Ted, he might provide some background that could prove useful.

After Jenny departed, I broke the stony silence between Ted and me. "You mentioned that you met Darla Diamond through some execs at Cirrus. Were they aware of her sideline as a hooker, or were they strictly looking for a concierge haircut and shave from a pretty girl?"

"The way these guys bragged about their female conquests would make Trump blush. They were married guys on road trips. And she *was* pretty spectacular. I'd say that had to be aware that she offered a little more than Floyd the barber."

"Anyone in particular introduce you?"

"I got her number from one of them over dinner. You know, it was a *nudge-nudge, wink-wink* sort of thing, now that I think back on it. "

"Who was at the dinner?"

"The regional sales manager, Bart Dawson. Campbell was there, the guy running the place now. The national talk programming director, Devon Mason. He made a crack about how my hair was getting a little shaggy and how I could use a trim. The other two laughed when he used that word. I never really thought about why it struck them as so funny until just now. So yeah, they must have known she was a working girl."

"Are they all still at Cirrus?"

"I know Mason was cashiered a few months back when they consolidated his position. The sales guy is still at Cirrus, moved up the ladder a peg to National. Campbell is the only one local."

"You on good terms with him?"

"Fair enough, I suppose. We're not what I'd call friends, but we've seen each other a few times since I sold the place. I hear from Stone and others that he's an insensitive ogre. A few weeks after the sale, he brought in a salvage company and they stripped the building. All those old leaded glass doors, original hardware, custom cabinets. Sold them for pennies on the dollar and replaced them with cheap crap. But he's been nice enough to me. Usually when we get together, he bitches about the staff, tries to pump me for information about them. I have to admit, I keep up with station gossip through him, so I'm guilty as well, I guess. Why?"

"Would he have dinner with you tonight if you said you just happened to be in town? Would that be an odd request?"

"Not at all. That's generally the way we've had contact since I left. I call him sometimes when I'm around and we have a meal or a drink."

"Try to set that up tonight. I'd like to tag along, but don't tell him that. I might have a surprise for him and I wouldn't want to spoil it."

SEVENTY FIVE

After my talk with Ted, I called Stone. It was just after sunup Pacific time and he was on his way to the set. He was enjoying his time in SoCal, although he was disappointed that Hef hadn't stopped by with a *Welcome to the Neighborhood* package. I can only imagine what he expected to find in that goodie basket.

Jaime would have been my first call, but I didn't want to wake her too early. Apparently, the lady writer was quite the star struck party animal and my strait-laced girlfriend was having a hard time keeping up. Both Rick and she were so caught up in their Western adventures that they had exhibited only polite curiosity about mine. That was just as well.

Next, I rang down to Hilton Head to make sure Anna was still okay with minding Bosco for a few more days. As always, she was up for the task. McCarver's former housekeeper said that if I ever got tired of the dog, she'd gladly take him in. No way would I ever let that happen.

As I sat looking out at the Atlantic, I reflected on how I had wasted so much time with all my ratiocination regarding motive and opportunity, when the answer that would lead me to the bad guy had to do with one simple question that I had yet to answer: *Who knew where Wally did his show while in hiding?*

This morning I could only think of two people who might have access to that information. One of them was steps from where I now sat --- Ted McCarver.

He knew that Wally was on the island. Although he claimed not to be aware of where Wally had gone after their argument, a man as bright as Ted might have found a way to trace him. Killing Wally certainly wouldn't fit into his professed desire for Josephs' reclamation. He claimed that a reconstituted Wally Josephs could be his legacy, his ultimate gift to radio. But an unbalanced mind might think that by eliminating the grotesquerie Wally had become, he'd be doing the industry and the world a favor.

His merciless beating of Elvis sure qualified as unbalanced. Maybe he feared that if I eventually got Elvis to talk, the trail might lead back to him. By rendering Crayton mute, he had short circuited that.

This was all speculation. I was giving Ted credit for playing three dimensional chess while McCullough and I were playing checkers. Or it could be that I had just run out of theories that made any sense.

Seventy six

The other person I had qualms about was Alison Middleton. She had the advantage of actually talking to Wally, both on and off the air. She could have figured out where he was broadcasting through sound cues or perhaps specious remarks that hinted of his whereabouts.

Why? Built up resentment over the way he treated her? Belief that he was overcompensated for his role while she was vastly underpaid? Jealousy that he had shown no sexual interest in her? No appreciation for her numerous interventions with management?

All possible but not provable, at least in any way I could figure.

So I contacted BS and he agreed to a phone call. He prefers other means of communication but I told him that speaking directly was the most efficient means. He is all about efficiency --- he considers time his most precious commodity.

"So King, you have questions?" he said, in the deep multi-tracked voice of Satan. It sounded like Howard Stern doing one of his pranks.

Minus the special effects, he already had a stilted manner of speaking, which led me to believe that he might be suffering from Asperger's. Or maybe he was just strange and socially awkward. He never uses contractions and chooses unnecessarily complex verbiage that often sends me to a dictionary after communicating with him.

I said, "Yes, I do have a question. Do you know anything about internet protocol for broadcasting? That's what my client is using to do his radio show on remote."

"I am familiar with the system. The main companies who promote this are Tieline and Comrex. The prevailing technology used to be ISDN or POTS, which stands for plain old telephone service. But increasingly, IP has become the standard, since it is generally reliable and inexpensive."

"What I need to know is --- can it be traced? In other words, can you tell the location where the broadcast is coming from through the machine?"

I felt stupid for my scant knowledge about a device that Rick had used countless times from my house. But then again, I have no clue how a micro SD card the size of a thumbnail can contain thousands of my favorite songs.

"Most home DSL providers use what are called dynamic IP addresses. That means that the chip latches on to the most convenient and strongest signal available at the time. So if you are broadcasting from Syracuse, the signal may be routed through Cincinnati. That makes it virtually untraceable since dynamic IP frequently switches when one signal is low and another more powerful one becomes available. It is similar to a technique I use to disguise my location, although I use it deliberately, whereas this occurs at random."

"So there is no way to know on the receiving end where a voice is originating?"

"That is not precisely what I said. Although dynamic DSL is readily available and inexpensive, it is by nature less reliable than what is known as static. That means that the provider employs a line which is dedicated exclusively. It is in a fixed digital location and is rock solid. I am not an expert on radio protocol, but I would assume that if someone were to do remote broadcasts from the same location on a frequent basis, static would be optimal. Any competent engineer on the other end would be able to pinpoint the IP address within seconds. He could determine the physical location using the equivalent of a digital phonebook."

"Would a hotel use this static IP?"

"If it catered largely to business travelers, that would be a wise choice."

"Thanks. Bill me double your usual rate. You've just cracked an important case I've been working on forever."

SEVENTY SEVEN

I had been pursuing a bunch of dead end clues, when the most obvious solution was staring me in the face all along. My old school stubbornness at not going tech as a first option was at fault and my next call confirmed it. I used *67 to mask her caller ID.

"Alison, it's Riley King."

The silence greeting me on the other end was expected. I said, "Listen, I know you're mad at me and maybe I deserve it, but if you still want Wally as a partner, I need your help."

"Wally's gone AWOL again and no one knows where he is. There's a rumor flying around again that he's dead. And before you accuse me of lying again, he hasn't contacted me."

"He's in a safe place. That's all I can tell you now, but trust me, he'll be okay."

"Trust *you*? Right. I'm at the station now. Recording promos. I can't talk."

"I don't need much time. Remember the first day Wally did the show from my house on Hilton Head and the kid engineer couldn't figure out how to hook up the remote?"

"Yes. So what?"

"Obviously, you did several shows with him after that day when I wasn't around. Did the kid figure it out?"

"What's this got to do with anything? I'm busy."

"Please, Alison, just humor me."

She breathed a heavy sigh of impatience. "After the show that day, I complained to Campbell. I said that I was offended that a major radio station didn't have someone competent to set up a remote. I told him we fixed it temporarily. I don't remember if I used your name or not."

"Doesn't matter. So what happened then?"

"As much as Campbell is a know-nothing jerk about a lot of things, he said he knew a lot about the Comrex unit from his days in the Midwest setting up remotes for sales events. He said that he would personally hook it up every day, and for once, he was as good as his word."

SEVENTY EIGHT

Honoring my request, Ted arranged dinner with Campbell that evening at a restaurant called *Wind on the Water*. It was a charming spot, hard by Barnegat Bay in Bayville, the next town south of Toms River. Stone and I had dined there many times when I lived at the shore, although it was now under new management for the third time in the last five years, never a good sign. I wasn't going there for the food.

I was finally going to meet BJ Campbell. The man was Stone's nemesis: he had fired my pal unceremoniously, not even having the decency to inform him to his face. He had left the dirty work to his secretary. In recompense for this less than appreciative denouement, Rick had deposited a pile of dog mess on the man's desk while he was out to lunch. It was an immature but satisfying way to say goodbye to a scoundrel for whom Stone had little respect.

Ted would likely be more objective than Rick so I sounded him out as we sat on Rick's wooden deck facing the Atlantic. We both wore heavy wool sweaters to ward off the late autumn chill. Temperatures were in the high fifties, borderline for eating lunch outdoors.

Ted had prepared a drink called a *Tom and Jerry* to help with the warming process. Boiling hot water, whipped egg white, cinnamon and nutmeg were the main ingredients I think, bolstered by a healthy ration of rum and Irish whiskey.

"Drink to your liking?" Ted asked as we unwrapped the sandwiches he'd picked up from a deli in Point Pleasant.

"Most refreshing," I said, savoring the slow burn the brew provided on the way down. "So, tell me about Campbell. Rick hates him. Any redeeming qualities?"

"We're setting the bar awfully low, aren't we? Let me give you some background. At first, Cirrus didn't want to buy the station for cash. They wanted to give me shares in the company instead. In exchange, I could still manage the place under their supervision. I talked to a few of my fellow owners who had taken that deal and to a man, they regretted it. I saw what was happening and I figured the stock, which was trading mid-twenties, would be down to single digits within a few years. No great genius on my part, I just read their quarterly reports and saw how leveraged they were. Yesterday they were trading under a dollar."

I've never had a head for these complex corporate maneuverings and was glad I never needed to tread the political minefield they entailed. The bureaucracy of the FBI was too much for me to handle. "So how did you finally get them to cash you out?"

"Another suitor entered the picture. Wealthy lawyer in Central Jersey. Big sports fan. Stone called him a jock sniffer. The fact he was willing to pay cash upped the ante. Rather than lose the deal, Cirrus borrowed against equity and came up with a check. I did accept a small amount in stock, just to keep my foot in and make my influence felt. But my tiny stake in Cirrus is hardly relevant these days."

I said, "So, what about Campbell? What can you tell me about him?"

"He's from the Midwest. Detroit was his base. Sales background, doesn't know programming, although he thinks he does. Strictly a bottom line guy. If I ever had any doubts about running the place under his supervision, one meeting was all it took."

"How so?"

"First thing he did was rip the staff. Said the morning team was boring. Wanted them out without having a clue as to who to replace them with. Hated Stone. Said he appealed to the wrong demo --- the sixty five to death squad. He thought Wally had potential. Liked Wally's sass, as he put it. Had some crazy ideas on how to take it further. Wanted to bring in a wacky black traffic helicopter guy from his old station to do what amounted to Stepin Fetchit routines."

"I have to ask, Ted. This place was your labor of love. You practically built it from the ground up. It was the key to your fortune. How could you let it fall into the hands of a bunch of fools that you obviously have no respect for?"

He pushed his thick mane of silver hair off his forehead, but the ocean breeze had other ideas and tossed it back into his eyes. "Money, plain and simple. My attorney suitor brought cash, but not enough of it. They topped his offer. In retrospect, I should have taken his deal --- for my own sake and the sake of the people working there. Campbell fired the morning guys right away. Rick had a couple more years on his contract. Of course, they canned him as soon as it was up. I protected Wally. Gave him a long term ironclad contract."

I said, "Speaking of protecting Wally, Tomey has kept his name quiet but that won't last much longer unless we can clear him completely. McCullough's made headway there and Logan will pitch in if need be. What about Allie? Why didn't you give her the same treatment?"

"I always thought she was an interchangeable part, like a spark plug. One wears out, you put in a new one. Wally drives the bus. She's just a sidekick. She can be replaced. The true talent, the stars? They're hard to come by and you lock 'em up if you're lucky enough to catch one on the rise. Like them or not, the Rush Limbaughs of the world maybe aren't as powerful revenue-wise as they once were, but they're still a force. To guys like BJ Campbell though, Wally is a piece of meat. Like cattle futures. As long as he gets numbers, he tolerates his antics. The minute that ends, he'd be gone. That's why *I* gave him that contract. Cirrus never would have. If Campbell saw a bad quarterly trend in the afternoon, Wally would be out quicker than a Syndergaard fastball."

"But the ratings *have* been down. You told me so yourself."

"I'm out of touch with day to day radio really, between the time in the monastery and the foundation work. I just see the 12 plus ratings in *Talkers Magazine*. That's all I know. You should probably call Michael Harrison at *Talkers* if you want to know specifics. I'll set that up for you."

He sipped his *Tom and Jerry*, which had lost its foam. "And in answer to your original question, yes, I do feel sad to see this once great station slip beneath the waves. If had I stayed, I might have kept it afloat a little longer. But once it hit the iceberg, the ship was going down, no matter how skilled the captain was."

SEVENTY NINE

I had a great circumstantial case against Campbell. He knew Darla Diamond. He easily could have found out where Wally was if he set up the Comrex unit every day. A quick call confirmed the Sonesta had a static DSL address. Campbell tells Darla, Darla calls Crayton, they fly down to Hilton Head and lay in wait to ambush Wally.

The hole in my theory was motive. If Wally Josephs is so important to WJOK, why would management want him dead? As always, it was *follow the money*. Michael Harrison of *Talkers* might be able to provide insight on that.

McCarver had told me that there wasn't anything that happened in talk radio that Harrison wasn't aware of. When I called this man who was regarded as the guru of the airwaves, I quickly established that Ted wasn't exaggerating.

"Cirrus is in big trouble," Harrison said. "It's no secret they are way over-leveraged and that their financiers are panicky. They have a big payment due next month and their practice of kicking the can down the road seems to have run its course. The bankers want to see progress toward profitability to re-finance the loans and I don't see how they can do that. I hear from general managers every day complaining how they've cut expenses to the bone. Sales people are working strictly on commission --- no draw for years now. They're paying techies minimum wage to run the board and screen calls. Using free intern labor in states where they can. And they still can't make enough profit, at least to the satisfaction of the money people."

I said, "What about WJOK? They seem to be inundated with commercials. They have to be making money."

"Not really. Everything on their rate card is negotiable. They're giving bonus spots to keep advertisers. Buy one, get three free. And a lot of those spots are network ones that they dump on the local stations. Then there are the *per inquiry* commercials. They pay a small fee for each response. So it costs the sponsor next to nothing unless they get big results, which they don't. So the airwaves may sound cluttered to you, but the revenue isn't close to what it was when they were running fewer spots."

I said, "And from a listening standpoint, those commercials can't be very effective. I know when they go into those ten minute breaks, I'm gone and I may not come back if I find something better."

"You're pretty typical, Mr. King."

"Call me Riley."

"Okay, Riley. I don't know how old you are but Millennials in particular can't abide commercials. They're used to free podcasts and they tune out the second they hear advertising. That's why agencies are trying to sneak in product mentions, like during ballgames when you hear things like 'the first pitch is brought to you by', et cetera."

I had no idea things were this bad. Ted had given me the terms of Wally's contract. I ran the numbers by Harrison. "So Michael, could the Allie and Wally show be profitable if they're paying him that kind of dough, in addition to what she makes and what the support staff are getting?"

Harrison grunted in skepticism. "There's no way. They must be hemorrhaging money every second that show is on the air. When McCarver signed that deal a few years back, it might have made sense. But the industry is collapsing under the weight of these contracts and the debt service on the loans. When someone's deal is up, their agents don't even bother to talk about raises. They just try to minimize how much they'll be cut. Cirrus was foolish to buy the station with that kind of obligation to Wally Josephs, no matter how good he is. McCarver ran a tight ship and made good money and he paid his air staff generously. That's how he kept major talent in middle Jersey. But he saw the writing on the wall early and had to realize it wasn't sustainable."

"He's good that way. So Wally's contract is a burden WJOK can't afford? What can they do about that?"

"They're in a tough spot if the deal is as ironclad as you say. They could appeal to him that the whole chain could go under and he'll get a small percentage on the dollar if they declare bankruptcy. Try to negotiate a lesser number or a buyout over time. I doubt a jock with a decent agent would go for that. He'd probably figure they'd find new money somewhere. They always have in the past. But now, I fear the chickens have come home to roost. If WJOK doesn't pare expenses pretty severely, they could go dark. And to me, that would be a tragedy. A lot of people out of work with no prospects to get new jobs that pay anything close to what they were making."

"Desperate times."

"Indeed. Well, I hope I've been of some help."

"Oh, you have, sir. More than you'll ever know."

EIGHTY

The text message was terse and mysterious.

STARLIGHT.3.FM

Tradecraft? From McCullough. What kind of monster had I created? Now my ramrod-straight cop friend was resorting to cryptic texts which could have been culled from the pages of MAD magazine's Spy vs. Spy comic strip.

Regardless, I complied with his invitation, driving Stone's old F-150 pickup to the Starlight diner in the mid-afternoon. The bright sun had warmed things up a bit, but the offshore breezes were pushing things in the opposite direction. I was grateful that Stone had left a light down jacket in Mantoloking that almost fit me.

Seated at his usual spot in the back booth was McCullough.

"Greetings, 007," I said, sliding into the seat opposite him. "We've got to stop meeting like this."

I didn't get his customary smirk as an acknowledgement of my wit. He didn't even look up from his smart phone. I'll have to stop using clichés and come up with something original.

I said, "So you send a coded text, then meet me in a public place. Overly careful and then sloppy. Pretty schizophrenic, even for you. What gives?"

He looked up. "I'm now interviewing a source. Trying to gather information regarding the attack on one

Elvis Crayton, who will soon be a permanent resident of the Wedgewood Gardens Care Center."

"Sorry to hear that. Can I speak freely or do you prefer Aramaic?"

"Cut the shit, King. None of this is funny."

"Okay, plain talk. I know who's behind this whole mess. I was going to call you but you beat me to the punch. Great minds and all that."

Reverting back to old bad habits despite doctor's orders, he motioned to the waitress to refill his chipped coffee cup, an indication of how much he valued my investigative prowess. After she left he said, in a voice filled with disdain, "Well, don't keep me in suspense, buckaroo. Who?"

"BJ Campbell." I went on to explain how I had pieced things together and he listened with passing interest.

When I was finished he said, "Could be. I'm sure you realize, you've connected a bunch of random events, but it isn't enough to take to an ADA. Campbell can say that he only knew Darla as someone who cut hair and you can't prove otherwise. He can say that as someone in charge of a radio station, he was just doing his job making sure his star player got on the air every day. And he can laugh off the idea that he'd actually hire someone to kill his afternoon host because he was making too much money."

"I know that. That's why I told Ted to set up dinner with him tonight."

"King, let me give you an alternate theory. McCarver knew where Josephs was. McCarver signed that noxious contract. McCarver told you he was ashamed of Wally on the air. And he beat Crayton to a pulp, maybe so that he could never be linked to the crime. And by the way, he knew Darla and not just as his barber."

"Do you think I haven't considered that? Do I worry Ted's gone off the deep end? Absolutely. That's one reason I want to meet this Campbell character in person. Get a read on him. Firsthand."

"Does McCarver know that you think Campbell is the man behind the curtain?"

"I never told him in so many words, but he's no fool. He knows why I want to meet Campbell for dinner."

"All I'm saying is that if you want me to arrest someone, there's just as strong a circumstantial case for McCarver as there is for Campbell."

"What about the money? Campbell stands to lose his job and a big company might default on a debt payment. We're talking billions. Ted owns a stake in the company worth chump change for him. And if he really wanted Wally dead, Ted could have arranged it while he was staying at his condo. He could have sent him out to pick up a pizza and had him knifed in the parking lot and made it look like a mugging. That's how Ted would have arranged it."

Flint tilted his head to one side and looked me in the eye. "So what do you want from me?"

"You texted me to meet you. What did you have in mind?"

"I was going to tell you that I talked to that female detective down on your island. They're releasing Josephs later today. They're going to keep an eye on him, but they bought the self defense argument."

"Talk about burying the lede."

"If were you, I hop the first flight you can book back to the island and babysit Josephs. God knows what that asshole will do now. He might be safe for the moment since Diamond and Crayton are out of commission, but I'm telling you, papa Costello is not going to stay uninvolved. There's also the possibility that whoever took out that sanction did it through him."

That would escalate the stakes. It is one thing to suspect that a rogue hooker took on a murder contract and enlisted a partner whose father happens to be a crime boss. It's another matter that the boss himself was given the contract and delegated the job out to his son.

I said, "That's a disturbing thought. Thanks for putting it in my head. But Crayton insisted Darla set this up, and I think he was in too much pain to lie. Okay, here's what I'm thinking. I go to dinner with Campbell and wear a wire. You listen. I'll try to trick him into admitting something, or at least giving us more to go on. Worst case, I get a feel for what this guy is capable of. I'm not always right, but I'm never wrong."

"Save the cornpone wisdom, huckleberry. I'll admit it's not the worst approach I've ever heard. I'll hook you up with the wire. But I don't want McCarver at this dinner. It could be that he and Campbell are in this together. Mutually beneficial. Ever think of that? In any case, after tonight, you get your ass down to Hilton Head. Let me handle things here."

"Let's see what tonight yields before we make that call."

"I'm telling you King. Get thee to Hilton Head. And take frigging McCarver with you before I bust his ass."

EIGHTY ONE

Ted wasn't thrilled that his presence was not welcome at dinner, but it was not up for debate. I made him promise that he would not intrude under the guise of protecting me, as he had with Crayton. He agreed after making me swear that I'd call on him if things got sticky. It was an easy condition to accept, one that I would never honor, since I had all the backup I needed in McCullough.

Flint outfitted me for the wire and we discussed some last minute contingencies. Without telling him, I brought along my digital recorder. I tucked it into my jacket pocket to have my own record of the conversation. Not that I don't trust Flint, but sometimes evidence has a way of disappearing when corporate politics are involved.

Wind on the Water had changed since a year ago, when last I visited. The mustiness from decades of salt water and hidden mold was replaced by the clean smell of fresh paint and newly milled cedar, which adorned the high ceiling. The whitewashed shiplap was a marked improvement over the yellowing cracked plaster. The new owners had opened up the design so that the kitchen space was partially visible. The pungent aroma of the wood fired grill wafted into the dining space. Bosco would be drooling.

White wainscoting had been installed around the perimeter and old fogged windows had been replaced by larger ones that took full advantage of the long view of

Barnegat Bay. The walls above the wainscoting were tinted a pale blue and adorned with impressionistic paintings of the Jersey shore. All and all, a vast upgrade over the dank atmosphere of the previous iteration.

Immune from all these upgrades was the bar area and I hoped it would stay that way. It was dark and masculine, all mahogany and leather. It reminded me of a London gentlemen's club in those classic British mysteries, an atmosphere of pipe tobacco smoke and cognac. A snug enclave of quid pro quos and sub-rosa pacts never graced by signatures.

I pulled in a few minutes before six and waited at the bar. I ordered a Glenfiddich for me and a bourbon and branch water for Campbell, his beverage of preference according to Ted. Moments after the drinks arrived, a slender fellow strode through the main door, glancing around furtively as if casing the joint.

This had to be BJ Campbell.

"Mr. Campbell?" I said, as he entered the bar. "Ted McCarver sent me. He's been detained on a conference call and he'll be a few minutes late."

"He couldn't have told me that himself?" Campbell said, not bothering to disguise his displeasure. "Who are you?"

"My name is King. I've ordered you a drink. Why don't we sit over here while we wait? I'm sure it won't be long."

Without thanking me, Campbell whisked the whiskey off the bar and walked over to a corner booth. The seats were clad in burgundy colored leather, well worn from the fannies of the Central Jersey dealmakers who had conspired there.

Campbell wore a dark brown suit, not custom tailored but it fit him well enough. A cream colored button down shirt, no tie. The man was not unpleasant to look at, in an androgynous sort of way. His skin was smooth and bloodless. Eyes wide set and dark, mouth small and thin lipped. His most notable feature was a strong curved nose, which gave him a hawk-like appearance.

He sat. Took a short pull of the bourbon and stared out at the room. No pleasantries. No words, period. Just boredom. He'd have to waste his time engaging a lesser being until someone more consequential came along.

"Actually," I said. "Ted isn't on a conference call. He wanted you and me to speak privately on a matter of concern to you both."

"Concern to us both? I haven't seen or spoken to the man since he got out of jail last year. I can't imagine what the hell you're talking about."

"You *are* aware that Ted still has a stake in WJOK?"

"I don't know the particulars but yes, I know he got some stock as part of the sale. How is that skin off my back?"

"Ted tells me that you two don't really know each other all that well. Let me just say that Ted McCarver is one of the smartest people I've ever met. He knows a lot of secrets. I have no idea who his sources are, but the way he operates in the shadows makes the CIA seem transparent."

"So?"

"So. He knows that that WJOK has money problems. And he'd like to help solve them."

Campbell downed the remainder of his drink and waved to the barman for another, not asking if I wanted a refill.

Campbell said, "Look, McCarver sold the place years ago. I *do* know that he was offered a chance to stay in charge, working under Cirrus' supervision and he declined. So however well-meaning this gesture may be, it is totally unnecessary and might I add, unwelcome. Much of our current problem stems from the poor decisions he made when he owned the place."

"Exactly. Which is why he wants to help."

"Again, not needed." To him, it was *game over*.

"I had hoped we could hash this out without getting too specific. That I could provide you with some professional assistance on something that you attempted on your own that reeked of amateur bungling."

He gave me his best sneer.

"King." He squinted, rolling my name around. "You wouldn't be Riley King, would you? The man who helped get Ted out of jail on that murder rap. A friend of Rick Stone's too, I believe."

"Guilty on both counts, although Stone and I aren't close. His childish behavior put a crimp in what was once our friendship."

Not exactly true, but technically not false.

Campbell scoffed. "I owe him a punch in the mouth for what he did when I fired his ass. That bastard is on my shit list."

And you on his, literally. He hadn't forgiven Stone for leaving dog poop on his desk. Some people just can't move on.

"An example of his frat boy immaturity," I said. "In any case, you were right about the other thing. I did fix matters for Ted last year to get him sprung. That's what I do."

"Wait a minute. Are you saying that Ted *did* kill that girl and you found a scapegoat to take the rap? That sick old man who died in prison?"

"No comment."

"Wow. Holy crap. I kind of knew Ted had brutality in him. I saw him lose it one night before the sale went through. Almost cold cocked a bouncer at a club. Guy seems calm on the surface, but there's a volcano bubbling underneath."

"Again, no comment."

So far I had made a great case that Ted was an out of control killer who had engineered Stevie Perry's murder, when nothing could be further from the truth. He was broken up by it, and still hadn't fully recovered. Time to shift gears.

I said, "Past is past. I'm talking about now. And *your* problem. Wally Josephs."

Now it was his turn to be coy. "Wally. My afternoon star. What about him?"

"Let's just say his contract is not conducive to making your revenue projections. Would that be a nice, sanitized way to put it?"

"Go on."

The barman arrived with his bourbon. He raised his eyebrows in my direction; I shook him off and he went back to his empty post. I guess word hasn't gotten around about the improvements to the place.

I said, "Ted is aware that you engaged a mutual friend to attend to the problem. He also is aware that said friend failed to complete the assignment and she paid dearly for it."

He said nothing. Smart.

I said, "Ted feels responsible for your dilemma since he negotiated the contract in the first place. He authorized me to propose a solution. A final one."

Campbell glanced around, head on a swivel. He spoke in an agitated whisper. "Why did Ted, a man you claim is so smart, make such a bad deal? What was he thinking?"

"At the time, Ted considered Josephs his protégé. He wanted to protect him. As you are very aware, Wally is a loose cannon."

"You got that right." Campbell swirled the ice in his drink.

"Look at the way the corporate bigwigs canned Imus. The man had done much more offensive stuff and got away with it for years. Wally is prone to overstep occasionally; that's his appeal. The suits are too PC to understand that."

"Why is Ted suddenly willing to have you do this? What's so different now?"

"Wally betrayed Ted. Let's just say that he repaid Ted's generosity with insolence and that's one thing Ted can't tolerate. So, he's offering you a solution that will settle this thing once and for all."

"You?"

"I do have certain talents."

Campbell wasn't a total fool. There was no chance he knew about the wire, but he wasn't about to confess his sins to a man he'd just met ten minutes ago.

"So if Ted came to this conclusion independently, why even involve me?"

I said, "We weren't sure if it had gotten back to you that your efforts had failed and if so, if you've hired backup. And we need to make sure that you're still on board with fixing the problem. Or does this exceed your pay grade and you need approval from the high command at Cirrus?" I appealed to his ego, hoping he'd fall into the trap.

"No. This is my call. You're right, the big bosses are too chickenshit to do what needs to be done. This is all very interesting. All I can say is if something happens to Wally-boy and it helps me with my *dilemma*, as you so delicately put it ..."

He paused and shot me a stern look. Bad playacting --- a pitiful attempt at portraying a ruthless cutthroat. I stayed quiet to see if he'd hang himself further.

He did. "No need to worry about your efforts getting in the way of anything. I haven't taken any steps beyond the ones I took initially. If everything went sideways, well, this is not my area of expertise."

He finished his bourbon and gave me a thin smile. "Ted never was going to join us, was he?"

"Mr. McCarver didn't get to where he is by getting his own hands dirty. There's always been a buffer. So you're on board?"

He shrugged. "Like I said, whatever works."

EIGHTY TWO

I never did get to sample the new menu at *Wind on the Water*. I wasn't up for sharing a meal with Campbell, and he felt the same. I tried to get him to admit more, but he wasn't about to go there. He skipped out, leaving me with the check. The payback I had in mind would far exceed the Hamiltons I left on the table.

I made a couple of stops on the way back to Mantoloking. Best Buy sold me a few SD cards, and a visit to a Wendy's drive-thru satisfied my hunger. When I got back to Stone's place, I found Ted in the great room, watching *Patriot Games*.

"Never get tired of this one, Riley," he said as I came in. "I've seen it a dozen times but whenever I stumble on it, I can't turn it off. So, anything you can share regarding your dinner with Campbell?"

I wasn't about to play the recording for him, but I did go through a quick summation. I told him the only reaction I got from McCullough was a text telling me I'd done a nice job and that he'd be speaking with an ADA first thing tomorrow.

After my monologue concluded, he said, "I picked up a Joseph Phelps Insignia cabernet while you were out, and a liter of 21 year Gran Reserva Glenfiddich. Your choice."

I chose the scotch, savoring its floral and toffee aroma and the warm, lingering finish while watching H subdue Sean Bean and his merry band of Irish splinter group terrorists. As the credits rolled, I made my apologies to Ted and took off for bed.

It was just past suppertime in California so I dialed Stone on the off chance he wasn't wooing some wannabe starlet. He was headed out for a late dinner with Jaime when I reached him.

After I related the day's events, he said, "That shit Campbell was behind this all along? Great. It'll be a pleasure seeing that bastard behind bars."

"It still amazes me that someone could be that desperate to save his job. I mean, contracting a hit on your star employee? Man, that is cold. You got off light, just getting fired, pal."

"I suppose. Hey, I'm headed back to the island tomorrow. Wrapped my scenes today. They really liked me, even gave me a couple of lines that I hope make the final cut."

"Good for you. Is Jaime doing okay?"

He stammered for a moment. "Uh, she'd probably want to tell you this herself, but she's going to be out here for quite a bit. Her dad ain't on board with the way this shoot is going. No nookie for little Riley."

"You know, I told Campbell you and I weren't that close anymore due to your childishness. I was trying to bond with him by saying that, but it's not all together false. For your information, Jaime did tell me she'd be out there for quite a while."

"Rarse, man. You miss me. I know it and you know it. When are you going back to the island?"

"Depends on what McCullough tells me tomorrow. I may need to do a deposition about the recording, to verify it and all that. Hopefully, back to Hilton Head in a day or so. If you get back before I do, cut a check for Anna and thank her for minding Bosco.

And give the boy some extra treats and tell him daddy will be back soon."

"At least you won't be coming back to an empty bed. Bosco is handsome enough to be in the movies, but Jaime has a few advantages over the boy."

I said goodbye and turned off the light. I lay awake for quite a while, contemplating what life would be like without Jaime.

EIGHTY THREE

BLT.12P.FM

The text message read like an ad for a soft rock station. Our man Flint was tinkering in tailored spy lingo again.

The BLT referred to the sandwich McCullough had ordered for me at the Starlight a year ago as we wrapped up Stevie Perry's murder investigation. He even picked up the tab in gratitude for dropping the solution onto his lap. My leg work got him a promotion and even more respect than he previously enjoyed with his superiors. I took the message to mean I should join him for lunch at his favorite booth, usual time.

I spent part of the morning transferring the Campbell recording into the MP3 format and making copies on separate SD cards. The rest of the time, I mindlessly read the papers online and answered some email.

Ted stumbled out of Stone's guest room just after ten, an extremely late awakening for a man generally up at the crack of dawn. He confessed to having stayed up until the wee hours watching the Jack Ryan marathon on TCM.

"*A Clear and Present Danger* is my favorite," he said, after shaking the cobwebs out. "That line from Defoe about the Lindo brand of coffee going for 6200 dollars a pound always gets me."

More cryptic spy references. Maybe I'll come back as James Bond in another life. I told Ted I was meeting McCullough and that I expected good news. He should have the Socata fueled up and ready to go. Hopefully we could fly home later that afternoon.

But when I arrived at the Starlight, Flint wasn't smiling. His trademark smirk was not in evidence either, and it didn't take thirty years of detective experience to observe that all was not well.

"BLT's on the way, King. Still holding the fries," he said. To describe his manner as funereal would insult the dead. "Wouldn't want you to put all that weight back on."

He'd never let me live down the twenty pounds I'd put on a few years back when I was depressed over Liz Huntington, my murdered client/lover. Food was my pacifier during that extended period of self pity. Six months in a monastery was the cross McCarver bore. Stone walked into a bullet in his anguish over a broken love affair. I wondered if McCullough's divorce would exact a similar toll, although I couldn't imagine what form it might take with this resolute chunk of granite.

Hoping I'd misread his mood, I said, "Still on the kale salad kick or are you splurging with an egg white and greens omelet today?"

Before he could answer, the waitress materialized with our food. The eggs won. An indulgence. Not a good sign.

"Don't keep me in suspense," I said. "What did the ADA say?"

"Before I even played the recording, she called in her boss."

Her boss was Ocean County District attorney Miles Messervy. We had only crossed paths once, when his office decided not to prosecute me in an iffy self-defense situation that easily could have gone the other way. He refused to accept my attempts to thank him which made me think that the edict was dictated to him from above and he resented me as a consequence.

McCullough didn't elaborate on what happened next, picking at his food instead. I tried to coax him along, expecting the worst. "And?"

He looked up from his plate and said, "Bottom line? As he put it, he's not inclined to prosecute. In fact, I had to talk him out of re-opening Stevie Perry's murder based on your implication that old man Jackson was a scapegoat."

I said, "Really? A smart DA didn't understand that I was lying about that to set BJ up?"

"All too well. He said that he'd having a hard time arguing that it wasn't entrapment. A top lawyer like League or Furlong would cut that to ribbons in a courtroom. Campbell never actually admitted to hiring Darla to kill Wally. It could be taken that McCarver had a secret way to get out of the contract. If anything, it sounded like you were planning to do the deed, and he just went along without protest."

"Come on, Flint. It's right there on the recording. I listened to it again this morning. He said he hadn't taken *additional* steps. That implies he had taken prior action. He admitted that it had gone sideways because he's not an expert at that sort of thing. He had motive and opportunity. He knew the hitter. Connect the dots."

His voice was gruff. "You're preaching to the choir. *I* know Campbell did it --- you don't need to convince me. But we have no evidence of money changing hands. No proof of any direct contact."

"What about the fact he knew where Wally was? That wasn't common knowledge. Even Allie didn't know."

"But as you pointed out earlier, she could have. So could anyone with half a brain who knew how that Comrex machine works. Listen hard to that recording again. Campbell was smart. From his reactions on the wire, he could claim that Ted was the instigator."

"Can't you subpoena his bank records and see if there's an unusual withdrawal? Something big to pay Diamond off?"

"Already did that. You're not the only one with hacker contacts. Nothing in his personal financial records shows anything fishy. Money could have come from anywhere. Could have come out of the station's discretionary budget or laundered through some deal with an advertiser."

"So now what? Do we fake Wally's death and tell Campbell? See if he cops to more after he thinks the deed is done?"

McCullough gave me an impatient sigh. "Look Riles, after he heard the recording, Messervy dismissed the ADA and closed the door. Gave me a lecture. Said that you and I aren't looking at this objectively. The way he sees it is: *Where's the damage here?* A dead hooker eight hundred miles to our south. Not our problem. A low level gangster beat up in our jurisdiction. A waste of taxpayer money chasing that down. One less bad guy, so what? Then the original sin --- an alleged pimp roll where no charges were filed by the vic. Nothing there. The Hilton Head cops were on top of the hooker situation and have chalked it up to self defense. I'm in charge of the investigation on Crayton and we both know where we need that to lead. Messervy's up for re-election. A charge involving a major media company that isn't airtight could make him a lot of enemies."

"I get it. But since I don't plan to kill Wally, what keeps Campbell from hiring another hitter down the road to finish the job?"

"Me. I'll let him know I'm on to him and that if anything happens to Josephs, he'll be in my sights. He can't be that bold, can he?"

"It sounds like you're saying that we should just let it go."

"Sherlock, you know me by now. I'll keep my eyes and ears open. If something promising comes my way, I'll look into it. Or at the very least, send it in your direction."

"So in the end, he gets away with it. Unscathed."

"Again, a dead hooker who may have killed for hire in the past. A mob creep who got what's coming to him. My advice to you, my friend, is quit while you're ahead. Take the win and call it a day."

I couldn't believe I was hearing this from the once stalwart Flint McCullough. He had been corrupted. I started that train rolling, and the DA had just opened up the throttle.

I'd lost my appetite and didn't touch the BLT.

EIGHTY FOUR

"I've got this." Ted McCarver was insistent.

"No, you don't," I said, trying to sound equally insistent but his booming baritone overwhelmed my protest.

We were back at Stone's place. When informed of the District Attorney's decision, he suggested alternatives --- some legal, some not. When I shot them down one by one, he decided to take matters into his own hands.

As always, McCarver was elegantly dressed. He wore brogues, grey worsted trousers, and an oversized Irish fisherman's sweater which gave some heft to his slender physique. He could have hidden a small puppy within its folds and no one would notice.

"This whole thing is my responsibility," he said. He voice was measured. "I sold the station to these people. I was sure at the time that the pendulum on terrestrial radio was headed down and wouldn't be coming back up. I opted to take the money and run. I knew Cirrus would rue the day they paid me so much for the frequency. I was aware of the way they managed their properties. What Campbell did was just the logical extension of that philosophy."

"Please! That's like saying that if you believe in capitalism, the strong have the right to murder the weak if it suits their purposes. Listen Ted, I'm not going to argue Ayn Rand with you. There's no way that even someone with your genius for business could have anticipated that a mid level hack would order someone killed to get out of a contract."

"I made that necessary. I designed that deal to be so that they couldn't see another way out of it. I tried to protect the people at the station who had given me their trust and loyalty and obviously I took it too far."

"Again, you're playing God. You made a business deal that worked out in your favor. There were unintended consequences. Things you couldn't control. Cirrus had the chance to review Wally's contract before they closed. They could have backed out, or demanded that the contract be renegotiated as a condition of the sale. They either didn't do their homework, or they decided that they could live with the terms. This is entirely on Campbell, not you."

"Excuse me. Nature calls," he said, leaving for the powder room. I welcomed the break. This argument could go on for hours and branch off into religion, philosophy, psychology, sociology, mysticism, or any number of other isms or ologies. Ted is a skilled debater and light years ahead of me in smarts. But when pushed against a wall, he reacted with brutality, the basic instinct of an unschooled primate. I wasn't about to let loose *that* Kraken again, not if I had the means to stop it.

Ted returned a few minutes later, frustrated at his inability to sway my position. "All right, regardless of who's to blame, would you agree that Campbell can't go unpunished?"

I'd spent the drive back to Mantoloking thinking of an appropriate way to deal with Campbell, but my only solution was just a small step above Ted's response to Crayton.

I said, "Yes. But you and I just went through all the legal steps. I did the same with McCullough at lunch.

We need more evidence. I called my computer geek and he couldn't come up with anything. I hate to admit that Campbell outsmarted us, but it seems he did. He left no trail, paper or cyber. Maybe if you hadn't beaten Crayton to a pulp, he could have helped. Or if Wally hadn't killed Diamond. I had my guy check her phone and financial records and he couldn't tie her to Campbell. That's where it stands."

He hit the reset button. "Let me propose some new alternatives then. Let's start with physical punishment. We could engage someone to beat the tar out of Campbell. This man Moses Ginn sounds like a candidate."

"Back to the Wild West? I can't go there and if you do that on your own, I'll turn you in. You're lucky you skated on Crayton. That's already caused a really bad thing to happen. It's compromised a good cop in McCullough. I'm not going to suggest that *I'm* not already damaged goods, but I can't let you go there."

He said, "I thought you'd say that. Riley, I'm sorry about Crayton. I did it for you. If you made an enemy of his father, you'd be a dead man walking. You told me about that man Serpente and how the mob never forgets. He stole from them. He moved hundreds of miles away and changed his identity, but twenty years later, they found him and killed him. You're a good man. I couldn't let you live under that threat the rest of your life."

"There had to be another way, Ted. You didn't have to almost kill Crayton."

"I didn't do it just for you. If they came after you, they might have tied me to this as well and I'm not brave enough to live with that. I did what had to be done."

He truly was a man who thought several moves ahead of the rest of us. I knew that some danger existed by talking to Crayton and showing our hand, but I had faith in my ability to figure another way out. Maybe my threat of arrest would have sufficed, or maybe Ted was right and had done the only sane thing. Elvis was a low life criminal and I won't lose much sleep over his fate. But if someone up above is keeping score, I deserve a big black mark for my role.

I rose from Stone's tattered wing chair and stood in front of Ted. FBI training. Take the superior position to dictate terms. "What's done is done. But I can't let it happen again. McCullough promised to tell Campbell that if anything bad befalls Wally, he's coming for him. BJ may have slithered away once, but he'd be tempting fate to try it again, knowing he was under police scrutiny."

Ted was apologetic. "I've compromised both you and McCullough and for that I'm truly sorry."

He stood to shake my hand. I didn't see the TASER. But damn, I felt it.

EIGHTY FIVE

I've never been TASERED before and I'm not eager the repeat the experience. I was out for maybe fifteen minutes, unable to speak or move, other than the convulsions that spread throughout my body. I was sore where the two barbs had penetrated my tee shirt. I knew I wasn't going to die, but during that period, I would have welcomed it.

I never saw McCarver leave. When I finally gained a semblance of consciousness, I managed to make it to the sofa.

My phone. That was my first thought. But who should I call?

Sentences were starting to form in my brain, but they were interrupted at their midpoint, snapping onto disparate tangents. I couldn't stay on one thought long enough to figure what to do next.

Somewhere buried deep, I recalled that TASER stood for Thomas A. Swift's Electric Rifle, the acronym honoring the hero of a series of young adult novels. Tom Swift was a teenage inventor who inspired kids of my generation to study science, and perhaps planted the seeds of the digital revolution.

Unsteady on my feet, I walked to the refrigerator and managed to get a bottle of water.

After a few minutes, my thoughts began to coalesce into something resembling normalcy. I found my phone on the sofa. I stared vacantly at it for a moment and then began to scroll down my list of contacts, hoping that one of them would spark an idea. Halfway through, McCullough's name popped up.

I didn't hit the send button right away, but the name started me thinking more cogently. Ted had TASERED me, why? He was going to do something he knew I wouldn't go along with. What was that?

Direct punishment for BJ Campbell.

What form would that take? He had a zapper. Might he use it to kidnap the man and torture him into a confession? Incapacitate, then kill him?

Ted McCarver was a mass of contradictions. A keen intellect, a man seemingly emotionless and in total control most of the time. Yet he was prone to sudden violent outbursts when I least expected them.

One of Stone's lyrical references flew into my brain and I was able to capture it before it could depart. It was the Dylan line from *Like a Rolling Stone*, about having nothing to lose when you ain't got nothing. Rick had applied it to himself when he walked into a bullet to save Jaime and me, while he was mired in a depression over his lover's betrayal. At seventy years of age, with the ashes of Stevie Perry scattered over Barnegat Bay, did Ted feel the same way?

He told me he was a coward, afraid to fess up for what he did to Crayton. But last year, he said he was willing to take the rap for his fiancée's murder if Rick was going to be unjustly accused. Did the desire for revenge against Campbell qualify as justification for the personal sacrifice at stake?

While all this speculative probing into McCarver's state of mind might prove of value down the road, I needed to do something *now*.

I called Flint. He was in his car, a few minutes away from WJOK. I told him to get over there ASAP to keep an eye on Campbell and be wary of Ted if he showed up. I rang off before he could ask why. I trusted that McCullough would act first and pepper me with questions later.

A lot had happened in the last couple of hours. I turned on the radio. The Allie and Wally show was just beginning and Wally was on the air. From where, I had no idea but I assumed it had to be somewhere on Hilton Head Island.

I called Stone. Voicemail. Maybe Jaime knew how to reach him.

"Can't talk now, hon. Dad and the director are arguing and I need to get in the middle," she said in a hushed voice.

"Real quick. Any idea where Rick is?"

"In the air. Flew out a couple hours ago. Back to Hilton Head."

"Okay. You take care of business. We'll talk later."

"Everything okay?"

"Don't worry, I'm fine," I lied, then hung up.

If Ted had truly gone off the deep end, McCullough would stop him. On the off chance that Ted would try to harm Wally, I'd dispatch Stone or Ginn to protect him.

But what should *I* do? Where should I go?

Preparing to take Stone's truck to the station, I grabbed the keys and my leather saddlebag. The bag felt light. I opened it and immediately saw that the manila envelope containing the SD cards wasn't there. But that wasn't the biggest problem.

My Beretta was missing.

EIGHTY SIX

Stone kept a small arsenal and I knew the combination to his gun safe. I chose a Glock 27 with a ten round clip and headed for Toms River.

When I got to WJOK, Flint was standing on the front porch of the crumbling old building. His eyes were shooting death rays at me as I walked up the broken concrete walkway. I hoped that the TASER hadn't emptied my cache of droll greetings, because I surely needed one.

"A little chilly to be standing outside, Flint," was the best I could come up with. "Taking a cigarette break? I thought you kicked the habit years ago."

I couldn't tell from his face if he was going to scream or just punch me, but he did neither in a marvelous display of self control.

I said, "Is Campbell inside?"

"No, he's not."

"Any idea where he is?"

"They said he's on a sales call. Due back in a few minutes." His manner was clipped. He was hiding his annoyance as best he could. "Are you going to tell me what's going on or do I have to beat it out of you?"

He wasn't kidding. Much.

I told him about Ted, the TASER and my gun. When I was finished, he said, "So you thought McCarver was coming here to kill Campbell? And you didn't think I needed to know that little tidbit in advance?"

"I was just zapped. I wasn't thinking clearly. I'm still not a hundred per cent."

"You never were." The tart put down indicated he was at least a *little* sympathetic.

I said, "I didn't think he would outright shoot the guy. And there's no way he'd go after you. Fact is, if he saw you standing guard, he'd probably just turn around and wait for better opportunity."

"Maybe he already did just that."

"Look, this all may be a false alarm. He might have just gone out for a late lunch for all I know. But he's got a gun, and he knocked me out. I'm just being careful."

"So now what? You want to press charges against him for assault? I could put out a BOLO."

That was wading into dangerous territory. If a cop stopped Ted, knowing he was armed, deadly force might be in play. I was pissed at McCarver, but not enough to put him in harm's way without giving him a chance to explain.

"Let's hold off on that. I need to find out where Wally is. Just in case Ted is thinking of doing something to him. Unlikely, but we need to cover all our bases."

"I've saved you the trouble. Alison told me. Apparently Wally decided to trust her a little. He's at Ted's place, the condo on Hilton Head. He's probably safe there, at least for now."

"Would you call Detective Tomey on the island and ask her be sure to keep a man on him, at least until Rick or I get there? You said they already have someone watching him."

"I can ask. Look, I need you to be honest with me. Last year, you got Ted off on that murder rap for killing his fiancée. Flash forward. You've seen him lose his mind and beat a man senseless with a baseball bat. He just TASERED you, the man who saved his bacon. Are you sure that the old man who confessed to killing Stevie wasn't paid off by Ted?"

"No way. Why would Jackson do that?"

"The man had cancer. Just months to live. McCarver arranged to pay his legal fees. And take care of his adopted daughter for life. That poor broken woman."

I knew that Stonewall Jackson hadn't killed Stevie Perry. He was protecting his ward. But could Ted have set the whole thing up, killing Stevie for dumping him twenty years ago?

I said, "No one is that smart, even Ted. Look Flint, I don't expect you to be Campbell's bodyguard but is there someone you can assign to watch him? Someone you trust not to shoot Ted on sight?"

"I couldn't trust *myself* not to do that. Frigging guy's a thorn in my side. Why couldn't he have just stayed in that god damned monastery? Oh, shit."

He kicked the side of the building in frustration, and flecks of paint came scaling off it. He said, "I'm going to have a little tête-à-tête with Campbell and let him know we're hip to his tricks. Then maybe I'll get someone to cover his sorry ass."

"Thanks. I just thought of something. Hang loose for a second. It may save us some aggravation."

I dialed BS, my computer geek. He answered right away, in his normal voice. He was starting to trust me. A small victory.

"I need to know if McCarver's plane is still at the Monmouth Jet Center and if not, where it is. Can you call me back?" I said.

"There is no need to call you back if you can wait forty seconds."

"Clock's ticking."

Keystrokes. Incredibly rapid typing. McCullough stared at me impatiently. After thirty six seconds BS said, "The Socata with the tail number in question took off for the DeKalb-Peachtree airfield, just outside of Atlanta, Georgia approximately five minutes ago. Theodore Chesterfield McCarver, pilot."

Atlanta?

EIGHTY SEVEN

I asked BS to text me when Ted's plane touched down and to keep me apprised of any further flights.

"Manpower is scarce, King. Since McCarver's headed to Atlanta, I'm going to assume that Campbell's not in any danger," McCullough said.

"For the next few hours. But he could easily take a commercial flight back and leave his plane down there…" I stopped myself, realizing how crazy this made me sound. "We're really over-thinking this, which might be exactly what Ted planned. Get us off on some misdirection counter-play and then do something out of left field."

"Nice mix of baseball and football metaphors," McCullough said, incorporating a term he likely hadn't used since high school. "I'm going to go up to Campbell's office. I'll call Tomey while I wait for him to get back. Where are you and that rust bucket headed next?"

"I'll go upstairs to the air studio and try to talk to Wally."

No one stopped or questioned either one of us as we entered the station. I took the stairs to the third floor and waited in the control room while the Allie and Wally show sizzled with frenetic energy. The twenty four channel audio console was alive with irate callers, but Wally was subdued, off his game. It was Allie whipping the fans into a further frenzy. She almost got me caught up in the madness until they threw to a break. Her producer said that she'd be free for at least eight minutes.

"What do you want, King?" Alison said, as I poked my head into the studio. "Whatever it is couldn't wait until I got off the air?"

The flashing lights in the control capsule had made my dizziness worse. I suppose if I was a radio programmer, I would have waited to impart bad news until she finished her show. But I really didn't care what happened for the rest of her program. I told her about everything that even peripherally affected her --- from Campbell's culpability to McCarver's foray into insanity.

When I was finished, for once in her life, Alison Middleton had no comment.

"Allie, I don't think you're in any danger from Ted or Campbell or anyone else. I feel for you. I don't know how you can go on working for someone who tried to get your partner killed."

She was numb. "Sounds like you're telling me there's nothing you or the police can do."

"We tried working it through the system. No go. For right now? Your boyfriend is telling Campbell that if anything happens to Wally, he'll be the first one he hauls in."

"My boyfriend?"

"McCullough." I welcomed the change of subject. "He said you two had dinner the other night and it went well."

"We didn't throw the silverware at each other if that qualifies," she said, scoffing at the notion. "Actually, I'm not being fair. He seems like a good man and we had a few laughs, but that's it. First, I don't see myself getting involved with a cop. And second, he talks about his ex-wife a lot. I don't fancy being somebody's rebound. The first person you date after a long term relationship breaks up is usually eating dust after a few hot weeks of revenge sex."

"I'm not one to give advice on matters of the heart," I said, not wanting to pursue this particular thread either. "Can your engineer hook me up so I can talk to Wally off the air?"

She walked across to the control room, which was separated from the air studio by a large window and a sound isolating door. I was again shocked by the shabbiness of the studio. I'd been there many times when Rick worked at JOK, and it always had been impeccably maintained. Now the fake leather seat cushions were spewing chunks of yellow foam, barely held together by strips of duct tape. The delaminated Formica desk was mottled with coffee, soda and booze stains. Even the microphone screens were discolored by some unknowable brownish filth. Every horizontal surface was sheathed in a layer of dust and the threadbare blue carpeting was worn to the nub in high traffic areas.

After giving her producer instructions, Alison shot me a thumbs-up through the glass. Given the time limitations, I was quick to the point with Wally. I told him that the HHPD was monitoring his every move. I said that after his show, he needed to get to my house as soon as he could. I gave him the combination to our electronic lockset and said that he should stay clear of Ted for the time being. I'd explain later.

To my shock and surprise, he agreed without protest or additional inquiries. Off the air now, he sounded like a beaten man. A couple of nights in custody will take the starch out of most people, but I expected him to react defiantly with even more outrage than he normally displayed. Instead, he passively accepted everything I suggested and even said "thank you, sir" at the end of the exchange.

Alison came back into the room, donned her headphones and hummed along with the insipid theme music until the vocal ended. Then she began her spiel. I was amazed that after all she had been told in the last ten minutes, her on-air demeanor was unchanged. She launched into a scathing critique of the previous night's Knick game, her muscular attack showing no signs of the distress she must be feeling. Wally had little to add. I listened for a minute and then slipped out of the studio.

As I exited the building, Flint was waiting, his face red with anger. I was ready to turn around and go back inside if his wrath was directed at me, but I wasn't the target.

He said, "That son of a frigging bitch. Before I could even start, he tried to kick me out of his office. He came *this* close to putting his hands on me. I wish he had. I'd run him in for assaulting an officer in a New York minute. That is, after I beat the shit out of him."

"I take it that it didn't go well."

Flint was fuming. "Oh, I got my message across. I told him we had the goods on him but were withholding prosecution for now. Warned him about leaving the area and all. He practically spit in my face. You know what, we'd better get out of here before I go back in there and clean his frigging clock."

There were no direct flights to Savannah/Hilton Head until the next morning. I didn't want to wait that long. There was a late afternoon departure to Charlotte, and from there, I could drive down to Hilton Head. If there were no delays in the air or on the roads, I could be on the island by ten.

Flint McCullough insisted on running me to the airport, possibly to make sure that I actually got on the plane and didn't double back. Or maybe he was just doing me a kindness. Whatever. He calmed considerably on the ride up the Garden State Parkway and New Jersey Turnpike. Exit 13, if I was tempted to repeat the stale joke.

Two hours after our encounter at WJOK, we sat in the American Airlines VIP lounge at Newark/Liberty. The flash of Flint's badge got us into this exclusive area and *whoop-de-do*, they served free coffee and appetizers. That made us happy. My flight was due to depart shortly, and I told him it wasn't necessary to babysit until take-off. But he stayed with me the whole time. I'm not sure whether it was the engaging company or the free eats.

As I got ready to leave for the departure gate, he said, "I just want to let you know. I've decided I'm not going to put a man on Campbell no matter what. If somehow Ted comes back and shoots the bastard, it'll serve him right."

"I didn't really want you to cover Campbell for *his* sake. I just wanted to keep Ted from doing something extreme that'll land him in prison for the rest of his days."

"Him, too. I say good riddance to them both. McCarver almost killed Crayton. I looked the other way for him once, I ain't doing it again. I'm still not sure he didn't kill Stevie. Your friend just might be totally psycho. If he comes back here to kill Campbell, he'll either get shot resisting arrest or he'll get locked away for good. The way I see it, it'll be two fewer creeps I have to worry about."

EIGHTY EIGHT

When I got back to the house on Hilton Head, Bosco greeted me at the door, jumping all over me with his tail wagging. At that moment I felt that my dog was the only friend I could fully depend on, who'd be there for me no matter what. All my human friends, including Jaime, had other business which took precedence over my needs. Bosco was dependent on me for his very existence, and in a way, I needed him almost as much.

The door to Stone's room was slightly ajar. I eased it open to see if he was there. He was snoring gently and I was relieved to see that no naked presence occupied the other side of the bed. A gun was on the night table. Hooray! He was capable of learning. I let him sleep.

I walked down the hall to the room we had previously assigned to Josephs. I assumed he was there, since the old Toyota that Paul Esposito had loaned him was parked in the driveway. I heard the faint sound of an NBA game on television coming from the room. I knocked and a muffled voice invited me in.

Wally said, "Watching Golden State beat up on the Lakers. Couldn't sleep. Just get in?"

The room smelled of whisky. I hoped it wasn't my good scotch.

It was almost midnight. I was delusional in thinking that the trip from New Jersey would go smoothly, but here I was. "Yeah. There's still a cop parked a couple doors down. You awake and sober enough to hear what's going on, or would you rather wait until morning? I'm kind of beat myself."

"No, tell me now. I got some news of my own."

Josephs was propped up on top of the covers, wearing a tee shirt and sweat pants. He looked helpless, a far cry from the frightening demon I'd first encountered. I told him about how Campbell was behind the attempts on his life and how I was planning to play the recording for Alexandra Tomey, which should remove any doubt that he had killed Darla Diamond in self defense.

"That's good," he said in a small voice. He wasn't drunk enough to slur his words. I was stunned by how the short time in custody had changed his demeanor. He'd morphed from an unthinking cretin to a frightened child.

I said, "Even though it's Friday night, I expect that I can clear this up over the weekend. By the time you hit the air Monday, everything should be resolved."

"I won't be on the air Monday or any other time."

"What are you talking about?"

"My agent called me a few hours ago. He got a call from the national head of programming at Cirrus. They want me to do mornings, starting Monday. I told him there was no way I was doing that. He said that if I refused and didn't show, they could make a case for voiding the rest of my deal. I said go ahead and tell them that I quit."

"You quit? Wally, you're giving Campbell what he wanted all along. You can't do that."

"This isn't about him. I wasn't sure I wanted to keep doing this anyway. I'm seeing this move by them as a sign I was right. I'm done. King, I fucking killed a woman. Shot her dead. And now you're telling me it was because I was making too much money? What a fucked up world we live in."

I couldn't disagree with him on that score. "I know you're not asking for advice, but this isn't a great time to make a big decision like this. You've been under a lot of stress. You need to step back and breathe a little."

"That's what my agent said. He told me that I should sleep on it and that he wouldn't give them an answer right away. But I don't give a shit, my mind is made up."

"You're going to lose a ton of money."

"So what? What's more important, my money or my life?"

The famous Jack Benny line came to mind which Wally was too young to appreciate. The great comedian, when faced with the same choice by a mugger, paused for a long beat and then deadpanned, "I'm thinking it over."

I forced myself back into the moment and said, "It doesn't have to come down to that. I told you Campbell has been put on notice."

"Yeah, you say that Campbell won't try anything because your cop buddy warned him. Yet you hustled down here to stand guard. You think I want to live like that?"

It struck me for the umpteenth time that I was the one acting irrationally, as I had been all along. I hated what Wally did on the air. The world would be a better place if he no longer had that fifty thousand watt megaphone. But something in me couldn't abide Campbell winning.

"I didn't come down here to protect you from Campbell. He said on the tape that he hadn't come up with a plan B so you're safe from him for now. Trust me, I'm not going to let this go."

"That's not the only reason. Ted gave me shit the other night when we argued about my show. I gave it right back to him and I ran out. I was thinking he betrayed me. But while I was in that holding cell after I killed that woman, I realized he was right. That guy on the air isn't me. It's like Jekyll and Hyde, man. He was the worst part of me. The dumbass part. I just said whatever came into my mind. I didn't care who I hurt or who I offended, as long as I got applause or some idiot caller agreeing with me. I'm frigging better than that. That's what Ted said and he's right."

I hadn't told him how his wise mentor had beaten a man senseless with a baseball bat and that there was a chance he might be next.

"Wally, I can't say that I'm not happy about your *Come to Jesus* moment, but why don't you unveil this new persona on the air Monday morning? Best of both worlds --- you keep the dough and re-invent yourself for the better."

"You know King, if I was still on with Allie in the afternoon, maybe that would fly. Although I doubt it. There wouldn't be enough spark to make the suits happy. But they weren't talking about bringing her to the morning with me anyway."

"So she'll do afternoons solo?"

"I don't know. All my agent said was they were making big changes at JOK, none of which he was privy to. It doesn't matter. The bottom line is, I can't do mornings. I'm a night owl. I can't be getting up at four thirty every day. No frigging way."

"But your whole career is on the line."

"I couldn't care less about that," he said, his voice echoing despair coming from deep within. "I don't know who I am. I never would have thought I could kill somebody. I mean sure, I figured I was a tough hombre and all, but this is real and I'm having a hard time with it."

"She would have killed you. You were just doing what anyone would have."

"Yeah, in my head, I get that. And maybe someday, I'll get my shit together. But for now, I'm just planning on getting lost. Get my Porsche back from your friend in Forked River and head out on the highway. If I'm not at WJOK anymore, Campbell has no cause to come after me."

"Maybe you can get Cirrus to buy you out, at least get you something."

"That's agent talk, King. Look, it's none of your business, but Ted set me up with a great money guy after we did the contract. I only got maybe like a tenth in cash, the rest got directly transferred to this dude to put away in a safe fund. I can probably go ten years without earning another dime. And it sucks to say it, but my folks are getting up there and they're rich."

"I'm not going to try to change your mind, kid. Just wait until I clear everything up with Tomey before you go."

"I will. Hey, I got some good news for you. I made my peace with Stone before you got here. He and I had a talk and we're cool. I don't see us hanging out on a regular basis, but I think we got more in common than what we got different. No matter what, I'm checking out of here in the AM. Got a room at the Disney resort down near Shelter Cove. If the cops or you need me, that's where I'll be. I figure no one else would think to look for me there, if you're wrong about Campbell."

"I think the coppers will still keep an eye on you until we square things a hundred per cent with Tomey. Just don't try anything stupid, like trying to give us the slip again. I kind of like the new Wally and I wouldn't want anything to happen to him."

I punched his arm gently and headed off to bed. I wasn't totally convinced that this transformation would last, but it was possible that Walter Josephs had finally seen the light and would one day make us all proud.

Waiting faithfully in my room, head snuggled deep into my pillow, was Bosco the Wonder Dog. If he could forgive Wally, the matter could finally be put to rest.

EIGHTY NINE

By the time I got up Saturday morning, Rick was already in the kitchen. After taking Bosco out for his morning activity, I returned to the smell of coffee brewing and something sweet baking in the oven.

"How domestic, Rick," I said, as I ladled Bosco's kibble into his bowl. "What's cooking?"

"Cinnamon buns. Much as I'd like to take credit for my culinary wizardry, you just pry them out of the tube and pop them in the oven. Add frosting while they're hot and you're good to go."

I mentioned my late night talk with Josephs. "I saw his car is gone. Did you see him before he left?"

"Nope. He told me the same thing last night. He's crazy --- walking away from major bucks."

"Speaking of major, he said they're making big moves at the station. Although if he doesn't show up Monday, I wonder what they're going to do. And what happens with Allie if they're splitting them up?"

"One way to find out," he said. "She may not even know. Let's see."

Her number was on his speed dial and he put the call on speaker so I could listen in and interject.

"Allie, it's Rick. King's with me. We're in Hilton Head. How you doing?"

She was obviously over her boycott of Rick and me. "Pretty god damned bad, if you want to know the truth. When my doctor told me I had breast cancer years ago, that was the worst bad news I ever got smacked in the face with. This comes in a distant second."

"Why? What's happening?"

"I got an email this morning. Starting Monday, they want me to work overnights, midnight to six. I called Donna Parker on her cell to see if she knew anything. She was at the station. All hell is breaking loose there."

"Moneypenny. She always knows everything that goes on there before it happens," Rick said. He had told me numerous times that the station couldn't function without Parker, a throwback to the McCarver era and still a reliable ally.

Alison said, "She had no clue until this morning when they called her at seven a.m.. The national head of programming told her to get into the station within the hour or she'd be looking for work. They're going almost all syndicated, starting Monday. They're taking the SBS sports network feed except for mornings and overnights. They want Wally for mornings and me for overnights. She says they plan to dump me for good when my thirteen weeks are up in a month or so."

Stone was stunned at the news about the station he had grown up with, so I took over. I wasn't sure whether to tell Alison that Wally wasn't about to do mornings, but that was the least of her concerns now.

I said, "This was Campbell's call?"

"No. He was fired. They had security in his office, packing up his gear in boxes. They confiscated his computer. Donna said it's like an FBI raid, but it's company goons, not law enforcement."

Stone said, "So what are you going to do? It's an insult to ask you to do overnights after all you've done for the place."

THE LAST RESORT

"Tell me where you found that dog shit. I may need some of it," she said, showing that she hadn't totally lost her sense of humor. "I don't know who to call now but I don't plan to come to work. Maybe Cirrus will throw me a bone if I quit now and save them the trouble."

Stone and I expressed our sympathy for her plight and told her we'd call later after we found out more about how this had come down. I went to retrieve my phone from the bedroom as Stone went about frosting the rolls he'd taken from the oven. Despite how good they smelled, all of a sudden I wasn't very hungry.

As I picked up the phone, I noticed a text message from BS that had been sent a couple of hours earlier.

Socata registered to McCarver departed DeKalb Peachtree 7:20 EST Destination HH Island.

NINETY

If a passerby noticed the three men and a dog, walking on the beach in animated conversation, what would they imagine was being discussed?

a)Who will the Dems run for president in 2020?
b)Which two NFL teams had the best shot at the Superbowl in February?
c)Does a grain free diet have any tangible benefits for a Golden Retriever?

Ted McCarver, Rick Stone, Bosco King and I were bundled up against the November wind buffeting the shoreline. Bosco was uncomfortable in his dog sweater, although not because the psychedelic pattern was fifty years out of style. He wouldn't have cared if Ted had commissioned one of his Savile Row tailors to design a custom outfit. Any weather that his natural thick coat couldn't handle was a great excuse to sit home by the fire and play with his toys, while his master and friends braved the cold.

"So you blackmailed the CEO of Cirrus, Ted? Is that what you did?" I said.

"Blackmail implies criminality," Ted said. "I prefer to say I was merely using leverage to assure a favorable outcome. The art of the deal, to steal a phrase."

"I guess I should be happy this doesn't affect me directly now, but you *have* destroyed a great radio station," Rick said.

"This will affect you, but not like you think. I didn't destroy WJOK. It was destined to collapse no matter what. I only hastened the process along. Cirrus already had plans in the works to take syndication. I just forced them to do it a bit sooner. Either way, the company is headed for bankruptcy unless they succeed in monetizing their website, which they're frantically trying to do. This latest bit of chicanery might buy them some time."

I said, "Walk me through how you did this."

"It wasn't all that complicated. I flew to Atlanta where Cirrus is based. I met with Len Richie, the CEO and his brother Leo, the CFO. I told them what Campbell had done. Played an excerpt from the recording. They acted shocked, shocked that one of their charges could act so irresponsibly."

"So you're convinced that they didn't know about this in advance?" Rick asked.

"They pride themselves on being good Christians. At least, that's the way they position the company to the shareholders. They're ruthless businessmen underneath it all, big time hypocrites, but I do think they'd draw the line at murder. Regardless, they agreed to fire Campbell in exchange for my promise not to release the tape to the media. They also agreed to essentially blackball the bastard out of getting another radio job."

I wasn't sure that was enough punishment but I'd wait until we heard the whole story before going there. Ted always has a trick or two up his sleeve that he doesn't show in his opening gambit.

I said, "So they make out like bandits. They get out from under Wally's contract, which is what they wanted all along. Whether they sanctioned it or not, the pressure they put on Campbell to make the bottom line look presentable to the bankers called for desperate measures. He took it a few steps too far. These pompous bigwigs aren't blameless, by any means."

"Oh, they paid a price, which I'll tell you about later. The irony is that if they were really hands-on managers instead of paper shufflers who never take the time to get to know their key employees, this never would have happened. Wally's deal contained a poison pill. Even Wally's agent didn't pick up on it."

Bosco was behaving very well, unusually so. Maybe he was as eager as we were to hear about Ted's machinations, or maybe he just felt confined by the sweater and couldn't move about freely.

Ted continued. "I knew that Wally would never agree to do mornings. He'd done it once early in his career and hated it. He told me many times in his crude fashion that he'd rather clean the commodes with his tongue than do morning drive. So I deliberately didn't specify at what time of day his program would air in the contract. I loaded it up with tons of legal gobbledy-gook, as well as the protections for him, compensation, vacation days and such. Hidden amidst the clutter was the fact that it only said that the program would be four hours in length but never specified when it was to air. So rather than put out a hit on Wally, all Campbell had to do was move him to mornings. He would have quit on the spot, as he did."

Stone said, "If Cirrus had come to you early on and said that Wally had to go, would you have told them about that?"

"As long as he was under my direct supervision, I could keep him in check. But once I sold the place, my influence on him was minimal. Sure, we spoke from time to time, but he ignored my counsel for the most part. It's hard to blame him. He was making big dollars, had great ratings. The industry was trending toward what they call *guy talk* anyway. It was easy for Campbell to egg him on in that direction."

That was not what I asked but I let it go. I told Ted how Wally had finally seen the light after his bloody encounter with Darla Diamond and vowed to create a different persona if he ever did radio again.

"Wally has always been malleable. He takes direction, but he has to respect where it's coming from," Ted said.

Rick said, "Don't you feel bad for the rest of the staff? What happens to all those people who'll be thrown out of work?"

"The damage will be minimal. The morning show guys will go to work Monday as if nothing ever happened. They may never know they were in danger. They aren't making disproportionate money and a live morning show is still a viable money maker. As far as the rest, mid-days were already syndicated after they let you go. They have play-by-play on almost every night so no one was displaced except the part timer they use to fill in on the rare nights there is no game. The main difference is afternoon drive and Alison was a goner when her thirteen week deal ran out anyway. And I have plans for her."

"I hope it doesn't involve a baseball bat. Or a TASER, which I still owe you for," I said.

"Something a little different than that. In talking to the Richies, I learned that Alison wasn't the witch Campbell made her out to be. Rick, *he* was the one who turned you against Wally, not Allie. The big bosses and I wanted to team you up with Josephs. But Campbell hated you and the only way they'd accept Allie as a substitute was if they were convinced that you and Wally just couldn't work together. Campbell's lies made that happen."

Rick said, "All the more reason to not let that son of a bitch get off lightly."

Ted picked up an interesting looking shell, examined it for a moment and stuffed it into the pocket of his windbreaker. "I said before that the Richies aren't emerging unscathed. I released the stock I own back to them in exchange for something I think is wonderful."

He stopped and gazed out at the Atlantic. There was a late season tropical storm a few hundred miles to the southeast that was roiling the water. The dark clouds were barely visible on the horizon.

"Well, Ted, don't leave us hanging. What's this *wonderful* thing you have in store?" Stone moved between McCarver and the ocean, into his personal space.

"There's a small station in Bluffton that Cirrus owns. A five thousand watt FM day timer. It's mine once the paperwork clears. I've had an eye on it for quite some time, ever since I moved here. I've been doing some research. With the Richies' cooperation, I have a path to increase the power and the operating hours. It's a bit complicated, but WPHX's signal will eventually cover the entire Low Country --- from Savannah to Charleston."

I said, "Just like you did with WJOK. But you said that terrestrial radio is dying. Why would you want to get back into it?"

"It's a case of love over gold. I have some ideas I've wanted to try for a while now. A free form station, limit of eight commercial minutes an hour. Great personalities with the freedom to do whatever they want. Talk, play music, do interviews. Harkening back to the early days of FM."

"You're crazy, Ted," Rick said. "Those days are over. That'll never fly today. Who will listen to it? Kids have their internet music services and their phones. You can't sell advertisers on the old fart demo you *might* have a chance to lure. An air staff with that kind of talent will cost big dollars. You'd never be able to staff the place."

"I'll start with you. I know that deep down, you love radio as much as I do. Screw these bit parts in movies. Then I'll bring in Wally. I bet he jumps at the chance. Maybe even Alison."

He clapped his hands together. "You're right, I can't pay great money. At least, at first. I've set up a profit sharing model and if this flies, we can all do well. I know a bunch of retired or semi-retired radio people who are like us. They don't need a lot of money but they *do* need a reason to get up in the morning. Some of them don't even have to be local --- they can work from home."

Stone said, "Okay, you've covered your plan for the outgoing expenses. What about the incoming revenue?"

"I've still got money from selling WJOK, enough to operate the place for a decade without much coming in. I'll be eighty by then. I can't see planning much beyond that, although I *do* plan to live forever. And so far, that's working out well."

EPILOGUE

Christmas was almost upon us. A few weeks after our walk on the beach, things were falling into place at Ted's new radio station. I had no idea of the significance of the call letters WPHX, until he explained that it symbolized a Phoenix: new hope rising from the ashes of a bankrupt industry. As promised, he assembled a crack staff ready to hit the airwaves sometime after the first of the year. Rick would do the mid-day shift, like he had at WJOK. Wally hadn't committed to do the afternoon show yet, but Ted was optimistic. Allie was signed for evenings. Ted himself was going to do the morning show with a cavalcade of co-hosts. They ranged from the ranks of major radio personalities who were winding down but still had their chops, to celebrities from the world of music, politics, film and television. The list he had already gotten commitments from was impressive. Ted hoped that one of them would be so dynamic that he could convince them to take the position full time, allowing him to concentrate on the business side.

Alexandra Tomey filed her report on Darla Diamond's death after hearing the wire recording. The Beaufort County District Attorney accepted her conclusion that Diamond had been killed in self defense. How she squelched the details and kept Wally's name out of the papers, I'll never know.

McCullough had done his part in convincing Tomey of Wally's innocence. In addition to sharing the tape, he had scoured the five year file of *unsolveds* in Ocean County and found a connection to Darla Diamond in three of the murders. There was nothing strong enough to secure a conviction, which was academic since Darla was dead, but the arc was convincing enough to put Tomey's mind at ease that Diamond was not an innocent victim.

McCullough had come to terms with his DA's decision to let sleeping dogs lie, but his own role in the cover-up chafed at him. He was still adrift in his personal crisis. I didn't see any way that I could help, other than to be available whenever he needs me. I doubt he'd initiate the call, so I'll stay in touch, maybe even invite him down to Paradise for a vacation.

In mid December, Flint sent me a link to a story with Rasputin's byline. It said that BJ Campbell, formerly the general manager/program director of WJOK had been found in a mangled BMW Z4 just off Route Nine in Forked River. Both his legs were shattered. He was concussed and there were deep abrasions all over his body. He was expected to survive after a lengthy and painful rehab. The damage was consistent with what a large SUV would cause by crashing into the driver's side of the small sports car. No other vehicle was found at the scene. Police were investigating the incident as a hit and run but so far they had no leads.

I confronted Ted about it, sensing his handiwork at play. He admitted that he had assembled an email containing an excerpt from a certain recording. Along with the audio, it explained the context of the conversation, implying that Mr. BJ Campbell may have tried to eliminate the only person who could implicate him in a plot to kill a sports talk host. It was sent from the offices of WJOK by persons unknown. My guess was that Moneypenny may have done a favor for her old boss. Ted would not confirm my suspicion of her involvement.

He did let on that the recipient of the email was the co-owner of the Iron Horse Tavern. Families may be divided, but they usually take care of their own. Revenge had been served cold. It seemed about right.

As for me, I needed to get away from Hilton Head for a while. Although Ted had engineered a reasonably just outcome, death and destruction were again left in my wake.

Another thing that disturbed me was that McCarver was willing to go to places I couldn't. I have always hoped that intelligent people could find a way work out their differences without turning to violence as the last resort, if they took the time to understand one another's position and talk it through.

Ted McCarver is an elite intellect, superior to ninety nine per cent of the population. But he could come up with no way other than mayhem to settle a simple matter. Maybe this planet is such a cruel place that *giving peace a chance* is hopelessly naïve and we are doomed to be at each others' throats for all eternity.

My reputation is that of a hard-hitting PI, yet I had allowed a seventy year old intellectual to do the dirty work while I sat by and ruminated about morality.

I *am* tired of Stone's endless parade of chippies, which I can only imagine will get worse if he attains some measure of local fame through WPHX. Maybe his realtor, Jenny Lightower will capture his affection. I can only hope.

Jaime and I are planning to spend Christmas together in Charlotte. I have no idea what will come of it. She has already prepared me for the possibility that her film ventures will eclipse her literary efforts and she will need to spend more time in California and less time with me. The whole long distance experiment was under duress, and I wasn't really sure how I wanted it to work out. I didn't want her to stay home and bake cookies, but we were having a hard time coming up with an acceptable balance.

I still owe Moses Ginn a call. Another seventy year old tough guy who makes me feel like a wimp.

A week before the holidays, I took Bosco in for his annual checkup and the vet gave him a completely clean bill of health. At age seven, I'm hoping that my best friend will be with me for many more years of loyal companionship. It's the one joy I cling to, as so many of the others slip away.

ACKNOWLEDGEMENTS

This book was inspired by the WFAN family, which I am proud to be a part of since 1988. The management and air staff have always been supportive and stimulating. Frequent callers like Ira from Staten Island, Bennie from the Bronx, Bill from Massapequa, Rob from Lake Success, the late Bruce from Bayside, among others have made my work fulfilling on so many levels.

You may recognize the qualities of some popular broadcasters in the fictional characters contained in these pages. A few of the stories spun may bear a slight resemblance to actual events. They are at best extrapolations of what might have happened had they populated Riley King's parallel universe. I did borrow the call sign WPHX from a fine Florida station.

Many of the places described do exist, although sadly Villa Vittoria was severely damaged by fire in 2016. The Starlight sounds like a great diner and the Iron Horse a cool cop bar, but they exist only in the imagination.

My wife Vicky again was essential to bringing this book to fruition with her great cover photography and graphic design.

Novelist Reed Farrel Coleman is a bottomless well of wonderful ideas and wise counsel. Michael Harrison of Talkers Magazine is a friend of many years who might have spoken as depicted.

My golden retriever Duncan the Wonder Dog wants you to know that any loveable acts attributed to Bosco in the book were inspired by him, and any quirks or misbehaviors must have come from another canine.

ABOUT THE AUTHOR

The Last Resort is Richard Neer's fourth novel featuring Riley King and his radio cohort Rick Stone, as they investigate crime along the eastern seaboard.

His work of non-fiction, *FM, the Rise and Fall of Rock Radio*, (Villard 2001), is the true story of how corporate interests destroyed a medium that millions grew up with.

Neer has worked in important roles both on and off the air at several of the most prestigious and groundbreaking New York radio stations in history --- the progressive rocker WNEW-FM for almost thirty years, and the nation's first full time sports talker, WFAN, since 1988. He was instrumental in the birth of WLIR, the first suburban progressive station, in 1970.

Something of the Night was the initial offering in the Riley King series followed by *The Master Builders*, (May 2016). *Indian Summer* was published in the fall of that year.

His next, *The Punch List*, is in the final stages of preparation.

Made in the USA
Middletown, DE
12 July 2020